THE BLACK ROSES
MC
MASSACHUSETTS

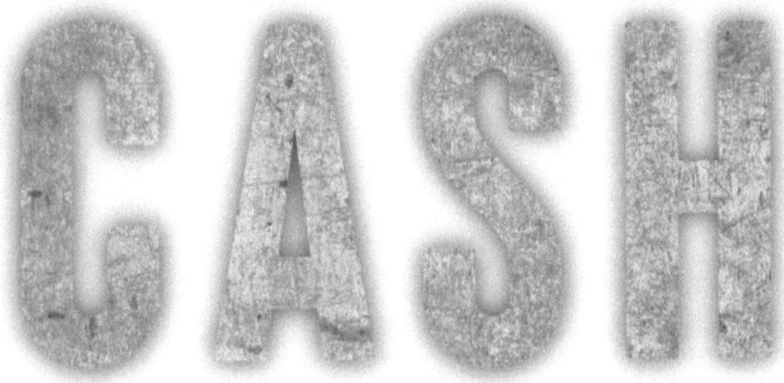

Book Cover by Y'all. That Graphic.

Photographer: Lindee Robinson

Editor: Victoria Ellis. Cruel Ink Author Services

Proofreader: Rose Puls. Your Fairy Proofmother

CHECK YOUR TRIGGERS

Your mental health and emotional well-being matters to me. You can find a list of possible triggers on the book's page on my website katerandallauthor.com or by scanning the QR code below.
Xoxo

As always for my amazing husband who keeps me fed, stocked on crispy Diet Cokes, and all around sane when I'm on a deadline.
Love you, babe.

CONTENTS

PROLOGUE
CECE

"Today is a good day, daughter," my father says at the breakfast table as he finishes the pancakes on his plate. He's already asked for seconds of the pancakes and thirds of the bacon. It's as though when my husband isn't here, he feels free to be as gluttonous as he wants. If Otto were present, my father would be grateful for the meals I cook with Otto's provisions, and he would never dream of asking for more.

That's the way of life on this compound, though. Or *homestead*, as they like to call it. In reality, it's a cult in the Nevada desert, just shy of the Arizona state line.

I've never been immune to the not-so-subtle whispers from the residents of the small town we would have to visit on occasion. I'd heard the word *cult* bandied about many times growing up. The horrified look on my mother's face when I asked her what that word meant was something I'll never forget. She told me we were living as God intended—not the sinful way others existed. She made our way of life sound glorious, but I soon came to realize it was anything but.

One day, while I was alone in the store, I asked the woman behind the counter where we were on the map. She looked at me with an odd expression and pointed to the town about thirty minutes from the compound I lived on. A smile stretched across my face. I knew where we were. It was a small thing, but never having known anything outside the compound I grew up in, discovering that this place really did exist somewhere gave me a tiny bit of comfort. Like I was really here in this world and not trapped in a nightmare—even though I truly am.

That was the day the thought crossed my mind. I could actually leave. There were places, cities, and other towns. I could run away like my sister Lucinda had. Maybe she was living a happy life in a town somewhere on that map. Maybe someday I would meet her there.

"My coffee is getting cold, Cecilia. I hope you take better care of your husband than me," my father barks, startling me out of my daydream as I wash the breakfast dishes.

"Sorry, Father." I grab the pot of coffee off the stand next to him, refilling his cup with my head down. If he thinks even for a moment that I'm being defiant by keeping my chin raised, he will report back to my husband, Otto, and my punishment will be...not worth it. My punishments never are.

When Otto started coming around, I was a naive little girl. My mother had passed away about a year prior, and I'd had to grow up quickly in her absence. Since my sister had run away by then, it was up to me to take care of my father and his house. Never in my wildest imagination did I think an elder, let alone the congregation's leader, would take an interest in marrying me—especially at sixteen. They all seemed so old. They had to be well into their fifties or sixties.

Otto wasn't the oldest living man on the compound. In fact, he was considered young for the position he held at fifty-three. His father was the leader before him, so I suppose he was born and raised to follow in his footsteps. But like I said, I was a naive little girl.

That naivety was smashed into a million tiny pieces on my wedding night while I lay in the marriage bed and Otto rutted into me like a dog in heat as I cried in pain and begged him to stop. That was the first night my husband punished me with a slap to the face that split my lip open. But it certainly wasn't the last time or the worst.

These last couple weeks without Otto here have been a godsend, though I'm not entirely sure I believe in any god at this point. But I've had a reprieve, and that's the most I can wish for. It's not as though some celestial being sitting on a throne in the heavens is going to save me now. No one has, and I don't expect that to change.

"Your husband returns today," my father informs me, and it feels as though a pit has dropped in my stomach. Of course, Otto would never deign to let me hear those words from his mouth, but he would tell an elder—the role my father earned by giving me away to the head of our community.

"It's a blessed day then," I say, like any dutiful wife should after such a long absence from her husband.

"And he's bringing a sheep back to the flock," he says as I turn to set the coffeepot back on the stove and return to the dirty dishes in the sink.

"Oh?" There's only one *sheep* that has ever made it out of here. Alive at least. One girl tried to run before my sister. She was caught and punished. There's an unmarked grave somewhere on the compound with her body lying six feet under.

"Your husband and his son have found your sister. She's on her way back to her rightful place to be Jasper's wife, as it was always supposed to be."

My hands begin to shake in the soapy water. I knew he was going to tell me it was Lu before he opened his mouth. It couldn't have been anyone else. But for one single split second, I was hoping it would be someone else—anyone else—even though I knew it was impossible.

Before Lu fled the compound—when she was seventeen and I was fifteen—she was going to be married off to Otto's youngest son, Jasper. There aren't many men who scare me at this point. I've met and have been brutalized by some of the worst. All at the discretion of my husband, no less. But Jasper? He makes my blood run cold every time his beady gaze lands on me.

I know what to expect from my husband and the disgusting bikers he makes me entertain. It's awful in ways I could never describe and rarely let myself think about. What's inside Jasper is something else entirely. If I believed in the devil the way we're taught to, then Jasper would be evil incarnate. And that's why Lu ran. She saw what her future would hold with him as her husband and refused to live what would most likely be a very short life with him.

When she left and he married another girl that the elders picked for him, they couldn't conceive. It wasn't more than a few years before there was an accident with a rifle, and his wife was shot and died. Honestly, I'm still not sure if he was responsible for her death or if she turned the gun on herself.

There have been many times I've wondered if I would meet the same fate, since I have yet to conceive a child with Otto. And the thought of taking matters into my own hands and leaving the earthly plane hasn't been far from my mind over the last couple of years.

"If there's anything I can do to bring her back to the fold and make her see the error of her ways, I'm more than happy to, Father," I say.

Though I am heartsick at the idea of my sister being captured, I'm desperate to see her. Desperate to wrap my arms around her. If there is a god, then maybe she was sent here as a second chance for me to make a different decision than the one I made all those years ago when I chose to stay. Chose to believe the teachings of Otto and the elders. I have to get out of here, and this time, my sister and I are going to find freedom together.

"I'm sure that would make your husband very happy. I'll speak with him about it." My father rises from the table and throws his napkin on his plate. "I have preparations to make for Lucinda's return," he says, then heads out the front door.

When he leaves, I collect his dirty plates from the table and bring them to the sink.

Lu's back.

A smile stretches across my face.

And together, we're going to find a way out of this hellhole once and for all.

My hands tremble as I walk up the steps of the church where my sister is being held. I kept myself busy baking bread, desperately trying not to run to the church the second I saw the truck carrying Lu, my husband, and Jasper through the town square. Otto came to the house briefly and told me that my father suggested I help Lu see the error of her ways. He decided that my father made a wise recommendation, and Otto told me to prepare something for Lu to eat and find her a change of clothes that were more appropriate compared to what they brought her here in. He was giddy when he swept into the house, and that was something that both confused and terrified me.

When I open the old wooden door of the church, the hinges release a high-pitched squeal due to years of use and the dry desert climate. Looking around, I don't see my sister or anyone else. Have they moved her somewhere else? Is she already gone again? The questions swirl as my head whips from side to side, looking for her.

"Lu?" I ask, my voice echoing off the walls.

A head with a tangle of black hair pops up from one of the first pews. So different from the light-brown hair she had when we were younger.

"Cece," Lu says, covering her mouth as she stands. She runs toward me, and I drop the clothes and food I brought her as she launches herself into my arms.

"Cece," she says again with a teary voice as though she can't believe this moment is real. I can hardly believe it myself.

We pull apart slightly, and her hands wipe the tears from my cheeks like she used to do when we were chil-dren. Lu was always there to wipe away tears, bandage scrapes, or tend to cuts and welts from our father's punishments.

"I thought I saw you earlier on my way through town," she says, her eyes roaming over my face.

"You did," I reply. I'd snuck away from the house when Otto came back, figuring if I got caught, I could make up some reason as to why I wasn't in the house waiting for him. All I knew was I had to lay eyes on Lu. "I didn't want Otto to see me, though. If he thinks I'm excited to see you, he'll become suspicious."

"Oh, Cece." Her arms wrap around me again. "I'm so sorry they married you off to that man. I'm so sorry I left and couldn't protect you."

"Shh, now, sister. It wasn't your fault. You know as well as I do there was nothing you would have been able to do to stop it." I lean out of her embrace and take a step back, holding her arms and pleading with my gaze for her to understand I would never—could never—hold it against her. "I'm glad you got out. Don't take this the wrong way, but I never wanted to see you here again. It would have meant you'd been captured and brought back. Imagining you in the world, living a life of your choosing, brought me peace." Looking at the bag and clothes on the floor, I bend over and pick up the food before handing it to my sister. "Here, I brought you some food and water."

She opens the bag, and we sit in the pew as she unwraps the sandwich, smiling around her bite of the bread I busied myself with making this morning.

"You always had a talent for baking, Cece. It's just as delicious as I remember," Lu compliments.

"The elders thought seeing a familiar face would temper your resistance to being here." I shoot her a wry smile. "Of course, I had to act like I wasn't chomping at the bit to come here. I told Father I'd help you see the error of your ways, and you would be more open to hearing it from me than them."

"I'm shocked they agreed with your plan."

A sad smile crosses my face. "I've played the obedient elder's wife for a few years now. I've earned their trust."

Lu's bright eyes become clouded as she swallows the mouthful hard before speaking again. "How did you end up becoming his wife?"

I take a steadying breath, hating that she was given that information by someone other than me. Not that it would have made it any easier for her to hear. "When his first wife died unexpectedly, he began coming for dinner more often and sending little gifts to me. At first, I thought it was on Jasper's behalf, but then Jasper's marriage was announced to one of the other girls, so I was a little confused. About a month after their wedding, Otto came to the house and had a meeting with Father. I was called in and told I was to marry Otto, and Father was going to be elevated to an elder."

Lu shakes her head. "What did Mama say?"

My eyes widen. "They didn't tell you?"

She gives me a confused look. "Tell me what?"

"Oh, Lu...Mama passed not long after you left. She fell ill, and her fever raged out of control. There was nothing anyone could do, and Father refused to let her go to a hospital."

Her head falls forward as more tears stream down her face. "Do you know...are you certain it was natural causes?"

"It was." I reach out my hand and rest it on hers. "I would have been suspicious if Father had remarried right after, but several members of the church fell ill around the same time. Even the men. Father never remarried. Even after I was married off and he didn't have anyone to cook or clean for him." I roll my eyes. "Of course, it still falls on me to help take care of him, his house, and my own house."

"Has it been terrible for you?" she asks.

"You know, at first, I tried. I tried to be a good member of the church and tried to be who they always expect us to be, truly believing I was doing right by God, but I don't know, something changed. I thought about all the ways I was made to feel inferior—the way they preached one thing from the pulpit while we were making drugs that killed people, then traded those drugs to gangs and anyone else who would supply the elders with weapons. The more I thought about it, the more I started seeing the cracks. Does that make sense?"

Lu nods with a knowing look in her eyes. "Perfect sense, Cece."

"I wish I would have come to the realization so much sooner, Lu. I shouldn't have let you leave on your own."

"You know I have to try to get out of here, right? There's no way I'm staying and putting up with any of this," she says in a low voice, determination wrapped around every word. It's the exact thing I was praying to anyone who may be listening that she would say.

"I know, Lu. And I'm going with you this time. I can't live like this anymore. Otto has been relentlessly badgering me about having a child. I'm just thankful it hasn't happened yet. No child should be raised in a place like this." Tears spring to my eyes when I think about bringing a child into this world. I can't help but think about the way my daughter would be treated, and it sends a violent chill down my spine. I don't think I would be able to stomach watching a boy be raised to believe that women are inferior, including his own mother.

"If anyone sees you or asks you about seeing me, you need to play the part of the disappointed sister. And you have to be convincing, Cece," she emphasizes. "The less suspicion anyone has about your motives for visiting me, the better the chance we'll have of getting out of here. They won't suspect you of being a traitor."

"You can't betray a cause that's done nothing but betray you since birth," I tell her. I simply can't believe this is how people are meant to live—what people are meant to believe. "Where will we go?"

A small hint of a smile tips the corner of Lu's mouth. "There's a little town in Massachusetts called Shine. I've been living there with my best friend, who I met while living in New Orleans. There're men there who treat women with kindness and respect." She clears her throat before continuing. "They would lay down their lives to protect their family."

"You love them," I state with a small smile of my own. Hearing that she found exactly what I'd hoped all these years brings me a small amount of happiness that I was right. I just wish, with everything in me, that she was still there instead of back in this situation.

She nods. "They're my family, and they'll be yours, too."

"They must be so worried."

"If I know anything about them, they're looking for me as we speak," she says with confidence.

We don't get a chance to say much more before Otto and my father walk into the church.

I immediately stand and give my sister a reproachful look. "She ate her food. I've been reciting scripture to her to show her the error of her worldly ways," I say in a haughty tone befitting an elder's wife—one who is convinced she is better than the sinful woman they've brought back to our community.

"I know you've done everything you could for her, wife. We'll take it from here," Otto says, and I turn to leave, knowing I've done all I can for now.

"No, Cecilia. You need to stay and witness this," Otto commands.

I silently take a seat in the pew while my father grabs my sister's arm roughly and hauls her to the altar.

"Time for your punishment, daughter."

"Father, put the gun down," Lucy says, turning to face the man who has the barrel of his gun pressed firmly to the back of my head.

Moments ago, the Black Roses—who are apparently the bikers that Lu told me she's come to know and love—rushed into the old church after my father and husband were told that the Great War was upon us and ran out of the building. A biker—who Lu called Jude—slit the throat of the elder who was guarding the front entrance. Gunshots rang out all around me as I ducked behind the altar at the front of the church.

My father must have snuck in through the back when he saw my husband and Jasper being dragged into the church.

Now it seems he's intent on seeing me die rather than losing the two men who are kneeling at the same altar where Lu was receiving her punishment. The same two men who have brought so much pain and suffering to the lives of me and the rest of the women on this compound.

"You think you can tell me what to do?" my father spits angrily. "A whore has no right to speak to a man of God."

Silent tears run down my face as the barrel of his gun presses into my skull. All I can think is *I don't want to die. I don't want to die. I just got my sister back. I just got the chance to live a free life away from here.*

"You aren't going to get away with this," Lucy tells our father.

"Maybe I die today, but I'll be welcomed into the kingdom of heaven, whereas you, daughter, you'll be going straight to—"

A shot rings out, and our father crumples to the floor while my eyes squeeze shut—waiting for the pain that never comes.

"If I had to hear one more word from that man's mouth, I was liable to turn the gun on myself," a man says with an accent I've never heard before. I turn and watch him walk over to me. I'm unsteady as fear and adrenaline swirl through my system, but he grabs me around the waist before I fall next to my father.

"Shh, now. I've got you." He leads me to a pew and helps me sit. His voice is so gentle, so soothing, and yet I just watched him kill a man without blinking an eye.

"Who do we have here?" he asks, walking over and standing next to Jude and Lu. Two other men hold Jasper and Otto in a tight grip as the monsters kneel at the altar. This time, it's their turn for punishment. The man who shot my father speaks in the same way that Jude does, and now that I see them next to each other, they look as though they could be brothers.

"Elder Otto and his son, Jasper. The ones responsible for Cooper," Jude answers.

The man nods and takes a step back with two other men toward the back. "Alright then, brother. I'll let you and yours handle this."

Jude walks over to a kneeling Jasper with hate burning in his gaze. "Look at my woman over there, Jas. She's beautiful, yeah?" The gun he's holding waves in Lu's direction.

Jasper nods stiffly but doesn't speak.

"You tried to take what was mine to love and protect. And for what? To turn her into a mindless shell of a woman who was only good for breeding and cleaning." He looks at my sister then back to Jasper. "Nah, mate. A woman like this was never going to bend to a boy like you. She needs a man who can handle her fire. And you?" Jude points the gun at his head. "You need to die."

When Jude pulls the trigger, the man holding Jasper lets him go, and he falls to the floor with a bullet between his eyes. I should be absolutely terrified, but with each body that crumples before the feet of these men, the only thing I feel is relief.

"And then there was one," Jude says, turning toward Otto, who is staring blankly at his son's lifeless body.

Lucy walks up behind Jude. Her hatred for the man on his knees in front of her is a violent thing, and she's so consumed by it that I can practically see it vibrating through her.

"How many times?" she asks my husband.

"What are you talking about?" Otto sneers.

"How many times did you rape my sister as she cried out silently, praying to your god to make it stop? How many girls did you give away to disgusting men like yourself to be used and thrown away?"

When she asks that, I want to scream. I want to cry. I want to vomit in this pew. God, if only she knew the truth about what he did to me—what he allowed other men to do to me. I don't do any of that, though. Instead, I sit silently and watch Jude slide the knife that my sister asked for into her hand.

"It was God's will. You have no right to interfere with that," Otto says, staring my sister in the eyes.

"You had no right to bring me here against my will or commit any number of horrific crimes you did in the name of God, yet here we are," Lu says, taking a few steps and planting her feet in front of my husband's trembling body.

"You'll burn in the pits of hell for this, Lucinda. Mark my words," Otto grits out.

She pretends to ponder his statement, tilting her head back and forth and looking toward the ceiling. When her eyes meet his once again, they're hard as steel and just as unforgiving. "I suppose I'll see you there, then."

Lu slashes the knife across his throat. She watches as the blood pours from his wound—a look of shock on his rapidly paling face. My sister is covered in blood, some of it hers and some of it Otto's. But all I see is a glorious avenging angel standing in front of me. When the men spoke of such beings, I highly doubt this is what they had in mind. A small smile plays on my lips as I watch Otto's life force drain away, his eyes fixed blankly on the altar of his church.

After walking out of the church, Lu and I gathered all of the scared women and the children on the compound. I knew there was no way we could simply leave them here. The man with the strange accent—who was introduced to me as Liam, Jude's older brother—made some phone calls so they could transport them all back to the small town my sister calls home.

With everyone now in the town square, Lu and I walk to one of the barns and collect every gas can we can find. We make several trips back and forth from the barn to the church, Lu quiet the entire time. Both of us seem to be lost in our own thoughts as we prepare to destroy the place that nearly destroyed both of us and everyone else living here.

"Ready?" she asks as we stand together, holding hands in the dead of night, with the smell of gasoline stinging my nose.

I nod and Jude hands my sister a book of matches. She releases my hand and lights a match before setting the entire book ablaze, then she grabs my hand again. Lu throws the burning matches onto the trail of gas that leads to the church, where we had poured gallons and gallons around the perimeter.

The church goes up in flames, the old dried-out wood taking hardly any time to erupt into an inferno. Lu and I stand hand in hand, transfixed as the fire dances against the backdrop of the barren desert I pray I never step foot in again.

Tears of relief fill my eyes.

I'm finally free.

CHAPTER ONE
CECE
TWO YEARS LATER

My blaring phone wakes me up. I groan and turn over, seeing Cash's name on the screen. Rolling my eyes, I decline his call and turn over to go back to sleep. It rings again, and again I decline it. What the hell time is it, anyways? I look at the clock on my phone. After ten in the morning. Shit.

Sitting up, I scrub my hands over my face. God, I feel like shit. My head pounds in time with my pulse, and everything I ate the day before is threatening to make an appearance. Not that I ate much to begin with. Pretty sure I consumed my body weight in wine—and then vodka—instead of putting anything of real substance into my stomach.

Yesterday was...not a good day. The memories were too much.

I had every intention of going to the barbecue at Elaine Dawson's house, or rather sprawling estate, and spending time with my family and friends. But the thought of being anywhere near a Dawson started fucking with my head. I love Elaine, and I love Mia—her granddaughter and one of my sister's best friends—but the Dawson name brings back too many memories, especially after finding out Mia's brother was one of the Bone Breakers.

I remember Nolan. He was part of the group who kidnapped me and Colby—Nolan's biological son—just over six weeks ago. Not that I'm counting or anything. I knew him when I lived in Nevada on the cult compound—the place I called home for my entire life. That was until two years ago, when the Black Roses stormed the property and took out the men who ran that godforsaken place.

Nolan was a member of the Bone Breakers—the MC who my "husband" was partnered with to sell the meth that was made on the property. They used the income from the drugs to fund the cult and prepare for the Great War the elders constantly preached about. I think that war came a little earlier than anyone expected, and it wasn't all that great. The Black Roses basically walked in and took out every piece of shit who had a hand in enslaving the women and kids who lived there.

Nolan was one of the men who regularly came to the compound to make the deals, and my body was usually part of that deal. When the man who claimed me as his wife started courting me, I thought it was because he wanted a young wife who could *bear his fruit*, as he liked to say. I had no idea he wanted me because I was young and pretty, and the MC who came to the compound had noticed me. I was a bargaining tool. An extra reward for helping Otto unload the drugs that he said were poison to the nonbelievers, which is why he wanted to distribute them to the outside world. Maybe he thought he was getting a jumpstart on weeding out the *sinners* for his god. Or maybe he was just a greedy bastard. I'm going to go with the latter.

It didn't come to light that Colby was the biological son of Nolan until right before the kidnapping. They wanted Colby, and I was picked up as collateral, but as soon as I was recognized as Cecilia, the wife of the elder who was murdered and therefore couldn't supply the Bone Breakers the drugs that turned them a nice little profit, they decided to take their payday from my flesh. Two years later, and Otto was still the reason disgusting men thought they could use and abuse my body.

Thankfully, they didn't get far before Cash burst through the door and shot the man on top of me. But it didn't change the fact that I was in the one place I never dreamed of being after the Black Roses saved us—under the sweaty, smelly body of a drunk Bone Breaker. Not that anyone knows the extent of the abuse I suffered under the eye of my husband.

Before Lu—or Lucy as everyone calls her now—killed my husband in the church on the compound, she asked him how many times he'd raped me. But that was the wrong question. She should have asked how many times he let the bikers he did business with rape me. Maybe he would've had an answer for that. Not that he'd kept track, I'm sure. I did, though. And it was no small number.

My sister doesn't know about the assaults. She doesn't know about the many times I thought they were going to kill me, or the times I wanted to kill myself just so I wouldn't have to go through with another "payment."

I shoot up from my bed and run into the bathroom, barely making it before heaving into the toilet bowl. I try to stay as quiet as possible. No need to alarm Lucy and Jude, who I've lived with since coming to Shine. Lu will fuss, and Jude will be worried about me and my sister. Honestly, I feel a little bad for the guy. It's doubtful he ever saw a future with Lucy that included living with her younger sister—who is a fucking drunk basket case half the time and an angry, raging woman the other half.

My phone rings again from my bedroom, and the sound grates on my frazzled nerves. I'm sure it's Cash again. He's been one of the few people, hell, the only person if I'm honest with myself, who I've been comfortable sharing parts of my life with. Lucy wants me to talk to her, to open up about what happened to me on the compound after she left. To tell her how I went from being so quiet and introverted when I got here, to the rage monster I am today. Those aren't her exact words, but the sentiment is there.

I lean back against the wall and grab a hand towel from above my head, pulling it down to wipe my mouth. Running through a few cycles of deep breaths to help calm my stomach, I relax against the wall and close my eyes. It's too damn early to deal with this shit.

When I came to Shine, I was a scared girl who was grateful for the chance to be free. I'm still grateful. But now I'm angry. So, so *angry*. I hate my father for trading me for a little power. I hate Otto for using me and hurting me and allowing other men to do the same. Especially now that I see the way these men protect and care for the women they love. I knew what was happening on the compound was wrong. That no one should be treated the way me and so many other women were. But witnessing every day what I missed by staying on the compound instead of running with my sister when I had the chance fills me with utter and total fury.

And Cash has just always...been there.

At first, when I would accompany my sister to the clubhouse, I would generally stay in the kitchen away from everyone. I baked. A lot. Shit, I still do. It was something to keep my mind clear. I'd concentrate on new recipes, and in some ways, it felt like it was my contribution to the family who risked their lives to set me and the other women free.

Cash was one of the only brothers who would venture into the kitchen when I was there. I think Jude or Lucy may have warned the other brothers to give me a wide berth. On one occasion, I overheard Lucy tell Jude to make sure the other men kept their hands and dicks to themselves or she would cut them off with a butter knife. She said I needed to heal and not be dragged into a violent life or be taken in by a man who was only looking for a good time. When Jude reminded her that she and her best friend were part of this life, she told him that I'm different. That I'm soft and deserve to stay that way—whatever the hell that means.

But Cash was apparently the exception. At first, he didn't try to talk to me. He was sitting at the small table in the clubhouse kitchen, simply drinking coffee and reading the newspaper, when I walked in one morning to start baking. Such a normal sight for a man who lives a life of riding a motorcycle and doesn't blink twice at the thought of breaking the law. The club lives by their own code. It's one I can respect, and the complete opposite of what I thought the MC life was. Of course, the only exposure I had was from the Bone Breakers, and the Black Roses are nothing like them. Lu told me I could trust them, and I chose to believe her. They've yet to prove us wrong.

He asked if it was okay if he stayed, and I nodded shyly. For the most part, I pretended he wasn't there—which isn't an easy feat with a man like Cash taking up the space at the small table. His presence is large, and so is he. Easily six foot three and over two hundred pounds of lean muscle. But his dirty-blond hair, always looking as if he rolled out of bed and ran a hand through it, gives him a carefree, almost youthful impression. However, what's behind his eyes gives away the fact that there's more than what most people see. There's pain there. A sadness that, though isn't the same as mine, is familiar nonetheless. He needed a place to just *be*. Same as me.

When the first batch of apple turnovers I'd ever made came out of the oven, I put one on a plate and set it on the table. He thanked me, ate it, and then used his fingers to collect the crumbs, sucking them clean. My lips tipped in a satisfied smile when I saw him do that, and that's when I decided I was going to start experimenting with more pastries and desserts. It wasn't something I ever had the ingredients for on the compound. They were considered frivolous. Food was only meant to nourish our earthly forms, not to be enjoyed beyond it simply being edible.

And that's how the unlikely friendship between a biker and a mess of a girl began. Before I learned to drive, Cash took me to the store if I needed ingredients, and then Lucy and Jude bought me a car of my own. Whenever I experimented with a new recipe, Cash was my taste tester. When I started watching Colby for Maizie, he often came to the park with us. I wasn't afraid to be out on my own—not like I was the first few months I lived here—but having him around made me feel safer.

We started talking, really *talking*. He listened to me rail on about how my sister wants to "fix" me, but she didn't know how deeply I was broken. No one did. I've never elaborated on what exactly that meant, but I've never felt like I needed to with him. I listened to him talk about the guilt he felt over taking in Cooper—the prospect who died while protecting Lucy. Cash and Cooper grew up together. When Cooper wanted more than what the little town in Louisiana could offer him and his sister, Cash brought him to Shine to have him prospect for the club. They were both kids who had families that didn't give two shits about them when they were young, and Cash had found a real family in the Black Roses. He wanted Cooper to have the same.

A knock sounds at my bathroom door, shaking me out of my thoughts.

"Cece. You okay?" my sister asks through the wood.

"Yeah, just getting ready for the day," I answer before standing and turning on the shower.

"Okay. Jude made breakfast if you're hungry," she calls over the running water.

"Be out in a minute."

There's no way my behavior last night isn't going to be the topic of conversation at the breakfast table.

I quickly wash my hair and brush my teeth before stepping into my bedroom. Jude and his brother Liam decorated it for me—or rather, for the version of me they thought I was. The pastel-pink and white comforter is soft and sweet. But not who I am. Not that I know who that is right now. The furniture is a white-washed farmhouse style that screams simple and feminine.

The only thing I really cared about when I came to live here was having a lock on my door. Though I believed Lucy when she said I could trust these people, there was still a lingering fear in the back of my mind. Men aren't trustworthy. They're driven by the basest of instincts, which usually means taking advantage of those they deem weaker. It's taken me a long time to dispel that notion.

Opening my drawer, I pull out a pair of cutoff shorts and a T-shirt, throwing them on before brushing my long, straight blonde hair. I was often told how pretty my hair was growing up. How I was lucky to have such natural beauty. I've lost count of the number of times I've almost cut the long locks to my chin. Even thought of dying them black like my sister had when she was on the run.

When I walk out of my room and into the kitchen, Lucy and Jude are sitting at the small table next to a large window that overlooks the backyard. Jude looks up from his plate and gives me a pitying smile while Lucy's is tight as she watches me pour myself a cup of coffee and lean against the counter, facing my firing squad.

"Well," I say after taking a sip. "Out with it." I wave my hand in my sister's direction.

Jude clears his throat and stands from the table as Lucy and I stare at each other. He grabs his plate and walks over to the sink, rinsing the dish and putting it in the dishwasher.

"We only care about you, Little Bit. No matter what, we want what's best for you," he says and offers me a smile. "Go easy on your sister, yeah? She loves you."

I nod as he turns toward my sister. He bends and gives her a kiss on the mouth. When he stands straight, his gaze darts between the two of us. "Remember, you love each other," he says, then walks out the door.

"Chicken," my sister calls after him.

"Self-preservation, love," he yells back before the front door closes behind him.

Lucy holds my stare as we listen to Jude's bike start.

"Listen," I begin. "I know I was a mess yesterday. It won't happen again."

I showed up at the barbecue drunk as shit and drove there myself. Not my finest hour, to say the least. Lucy was done at that point with my drinking and surly attitude.

I'll be the first to admit to myself that I've been using alcohol more as a crutch since the kidnapping. In the months following my rescue from the compound, I'd buried the feelings and memories. Then the anger started and so did the drinking and rage baking, as Jude likes to call it. It was something that everyone tiptoed around. But last night seemed to be the final straw for my sister. We started arguing, and everyone was staring, including the five-year-old boy I absolutely adored but couldn't bring myself to spend time with. Not after seeing his father and almost being raped again while he was locked in the bathroom of a dingy motel room.

Cash intervened, from what I remember—which isn't much—and took me home while I silently cried in my car the entire way. I vaguely remember him walking me into my room and setting a glass of water on the nightstand next to my bed. As soon as he left, I grabbed an almost empty bottle of vodka from underneath my bed and pounded the rest of it. Then I promptly passed out and didn't wake again until the phone rang this morning.

"It won't happen again?" Lucy asks, shaking her head. "It shouldn't have happened in the first place!" she yells. "You fucking know better than to drink a bottle of wine and get behind the wheel. You should have fucking known better than to show up at a family barbecue so drunk off your ass you were stumbling through Elaine's fucking rose bushes."

That would explain the tiny cuts I felt in the shower this morning.

"I know. It was a stupid mistake," I plead.

"You don't know. And I've been tight-lipped about everything I've seen these last several months because I know you have shit you're trying to work through. But Cece, you won't let me in. You won't let me help you." She runs a hand through her messy dark hair and blows out a breath. "Look, I'm not exactly the poster child for *well adjusted*, but sister, you are traveling down a dangerous path. You're out all hours of the night. You drink like a goddamn fish, and don't think I haven't noticed the bottles piling up in the trash—and you won't talk to me. Just talk to me, Cece. Let me help you."

Though her pleas are coming from a place of love and concern—and I know that, truly I do—her begging grates on my already frayed nerves.

"What do you think you can do, huh? Erase my past. Make the seven years I spent on the compound without you just disappear?" I hold up a hand and snap my fingers. "You have no idea what I went through. And you have no right to judge me for how I'm dealing with things."

"That's just it. You aren't dealing with anything. When you were babysitting Colby, that was the only time you weren't drinking, or blaring music and baking, or out doing God knows what with God knows who. Now you barely look at Colby, and you haven't watched him in months."

"Listen, I might be a fucking mess, but at least I know not to bring it around Colby. At least give me some credit."

"Oh, I give you credit for that, but he loves you and misses you. Maizie told me he thinks you're mad at him because he didn't fight off the bad guys."

My heart drops to my stomach, and if I wasn't leaning against the counter, I'm pretty sure my legs would have given out. Hell, they still might.

I clear my throat and fight back the tears that threaten to spill out. "There's nothing he could have done. He's just a kid who had no control over what was happening to us. Neither of us did."

"I know that and you know that, but you've disappeared from his life. That's not the Cece I know. No matter what you were going through, at least I knew you loved that kid and were always there for him. It was the only time I saw a glimmer of the sweet girl I remember."

"And there it is," I say, throwing my hands in the air. "I'm not the Cece I used to be. Well, no shit."

"That's not what I meant," she says, trying to backtrack. "It's that I don't recognize *this* version of you. When you came here, you were quiet and reserved. And I was worried because you wouldn't open up. I didn't want to push, but maybe I should have. Then, in the last year, you've been angrier than I've ever seen you. I still didn't push when I should have. Now you're running around, not telling me where you're going or who you're with, and I have no idea what to do with that." Lucy takes a deep breath and tries to settle herself the best she knows how, which, for my sister, isn't much. "Do you understand what could have happened yesterday? What if Colby was outside riding his bike? Or what if you'd hit a fucking tree because you were so drunk you couldn't keep the car straight? What if, after all these years, I had lost you?"

"I know. Jesus. I'm sorry. I never drink and drive. I'm not that stupid."

"Then what changed yesterday?" Lucy prods again.

So many things have changed for me in the last month and a half. Namely, the images and feelings I kept buried are all that run through my head these days.

"I don't want to talk about it," I reply.

Lucy scoffs. "You never want to talk about it."

"Oh, I'm so sorry my trauma is such an inconvenience for you. If I'm too much trouble, I'll leave."

"Is this the part where I get the petulant teenager?" she asks snidely.

"Sorry, *Mom*."

I blurt out the word before I have a chance to think about it. Lucy and I hold each other's stares as tears fill her eyes. She wasn't there when our mother passed. Not that she was much of a caring maternal figure, but she was all we had. I know Lucy regrets the fact that she and the MC were too late to save our mother. They saved the other women and kids from the compound, but they couldn't save her. I think both of us carry around a lot of baggage where our mother is concerned.

Lucy clears her throat and stands from her chair. Shutting down when the conversation veers into something neither of us is ready to talk about seems to be a family trait.

"I have errands to run before I head into work. I'll see you when I get home." She grabs her keys and bag from the counter then turns around to leave the kitchen. "You know," she starts, her back facing me, "you aren't the only one who went through hell. I wasn't there for seven years and didn't see what happened to you, couldn't protect you, but every day I thought of you and worried for you. My mind came up with the worst possible things, Cece, and I was scared every *single* day for you. I just want to help now that I have you with me."

She steps toward the door, and a moment later, I hear it shut, then hear the engine of her car start.

No matter what Lu imagined, I can guarantee my reality was so much worse.

And neither of us is ready to open that can of worms.

CHAPTER TWO
CASH

I gave Cece a day. My calls went unanswered, which isn't necessarily out of the ordinary with her. Throughout the last two years, our friendship has had many ups and downs. Cece has been through a lot in her short life, probably more than any of us know. You don't grow up the way she did without coming out with some oversized baggage.

When she first came to the clubhouse, she would hide in the kitchen, and I was more than willing to hide in there with her. The responsibility and crushing guilt I felt about Cooper's death were fresh. I thought I was giving him a family, and instead, I gave him a death sentence. It's not as though this life doesn't come with the possibility of an early expiration date, but he was on a simple protection assignment. Not a single one of us thought the assholes from the cult where Cece and Lucy grew up would be bold enough to run them off the road and kill Cooper to get to Lucy. But we should have. And not having the foresight to assess every possible outcome will haunt me until my dying day. Whenever the fuck that might be.

I needed a minute to wrap my head around losing a kid who was like a little brother to me, and I couldn't do it around the noise of the clubhouse. Instead, I'd take my coffee in the kitchen and sit in silence with Cece. We were two people who needed a little time to sort through the shit we went through. A little time to catch our breath.

Honestly, I thought she would run screaming from the kitchen the first time I met her in there. I knew she was a child bride and that her "husband" was an abusive piece of shit—as was her father. I knew the way the men at the compound treated women from Lucy's stories, but Cece's story had yet to be told, and I was perfectly happy letting her tell it in her time, or not at all if that's what she wanted. But she never acted scared of me or put off by my presence, so I simply kept showing up, drinking coffee, reading the morning paper and eating whatever she set down in front of me.

There were no ulterior motives behind the mornings we spent in the kitchen to get her to open up and give the MC an account of what she went through. The club didn't need to know the details of that shit. We saw and heard enough from the night we went in and took out every one of those assholes. Cece and I needed a quiet place, but I don't think either of us wanted to be alone. We found that in each other.

It's been a few weeks since our morning—and sometimes afternoon—routine started, and Cece isn't here. When I asked Jude where she was, he said she was still in bed. She hadn't slept the night before, so Lucy figured she was getting her rest.

I'm familiar with not sleeping when the shit on your mind is too much. Instead of letting it go, something is telling me to go check on her. I'm not sure how she's going to react to a man showing up at her home, but I figure since we've spent every morning in the same space, I'll be able to sense if something is off.

So I hop on my bike and head to her house. When she answers the door, the dark circles under her eyes clued me in that Jude was right, and she hasn't slept.

"I'm sorry I wasn't there this morning. I just..." Her words trail off as she stands in the doorway and blows out a deep breath.

"Not sleeping?" I ask.

She shakes her head.

"Then I was getting everything together this morning and realized I didn't have the preserves to make the turnovers I planned on, and I didn't want to inconvenience Jude or Lu by asking them to take me to the store. Then I remembered the first time I ran out of eggs when I lived with Otto, and the punishment I received for not being prepared, and well..."

"I get it. Sent you on a spiral?" I ask.

"That's a good way to describe it. I have coffee ready if you'd like some. I was never allowed to drink it on the compound. Otto said it was interfering with my ability to conceive, so he banned me from it."

That's a gut punch if I've ever felt one. And the first time she's outright given me a glimpse into her life in the cult.

"Sure, I'd love a cup," I reply, and she lets me into her house.

No one else is home. It's the first time Cece and I have been truly alone without anyone just on the other side of a door. It feels significant to me—that she trusts me enough to be here without Jude or Lucy.

"I really must get to the store soon so I can make you some cherry turnovers. I think I finally figured out just the right amount of filling-to-pastry ratio needed," she says while pouring me a cup of coffee before setting it on the marble kitchen island separating us.

I smile in thanks and hold up my cup, taking a sip. "I like anything you make. All the brothers do."

Her shy grin and the way she dips her head so that her hair covers the sides of her face—and probably her blushing cheeks—don't go unnoticed. Nothing with Cece ever does. She doesn't seem to know what to do with compliments. I doubt she's ever heard them.

"I can take you to the store," I offer. "I'm on my bike, though, if you're up for a ride."

She cocks her head to the side and looks out the window to where my bike is sitting in front of her house.

"I've never been on a motorcycle before," she says.

A light chuckle escapes me. "I figured, sweetheart."

This is the first time I've addressed her as anything other than Cece. Her surprised expression has me regretting that word slip. It was probably too forward for her, but feels natural slipping off my tongue.

"I like when you laugh," she says, then quickly turns around to busy herself by putting away the few dishes in the drying rack.

I don't think she meant to say that either.

"Well, if you're up for it, I'm sure Lucy wouldn't mind if you borrowed her helmet. Safety first and all that."

She nods, then she turns toward me with a wide smile on her face. It's the first genuine one I've seen, other than when I practically lick the plate when she shares her baking with me.

"You know what? I think I'd like that," she replies in a decisive tone.

The corner of my mouth tips up in a grin. "I'll finish my coffee, you go get ready, then we'll head out. Sound good?"

Cece nods and leaves the kitchen. I grab my phone from my pocket and shoot a text off to Jude.

Me: Taking Cece to the store.

Jude: And you're telling me this why?

Me: Because she lives with you and barely leaves the house without you or Lucy. Thought you'd want to know where she was in case either of you came home and she wasn't here.

Jude: Got it. That sounds reasonable. I'll let Lucy know.

Jude hasn't exactly known what to do with Cece living with him and his woman. It's not as though she's a child, but it's also not as though she's really capable of taking care of herself at this point, even though she's *twenty-four. She still needs guidance. Still has a lot of growing up to do, shit to sort through, and I don't think Jude knows how to handle that or what his role is in it.*

Cece emerges from the hallway that leads to her room in a pair of snug jeans and a long-sleeve T-shirt. Her long blonde hair hangs loose around her shoulders, and there's a glint of excitement in her light-blue eyes.

"You're going to want to braid your hair back, otherwise the wind is going to whip it all over the place," I tell her.

She nods and pulls the strands back as her fingers begin braiding the light locks. Her movements cause her shirt to tighten around her breasts, and I feel like the biggest asshole on the planet for noticing. This is a girl who came to live here because we rescued her from an abusive cult, and here I am, ogling her tits.

I clear my throat and turn toward the garage door. "I'm guessing her helmet's in here?" I ask, pointing to the door.

"I think so. Let me grab a jacket and I'll be ready."

When I turn back around, she's finished with the long braid that sways as she spins toward the closet.

"I'll grab it and meet you outside," I say, setting aside my wandering thoughts of Cece being any more than a friend.

That was the first time Cece was on my bike, but it wasn't the last. The first trip was to the grocery store and back, then when she needed something, we started taking the long way around town. It didn't take long before she would text me and ask to go for a ride for no reason other than she wanted to.

Cece was never stiff behind me. From that first trip to the store, she leaned into me and wrapped her arms around my middle as though it was the most natural thing in the world.

In fact, Cece has never been uncomfortable around me, not like she was around everyone else. On the rare occasions that she was in a crowd of my brothers and whoever else was in the clubhouse at the time in those first few months, I would notice tension radiating from her. Her gaze would find me, and I'd offer her a reassuring smile. That seemed to relax her a touch, and she would resume whatever conversation she was in.

There were times when I could tell a smile wasn't going to cut it. I'd nod toward the kitchen or the back door, and she'd head that way with me following behind her. Sometimes it was only for a quick breath. Other times, we would take a long walk around the property, sometimes talking, sometimes not. It always depended on what her mood was, and I was happy she allowed someone to at least *be* with her. That she allowed me to be there.

Then her anger started. It took about a year, give or take, but I noticed a change. She wasn't calling me as often to take her on the bike, and she wasn't at the clubhouse nearly as regularly as those first several months. Jude started complaining about rage music blaring through the speakers as she baked into all hours of the night. Anytime someone brought up her sister, Lucy would get a worried look on her face. Cece was pushing her away. Hell, she was pushing everyone away.

The only time she was the sweet girl I first met was when she was babysitting Colby. She loves that kid. We all do. I didn't push, but maybe I should have. At least a little. But that was never our relationship, and I think it's something we both appreciated. Instead, I would answer whenever she called, take her out whenever she needed some time on the open road, and hang out with her at the park with Colby. Being in the open still made her nervous, and having me there eased her mind.

Since the kidnapping six weeks ago, that's all changed. She doesn't watch Colby at all anymore, and she hasn't called me once to take her for a ride. She rarely answers the phone when I call, and when she does, she's usually in a rush to hang up. A couple of times when she has picked up, her words are slow and slurred, and it's obvious she's been drinking.

According to Jude, Cece and Lucy have been fighting like cats and dogs. Not that I would know, since she hasn't deemed it necessary to talk to me.

When she showed up at the party at Elaine Dawson's estate, she was three sheets to the wind and stumbling over herself on the way out the back patio door.

I clock her immediately, which is usual whenever she enters a room, but so has Lucy, and she's fucking pissed.

"I said I'm fine," Cece hollers as Lucy tries to grab her arm.

"You're drunk," Lucy hisses. "And you drove here. That is not even in the realm of okay."

"I had one glass of wine. I'm hardly drunk. You drink all the time. We can do that now. Whatever we want. No one is going to tell us no, right?"

"I never get behind the wheel. And I guaran-damn-tee it was a bottle, not a glass, unless you filled a fucking flower vase and consider that one glass," Lucy shoots back.

I have no intention of holding back this time. Cece is going to hear what I have to say, whether she likes it or not, just as soon as Lucy is finished reading her the riot act. But then I look at Colby and see the heartbreak and worry in his gaze. He has no idea what's going on. All he sees is someone he loves acting out of sorts and getting yelled at. Right then, I decide she needs to get the hell out of here.

Stalking toward the woman who can barely stand straight, I grab Cece by the arm and lean down, whispering, "Colby is watching and he's scared. I'm taking you out of here."

Cece's gaze finds Colby sitting with his mom, nestled in her embrace. She closes her eyes and nods before allowing me to lead her back through the house to her car to take her home.

She doesn't say a word, just sits in the passenger seat as silent tears stream down her face. When we get to the *house, she still hasn't spoken. Honestly, I don't think she knows what to say or how to spin this. It seems as though her actions are finally catching up to the part of herself that knows this is wrong. Everything she's been doing, the way she's been handling things, is wrong.*

Walking her inside, I lead her to her room. Cece lies on the bed and closes her eyes. I head to the kitchen and grab a cup of water, then walk back into her room before setting the glass on the nightstand. I know full well she isn't asleep, but I leave her in her room, letting her think she has me fooled.

Then I pocket her keys.

If she wants them back, she's going to have to talk to me first.

Which brings me to her doorstep.

Cece refused to answer my calls yesterday. She probably didn't even know I had her keys when she woke up. When she realized they were missing, she texted and demanded I bring them back. I answered that I was busy and would stop by the next day. It may have been childish on my part, but she needed a day to cool off, and quite frankly, I was still pissed. How dare she put herself in a situation where we could have been burying another family member because she's been angry? She has every right to her feelings, but putting herself and others in danger because she refuses to talk to someone who could help her isn't going to cut it.

I park my bike between Jude and Linc's house and hear laughter booming from the garage behind Linc's place. Instead of going directly to Jude's, I walk up Linc's driveway and spot the two men sitting in front of the bike that Linc has been restoring.

"I see you decided to brave Hurricane Cece today. Too chickenshit to do it yesterday?" Jude asks with a smirk playing on the corner of his mouth.

"Figured she needed a day to reflect instead of running off," I reply.

"Yeah, thanks for that, mate. She was storming around the house well into the early morning hours. Would barely look at me and Lucy when we got home last night. Just blaring that shit she calls music and baked. I don't know about Lucy, but I'm not touching the new batch of bread. Shit's likely to be laced with arsenic."

"This is Lucy's sister we're talking about," Linc says. "She's more likely to stick a knife in you than watch you die slowly."

I give him a flat look. "I don't know. I think Cece might be patient enough to watch the poison slowly cripple him before taking his life."

"Wow, you assholes are really making me feel safe in my own home. I have to say, taking her keys was a nice touch," Jude says with a chuckle. "Wish I would have thought of that months ago. Maybe we should start calling you Daddy Cash," Jude jokes.

"Please don't ever let those words be repeated. To anyone. Under any circumstances." The last thing I need is a reminder that I have over a decade on Cece. I've never felt particularly old at thirty-six. Until I started having some not-so-appropriate thoughts about a girl who's twenty-four. Those get shut down really fucking quick, though.

"Plus, with that text from Red the other day, I'm perfectly happy having her stick close to home. Kind of hard to run off when you don't have the keys to your car," Jude says.

"You don't have an extra set?" Linc asks.

"You know," Jude says, tapping his bearded chin. "Now that you mention it, I do recall seeing one in Lucy's nightstand drawer."

"You go into your woman's nightstand drawer? That can be dangerous territory," Linc comments.

"Ah, mate. The stories I could tell you about all the fun things I find in there—"

"Which you won't because you aren't one to kiss and tell, right, asshole?" Lucy chimes in from behind me.

"Damn, Lucifer," Jude says, eyes wide with surprise. "Every day I'm more and more convinced you really are a demon with the way you sneak up on people."

"I clocked her as soon as she stepped out of the door," I say with a grin on my face.

"And you didn't think to share that information?" Jude asks, quirking his brow.

"Nope," I reply, my smile widening. "Figured I'd let you dig yourself in a hole. More fun for me that way."

Jude rolls his eyes and Lucy steps up to him. "I'm going to coffee with the girls. I suggest you keep our *activities* to yourself if you'd like to keep having them."

"Now, love. Don't act like you can resist my charming personality." Jude grabs her around the waist and pulls her to stand between his knees.

"You'd be surprised what I can resist. I have a drawer full of little gadgets to keep me occupied." She leans down and kisses her man on the lips.

"Wicked woman," Jude says with a smile when she straightens and steps out of his hold.

"Have fun with your toys, boys," Lucy says as she crosses the garage to where I'm standing just on the other side of the threshold. "You going in to give Cece her keys?"

"Yeah. Just checking in with these two first."

"Scared?" she asks.

I shake my head. "Not at all." Not *entirely* a lie.

"Thanks for taking her home the other day. I was in no position to be in an enclosed space with her at that moment." Lucy looks toward her house and back to me. "Since the attack..." She shakes her head. "She's been drinking. A lot more than what I'd seen before. Lashing out at the smallest things. Charlie thinks she needs to talk to someone, but she refuses. I don't know what to do."

"You thinking rehab?" I ask.

"God, no. At least not yet. I think locking her up would do more harm than good at this point. No, I think if she opens up to someone about what happened, not just in the motel, but while I was gone from the compound, it would help. Maybe I'll try to talk to her again about seeing a professional. I think the anger we see is just scratching the surface. I think—" Lucy swallows hard—"I think she might be angry at me for leaving."

"She said that?" I ask, a little taken aback by Lucy's openness with me right now. She's always been pretty tight-lipped about her previous life with the brothers, well, other than Jude. Charlie has always been her confidant, not any of us. Not like I thought I was with Cece.

"No. And I'm too scared to ask." She looks away as though she's embarrassed by her admission. Lucy isn't afraid of anything, but the thought of her sister resenting her for escaping without her obviously leaves her unsettled.

"I'll talk to her. See if I can get through," I offer, and Lucy nods.

"Thanks, Cash. She's always been more comfortable around you. Hell, more than she is around me sometimes." Lucy releases an unamused laugh and heads to her car.

"She's been in knots for the last month, brother," Jude says, looking toward where Lucy walked off. "When Lucy left, she had to toughen up quick, and she did. But she's made of stronger stock than Cece."

"I don't think that's true," I say, shaking my head. "That girl went through hell and she's still here to tell the tale."

"Problem is, she *isn't* telling it. It's festering inside her," Jude replies.

I stare at the house for a few beats, then return my attention to Jude. "I'll see what I can do to help."

Jude looks at me for several moments. "I've noticed the way she looks at you, brother. Lucy has never said anything, and Little Bit is the last person to open up to me about her feelings, but she looks at you like the sun rises and sets on your blond ass."

"I don't know what you're talking about," I reply, brushing off his comment. "I'm just a person she feels comfortable with."

"Hmm. Just remember whose sister she is when you're trying to get her to open up."

"Are you threatening to beat my ass or something if I mess with Cece?" Not that I ever would, but I can't help but find Jude's protective nature when it comes to Cece a little comical. He was never one to give a shit about anyone or anything other than himself or the brotherhood before Lucy came along. Life was always one big party. He certainly wasn't one to have heart-to-hearts with any of us.

"I'm not going to do anything. Lucifer, on the other hand? She's more likely to dig your grave than tolerate you breaking Cece's heart."

I shake my head. No one is breaking anyone's heart. Cece is too young for me and far too soft and sweet. The only thing I've allowed myself to be to her the last two years is her friend. And that's all it's ever going to be.

Chapter Three
Cece

His bike is parked between the two houses.

Fucking finally.

I sit at the kitchen table sipping on my coffee and catch Cash talking to my sister before she gets in her car to leave. Cash turns and begins making his way to our front door. The sight of him doesn't give me the butterflies it usually does. Instead, I'm seeing him in a whole new light, and it's not one I'm particularly fond of. Turns out he thinks he knows how to *handle* me, just like everyone else around here.

Apparently after taking me home the other day, Cash decided to take my car keys with him. To give me some sort of time-out. Then, because I didn't answer my phone, he also decided I didn't need them back until today. To say I've been a little pissed at him is an understatement. He's always been on my side, always been there when I needed him. And now it seems he's taking the side of everyone else in this damn town.

Oh, poor Cece, she can't take care of herself.

Oh, poor Cece, she had a hard life and doesn't know how to deal with it.

Oh, poor Cece, we're so worried because she isn't opening up.

What the hell does anyone want me to say?

If I told them the truth about what I went through and what being in the clutches of those bastards did to me—made me relive—they would never look at me the same. I can barely look myself in the mirror these days.

Cash knocks on the door, then opens it without waiting for me to answer.

"Cece," he calls.

"In here," I say, and he walks in, closing the door behind him.

When Cash strides into the kitchen, he's wearing a tentative smile as though he's not sure what kind of reception I'm going to give him. As soon as my gaze latches onto his, I shoot him an icy stare and continue to sip my coffee. His smile disappears, and he nods.

"You're mad," he says. It's not a question, but a statement of fact.

Cash has become adept at reading me over the last couple of years. The years he spent being my friend and *not* acting like I was someone who needed to be fixed. Guess he's finally caught up with everyone else.

"Gee, you think?"

"Look, Cece—"

I slam my coffee mug on the kitchen table, causing liquid to splash over the rim. "Who the hell do you think you are? You had no right to steal my keys and not bring them back when I asked you to."

His jaw tightens. "You mean demanded? I'm not at your beck and call. I called you all morning and you refused to answer the phone."

I huff out an unamused laugh. "So you thought you would punish me by stealing my keys and making sure I couldn't go anywhere?"

"You needed a day to calm the hell down. A day where you couldn't run off and go wherever it is you've been spending your time, or go get more booze to numb yourself."

"That wasn't your call to make. How I handle my life is my decision," I say through gritted teeth.

"If you were actually *handling* anything, I would agree. But you're not, and it's become apparent to everyone that this has gone on for far too long."

"Again, not your call. I don't have time for this." I hold out my hand. "Keys," I demand.

Cash looks at me for several beats, then it's almost as though I see him deflate—see the fight leave him—as he reaches in his pocket and pulls out my keys.

"What is going on, Cece? Talk to me," he pleads.

Part of me wants to. Part of me is desperate to tell him all the awful things that have been going through my mind for the last six weeks since the kidnapping. How the only thing that I want in life is to wrap myself around him while I'm on the back of his bike. How it's the only time my mind is clear.

But I know it's not going to work this time. He saw me when that disgusting man was on top of me. He saw me curled in on myself after nearly being raped again. He saw a small part of what I went through for years before the Black Roses came to the compound. Before the kidnapping, he'd only heard small bits and pieces from me and possibly my sister. But he *saw*. Cash was my safe space, and now that's tarnished, just like everything else.

"You want to help? Or you want to fix me like everyone else?"

"We care about you. I care about you." He slaps his hand to his chest.

I shake my head. "Really? Because it looks like you want to manage me. You want me better, so everything can be wrapped up in this nice little bow for you. Just like my sister does. Newsflash—it's not going to work. Nothing is going to magically change me."

And you will never understand how badly it hurts that you can't fix this, that I can't fix this.

I stand from my chair and walk over to the counter, grabbing the keys before shoving past Cash.

"Where are you going?" he calls.

"None of your business."

And I slam the door behind me.

A little over a year after being in Shine, I was driving home from the store in Ayre. I'd picked up a bottle of wine, having tasted it for the first time at the clubhouse the week prior. I liked the flavor of the white—crisp and fruity—but I *loved* the effect. For the first time, everything dulled. I didn't even feel the pang of jealousy at seeing one of the dancers from Midnight Rose hanging on Cash like I usually did. He would never reciprocate the attention, but he never pushed them off either.

I'm not stupid; he's a good-looking man with his blond hair that always has a bit of curl at the end of the longer strands. I remember the first time I realized I felt something for him that went beyond friendship. How it wasn't something I'd felt before, though I recognized it all the same. I also remember thinking that my attraction didn't matter because he was a brother, over a decade older than me, and had no problem attracting other women. More experienced women. Women who weren't damaged like me. What could he possibly see in me other than the broken girl he'd sort of taken under his wing?

That's when I discovered how much wine helped numb those feelings—all of my feelings.

I'd gone to Ayre because there were ingredients that our local market hadn't stocked, and I needed them for the turnovers I was planning to make. As I was heading back to Shine—having learned to drive and been given my own car by Lucy only six months prior—I saw the sign for an old quarry and an arrow pointing down a gravel road off the highway. I'd passed it plenty of times, but never thought much of it. On a whim, I took a right.

When the trees opened up to a vast empty space surrounded by the gravel ground, I stopped my car and got out, walking to the edge and peered down into a deep, wide hole. Jagged rocks jutted around the sides of the giant pit. Looking over the edge was almost dizzying. If anyone fell into that thing, they'd never be able to get out.

It was silent. Completely empty. The place looked as though no one had been out here in years. I went back to my car and grabbed my bottle of wine, sat down at the edge of the pit, dangling my legs over the side, and unscrewed the cap.

From that day forward, the quarry became my place, my refuge. I never saw signs of anyone else, and I would go out there often. Probably too often, seeing as Lucy had mentioned me disappearing all the time. I'd bring a bottle of whatever I was in the mood for out here. I would drink, talk to myself, scream into the void, or sometimes sit and cry. It depended on my mood. But out there, I could do it freely. Then I would lay in my car for a while, sober up a bit, and when I felt up to it, would drive myself home.

And that was the extent of my existence for seven months.

About six months ago, I saw a flyer at one of the liquor stores I would frequent. Every time I would leave with a bottle or two—okay, three—my eyes would catch on the flyer advertising a self-defense course. It had these little pull tabs with a phone number. A few were ripped off. My fingers itched to take the phone number. To do something that would help me grow stronger, help me focus some of the rage I carried that, until that point, was only expelled at the quarry.

My sister often trains with her friends. They practice various martial arts, work out, and practice shooting at the outdoor range on the Black Roses property. She invited me along many times that first year. But I never took her up on it. Then after a while, she stopped asking. I never asked to go with her, though I liked the idea of training my body to get stronger, so that I'd never find myself in the position of being weak and unable to defend myself.

But one day, I tugged on that little scrap of paper and shoved it in my purse on my way out the door, with the bottles clanging in the bag as I made my way to the car.

It took me another month to call the number, and the warm voice of a woman answered on the third ring. I told her where I'd seen the flyer and that I was interested. She sounded pleased and didn't mention the shakiness in my voice. Her name was Monica and she said she was looking forward to meeting me. I couldn't remember the last time anyone told me that. *If* anyone ever told me that. My life had become so small. Until I called a number on that little piece of paper.

I shake my head to pull myself back into the present, turning into the parking lot of the small gym in a nondescript brick building. The gym is on the first floor. Monica lives on the second, where she also runs her nonprofit that helps place women in jobs or gives them training to get a job after leaving an abusive situation.

The first time I met Monica, I told her I was from Shine. She was familiar with the shelter and the work Matilda, the woman who ran the place, did there. I told her my sister helped out there sometimes. Jude and Lucy actually teach self-defense to the women at the shelter once a week. I would usually send something I baked with Lucy for the women there who came from the compound, but I only went to visit a few times. I was never close with the women at the compound. I was the wife of the man who doled out their punishments or their redemption, depending on his mood.

The three times I went with my sister, none of the women were particularly warm to me. It was almost as though they were still scared that Otto was there waiting in the wings, and seeing me only compounded that fear. I wouldn't exactly be excited to have me around after escaping that hell either. They had each other, and Matilda was helping them get on their feet. And I was happy for them.

Monica looked at me, and it felt like she could see right into my heart. Did she know who I was? Did she know I was one of the women who escaped the hell of living in a cult? Could she tell that the years of torment and abuse had warped the good parts of me into something twisted and ugly?

If she did, she didn't say anything or give me any sort of pitying look. She simply smiled and asked if I was ready to jump in. And that was that—until a little over six weeks ago. I couldn't stomach the idea of being around anyone. Of anyone seeing the mess I had turned into. The hole I was slipping into with each passing day. A hole I refused to pull myself out of. But I know sitting in my room or raging at the quarry isn't going to do me any good. It may be a small start, but being here with people who know what it's like to feel helpless at the hands of another person is a good place to begin. They don't know my family and have never met the brothers. Here I'm simply Cece. I can just be a woman who wants to learn how to defend herself. How to become stronger.

"Hey there. Long time," Monica says when I walk through the door.

I smile—my first genuine one in weeks—and slide my bag into one of the cubbies next to her desk.

"Yeah, I had some family things to take care of the last few weeks," I reply.

"Everything okay?" Her deep-brown eyes fill with concern.

"Good as can be right now." It's as close to the truth as I'm willing to get.

She smiles and nods toward the other girls warming up on the mat. "They've missed you. And your cookies," she says in a husky laugh.

My lips tip up in a grin. "I'll bring some next time." I was too upset and in too much of a rush when I left today after my showdown with Cash and forgot the box on the countertop at home.

Walking over to the other women, I sit down on the mat and start stretching with them. I look around and see one of the women missing.

"Where's Thea?" I ask the group.

"She's in the hospital. Her ex found her. Broken nose, orbital, and three cracked ribs," one of the other girls, Leandra, answers. Thea and Leandra are cousins, and Leandra is the one who brought Thea into the group.

I look around and see the faces of the other four women fall. Two look angry, and the other two look ready to cry. But all of them, including myself, know that it's a possibility. Maybe even only a matter of time. The justice system does fuck all to protect women, and considering Thea's ex works as a prison guard...yeah, needless to say, he's never been held accountable.

"Is he in jail?" I ask Leandra.

She scoffs. "Was. For about five seconds." She shakes her head and hops off the mat. "Come on. I need to beat some shit."

All of us rise from the mats. Two of the girls grab giant pads that cover their bodies and a huge, cushioned helmet. One of the girls dons the gear and the other starts practicing her moves as the other girl attacks her. There have been a few times that Monica has had a man come in and wear the padding so we could practice on someone larger, but I'm glad he's not here today. Two other girls head over to the corner and start practicing some form of martial arts similar to what my sister is adept at. Leandra is at the boxing dummy, working out her anger one resounding kick and punch at a time.

When I walk over to Leandra, she already has a slight sheen of sweat covering her forehead and dripping from her hairline, the long dark locks tied in a haphazard bun behind her head.

"I'm sorry about Thea. How is she holding up?" I ask as Leandra uses a combo, punching the dummy in the ribs three times, then in the throat.

"She's scared. She's mad. I think she's going to run. Her parents live in Virginia, and they've been begging her to come home since the first time he landed her in the ER." She throws another punch and a double kick to the dummy. "She's having surgery tomorrow on her eye. Her fucking eye." Leandra punches the dummy again in the face. "Fuck!" She steps back from the dummy, crossing her arms over her head and turning away from me.

I take that as a sign that she's done for the moment and needs a second to collect herself. I can relate.

I start landing a series of punches and kicks that I've learned here. We're taught to incapacitate an attacker so we can run. But I'm so sick of running. I want to do real damage to men who hurt women. Something that will make them think twice about touching someone when they don't have permission.

Blow after blow, kick after kick. Every second of the kidnapping replays in my head. I couldn't do anything that night. They had Colby. They were threatening to hurt him if I didn't comply. He struggled, I struggled, those assholes hurt Pepper, Wyatt's dog. When Pepper attacked one of the Bone Breakers, the dog took a chunk out of the man's arm. But the second they held a gun to Colby, I was done.

When that piece of shit had me under him in the motel, it was everything I could do not to struggle. He allowed me to lock Colby in the bathroom so he wouldn't have to witness what was about to go down. The bastard was going to leave him in the corner while he took a piece of my flesh like his brothers had done when I lived on the compound. Then Cash and the rest of the brothers stormed in before he could get my shorts down my legs and shot the asshole. But Cash saw. He saw what that awful man was going to do. Saw what men like him had done so many times before.

Tears leak out of my eyes as sweat drips down my face, mixing together. Punch after punch, I think about the things I could have done to him, think about the ways I wish I could have made him bleed. But my priority was Colby and getting him out alive. As for me? In that moment, I couldn't have cared less if I lived or died as long as he was safe.

"When Thea was at the hospital getting X-rays in the ER, the nurse had some interesting information," Leandra says as she walks up behind me. "She said she'd been on shift a couple of times when Thea was brought in. Asked me a bunch of questions. God, I was so pissed and scared." Leandra shakes her head. "Anyways, the nurse said she knew someone who might be able to help. Someone who 'handles' men like her ex. She gave me a phone number."

I'm not clueless when it comes to people breaking the law to save someone. That's how I got out of the cult, after all.

"Have you called?"

Leandra shakes her head. "Thea refused, and I didn't want to push. At least not yet." She pins me with her gaze. "Thea used to disappear for weeks at a time after her boyfriend had a 'bad night.' Then she'd show back up and tell all of our friends she had family stuff to take care of. Only problem was, I was family and knew she was lying. I overheard you telling Monica why you've been MIA." She shoots me a pointed look. "Here's his number." She slips a piece of paper from her pocket and squeezes it into my hand. "Just in case."

I open my mouth to argue, but Leandra shakes her head. "What we learn here is great, but sometimes you need more than getting away. Sometimes you need them to bleed, too."

Leandra steps away from me and grabs her towel. "I'm going to go visit Thea. See you soon." She waves at the other girls and walks out of the gym as I slide the paper into my pocket.

God, I wish I would have made them bleed that night. The men who kidnapped us were taken care of, though I'm not exactly sure what happened to Nolan. There's no doubt in my mind that he's dead. After what he put

Maizie and Colby through, I hope it was painful and slow. I begin hitting the dummy again—this time with a smile on my face. The thought of Nolan brutally losing his life is one of the only things that makes me smile these days, and I wonder, for the hundredth time, what that says about me—and why I don't really care.

Hours pass between punching the dummy and doing some light sparring and tumbling with the rest of the girls. It's dark by the time I leave the gym, and I already have three messages from Lucy asking where I'm at.

Me: *Be home soon.*

Lucy: *Where are you?*

I don't want to answer that question, so I toss my phone onto the seat next to me and back out of the parking spot to head home. Ayre is about thirty minutes from Shine. I'm sure Lucy will be fine waiting a few minutes if she texts again.

Thoughts of Thea and the kidnapping tumble through my head. This is the time of day the demons like to infiltrate. When the sun is just about to set, and there's nothing but darkness for the next several hours. This is the time when I start getting antsy. When the world quiets, the memories scream at me.

I pull up to a red light and look to my right, seeing the neon sign of a bar I've passed dozens of times. *Lottie's Tavern.* I didn't have one drink yesterday and told myself I would never get behind the wheel of my car drunk like I did the other night. I told myself I wasn't going to use alcohol as a crutch anymore.

But fuck, I can't stop staring at that damn sign.

Before I can give it more thought, my car turns right, and I pull into the parking lot of the small bar. I won't get drunk. Have maybe one or two then head home. My hair is a ratty mess in a high ponytail, and I'm wearing a pair of shorts and a baggy T-shirt. Judging from the outside, though, this place doesn't exactly scream *dress to impress*.

When I open the door, the inside is dark with low lighting coming from the tile ceiling. A few neon signs litter the walls. An old jukebox sits in the corner, but no one is playing music.

I walk up to the bar, noticing the scarred laminate. Not real wood. Nothing like the bar that the Black Roses own in Shine, but no one knows me here. No one can judge my choices, or my scowl, or the million other little things about me that Lucy and everyone else seem intent on analyzing. Here, I'm just a woman having a drink.

"What can I get you?" the bartender asks as he looks me over, probably trying to gauge if I'm even old enough to be sitting in a bar.

"I'll take a light beer. Anything you have in a bottle." Looking around at the dingy carpet and the worn seats, I'm not sure that I would trust anything on tap.

He sets the beer in front of me, apparently deciding that he doesn't need my ID, and I take a long pull from the bottle. I'm not exactly a beer fan, but that's probably a good thing. If I don't like the taste, I'll be less likely to drink too much and have to pass out in my car for a few hours before driving home.

"I'll take a whiskey on the rocks as well," I say. Two drinks is my max.

The bartender sets the drink in front of me, and I hand him a couple bills before sipping the fiery liquid that burns its way down my throat, warming my belly. I don't like whiskey much either.

Some game is playing on the TV behind the bar. I stare at the screen, but I don't have the faintest idea of what's going on. My head is too busy thinking about Thea sitting in the hospital and the number Leandra shoved into my hand that's folded inside my pocket. Why wouldn't she want her cousin to get a hold of these guys? It doesn't sound like the law is going to take care of it for her, not as long as her ex is an insider.

There's one thing through this entire ordeal that I have been grateful for—that those men were taken care of at the compound and at the hotel. And I'm sure the rest of the Bone Breakers are in for a rude awakening at some point. They threatened the club, and if I know anything about the Black Roses, it's that there is no way that shit is going to fly. I don't hate the idea of vigilante justice. Hell, I'm more than okay with horrible men meeting the fate they deserve.

"Hey, honey. Haven't seen you here before," a man who looks to be somewhere in his fifties but is probably only in his forties says at my side.

I turn and give him a flat smile, and his eyes light up as his beady gaze rakes over my body. Disgust rolls through me at the way he's ogling what he probably deems as fresh meat.

"Just stopping in for a drink and to watch the game," I say, nodding toward the TV.

"Let me buy you one," he says, sitting next to me.

"No, thank you," I reply and turn away from him. It's not that I haven't been around men who I don't know in the last couple years. But it's usually in Shine where everyone knows who I am and who my family is. It gives me a certain amount of protection from unwanted advances—not that I go places where those advances would take place.

"Oh, come on. That game is a repeat anyway. I'm much more interesting," he says, and I ignore him. "Or maybe you're looking for something a little harder than that beer?"

"I'm not," I say without sparing him a glance.

"Then another shot won't hurt nothing," he says as the roughened pad of his finger skates up my arm.

I jump away from him and throw his hand off of me. "I said no," I yell and grab my purse from the back of the barstool before running out of the bar to my car. I drive a couple blocks, my body shaking so violently that I have to pull over to the side of the street. That man's touch, his sour breath too close to my face, the way he wouldn't take no for an answer...brought it all back. That asshole being on top of me, his rancid breath making it hard for me to breathe, the way I begged him to stop, and his laughter at my tears. It was too much.

I think about all the women who are hurt by men like him on a daily basis. All the ways the system that is supposed to protect us fails us every damn day. Then I remember the phone number in my pocket. I don't need anyone to take care of the people who brutalized me. Most of them have been taken care of. But what if I want to be the one who takes care of *them*? What if I want to be the one to make all the others hurt and bleed like they've made so many others?

I grab the paper from my pocket and stare at the number for a moment. Then, before I can talk myself out of it, I pick up my phone and dial.

"This is Roman," a gruff male voice answers.

"Hi. I...uh...I got your phone number from a friend of mine. Thea." Partially true. That's who the number was meant for in the first place.

"Okay."

"I'd like to meet. To talk to you about something." What the hell am I even saying? What the hell am I even doing? There's no way this guy is going to meet with me. If what Leandra said is true, then he's not going to meet up with some random girl who calls him out of the blue, saying she got his number from a friend. It screams suspicious.

"I'll be at Delvines's Diner tomorrow. Back booth facing the front door. Say noon?"

My eyes widen, shocked that this is actually working—that this is actually happening.

"I'll be there," I say.

"Good. You got a name?"

"Cece. Cece Thomas."

"See you tomorrow, Cece." And he disconnects the call.

This is crazy. I'm crazy for even trying this. But goddammit, I'm so fucking tired of feeling powerless. The self-defense classes are great and all, but I don't want to just be able to fight someone off so I can run.

I don't want to run.

I want to make them bleed.

Chapter Four
Cash

I t's been two days since Red, the president of the Bone Breakers, texted Ozzy and threatened the club. There is no way he knows that we had anything to do with the death of his brothers. Not when they came to the clubhouse a couple years ago and tried to take Lucy, or when they were here six weeks ago in a failed attempt to use Maizie, Wyatt's old lady, to spy on the club. But even though Red is a fucking tweaker in the Arizona desert, he's not dumb enough to miss the fact that every time he sends a couple of his guys to Shine, they don't make it back.

Since the night of the kidnapping—when that dumb fuck Nolan got impatient and decided kidnapping Colby and Cece would get him what he wanted faster—we've all been on edge. Red wants a fight. Maybe retribution.

The fight is something we're more than willing to give.

Retribution? He won't find that.

Add in the shit with Cece showing up at Elaine's, drunk off her ass, and the fight we had yesterday—my brain is fried. But we need to figure out this Bone Breakers shit before they come after anyone else in our club. Seems those assholes like to go after those they deem weaker. Though they certainly missed the mark when they went after Lucy. Even if Jude hadn't shown up in the middle of the attack, we probably would've still been clearing her house of the three dead Bone Breakers.

Me and the rest of my brothers file into church. Ozzy called early this morning and was on the same page as the rest of us. We need to get a plan together. It's not enough to pick off those assholes a few at a time. We need to take out that whole damn club. They've decided to make us enemy number one, so the way we see it, turnabout is fair play.

Ozzy bangs the gavel, and we all quiet down, turning our attention to our president.

"Time to come up with a plan. Red has decided he doesn't need proof that we were involved with his brothers' deaths a couple years ago. He seems to want an all-out war, and I want a strategic attack."

"Like what we did in Nevada?" Jude asks.

"That's what I was thinking. We go in and don't leave a trace of any of those assholes behind," Ozzy replies.

"My brother said he and his guys will take care of the Bone Breakers. Free of charge, even. Little Bit is family, after all," Jude starts, shooting Ozzy a grin. Liam likes to think Ozzy owes him favors. What Liam should be thankful for is the fact that Ozzy hasn't fed Liam to the pigs. "Told him I would bring it to you."

"Absolutely not," I say. "This is our business, and we'll handle it."

Like hell am I going to give Liam the opportunity to act out my revenge. Cece—or Little Bit, as Jude and Liam like to call her—may be their family, but it doesn't sit right to let him take care of this for us—for *me*. I'll call dibs if I fucking have to.

"I had no problem with his assistance when we got Lucy from that cult, or for him helping with the Nolan situation, but Cash is right. This is MC business, and we'll take the lead on it. Everyone agree?" Ozzy looks around the room, and every single one of my brothers nods their head—even Jude.

"I told the wanker as much, but he made me promise to make the offer."

"Now if he feels so inclined to give us a helping hand, I don't think any of us would say no," Ozzy says.

"He and his team are out of the country for about another month," Jude says. "But I know he wants to be a part of this. Cece is his little sister. Well, sort of. It would be weird if she actually were."

Linc, who is sitting next to him, rolls his eyes. "We get what you're saying, numbnuts."

Lucy is as good as Jude's wife, at least in our world, though I anticipate they'll officially tie the knot at some point. Or maybe not. Who the hell knows with those two. But that means Lucy is family to Liam, and by extension, so is Cece.

"Which government are they overthrowing this week?" Barrett, our road captain, jokes, and we all chuckle.

Jude's brother, Liam, runs a company with several other former military and paramilitary friends he's met through his years of service in the Royal Marines. Even Jude served for several years before following his brother to the States and meeting Ozzy in a bar in Boston. No one knows everything Liam and his team have been involved in, but that man has toys we could only dream of and is owed favors by some of the most powerful people in the world.

"He didn't specify. Just said *Don't believe everything you see on the news*," Jude replies.

Jesus Christ.

"I, for one, would be perfectly happy waiting for Liam to get back. It gives us time to prepare. But I don't want to wait too long. It gives the Bone Breakers the opportunity to make their way out here again," Wyatt says.

When we found his boy and Cece in that dingy motel, he made sure Colby's biological father didn't make it out alive. It's really something what a man in love will do for his woman and the son he took on. It was a thing of beauty, if I'm honest. Frankly, I wouldn't mind giving Red, or any of those other fucks, the same treatment. Not that Cece is mine. But it's also not like I've wondered what would've happened if I met her under normal circumstances. If we weren't who we are. She would still be far too young for me, but I don't know that it would be enough to stop me.

There's a softness to her that I've never had before. A sweetness. Or there used to be. Not as much anymore, at least not toward me. But honestly, I don't hate it. Sure, I wish she wasn't shutting me out, but that girl needed to get mad, and I respect her for it. No one can walk through life with the rage she felt weighing on her and not be somehow affected.

"I thought of that when he brought it up," Jude starts. "Sawyer has someone working under him now, and Liam has tasked him with making his full-time job keeping an eye on the Bone Breakers. Basically, that means he's hacked into everyone's phone and transmitted location software onto their devices without them knowing anything or being able to tell, not that they have a tech guy who is able to catch that shit anyways. He gets an alert sent to his phone if any of those fucks walk outside of a fifty-mile radius of their clubhouse."

My eyebrows shoot up in surprise right along with the rest of my brothers. Sawyer is Liam's tech guy, and if I thought about it too much, knowing what that guy can do with a few computer keystrokes would keep me up at night.

"Not gonna lie, Jude. Your brother terrifies me a little," Knox jokes.

"At least he's on our side," Jude says with a smile.

"We still have the problem of not knowing who the hell Red's been working with to get info on us," Braxton says.

"They can't possibly know anything useful, otherwise Nolan wouldn't have pulled his shit," I say.

Ozzy nods. "I've put out a few feelers around town, and Finn has been quietly asking around Boston since Nolan mentioned the Monaghans. So far, we haven't come up with anything." He looks around the room at all of us sitting at the table where his grandfather used to sit with his closest brothers and have these same discussions. "Look, we've had plenty of other clubs and organizations try to weasel their way into Shine throughout the years. But none of them have made it very far. You know why? Because while they're fighting for money and greed, we fight for family. They have limits. When someone threatens our family or our people, we have none. I don't love some unknown threat lurking around, but until they scurry out of the dark like the cockroaches they are, we sit tight and handle our most pressing problem, which is the Bone Breakers."

"We'll have them buried in no time, Prez," Braxton says across from me. Like the rest of us, our sergeant at arms isn't afraid to get his hands dirty any time it's needed. Especially when it comes to assholes who threaten our people.

"Let's put it to a vote. All those in favor of waiting until Liam gets back then heading out to Arizona to put those bastards six feet under where they belong, say *aye*."

Every brother yells the word while pounding their fists on the table.

"Ayes have it," Knox says with a wide smile.

Ozzy pounds the gavel, and we all get up from our seats to head out to the main room now that church is over.

"Cash, hold up," Ozzy says as the guys file out.

He waits for the room to clear before sitting back down, and I take a seat next to him.

"Heard you went to talk to Cece the other day. How's she doing?" he asks.

I frown. "Why aren't you asking Jude? He lives with her."

"Because I'm asking you, asshole. I've seen how close you two have become over the last couple of years. I don't think she talks with Jude like she talks with you. And vice versa."

I scrub a hand over my face. Fuck, I hate being asked about Cece. But this is my prez, and it's not like I can deflect his questions, even though I want to brush it off with a joke.

"She's not doing great. She's shutting everyone out, including me. I was hoping if I got her alone, she would be honest with me, but she shot me down."

"The Thomas sisters aren't exactly known for being open and communicative," Ozzy says.

"True. But we were different. Cece was different with me."

"How different?" Ozzy raises a brow, obviously thinking there are things I'm not telling him.

"Not like that. I would never—"

"Treat her how she deserves to be treated? Listen to her with an open mind? Be a calming presence in her life when she feels nothing but chaos?" Ozzy's eyebrows are raised in question, though it seems as though he already knows the answer.

I stare at him wide-eyed, finally allowing my eyes to blink after a few silent moments.

"Who the hell are you, and what have you done with my prez?" I ask, only half joking.

"I'm your prez, but I'm Freya's husband. Or *almost* husband. I know a thing or two about being a partner to someone who lives in chaos. Different kind, but there have been plenty of times I've had to be Freya's calm, especially when she was in the middle of her case against Cataldi." The two have been engaged for quite some time, but neither seems to be in too much of a hurry to walk down the aisle. "Don't think I haven't seen the way you're attuned to her at parties. At the slightest hint of anything uncomfortable for her, the two of you disappear."

"Crowds can be tough for her sometimes, and she doesn't like relying on her sister for every little thing. Her words, not mine."

"No. But neither of you has a problem with her relying on you."

"*Relied.* Past tense," I grumble.

"And you fucking hate it," Ozzy surmises from my tone.

"Yeah, I do."

He tilts his head, studying me. "Have you thought about telling her how you feel?"

"I did. I told her that I wished she would talk to me. Let me help her."

My prez scoffs at me. "Not that part, dumbass."

My brow crinkles. I'm not understanding what the hell he's talking about.

Ozzy shakes his head. "When she came here, you were both going through a lot. We'd just lost Cooper, and I know that shit hit you hard. The kid grew up with you. You felt a responsibility toward him, probably more so than the rest of us. Cece had just come from that nightmare in the desert. Both of you needed the quiet the other offered. The peace. There was a time I thought you were going to claim her. And then..."

"She got fucking pissed and pushed everyone away. Eventually even me," I finish.

"So what are you going to do about it?" he asks, cocking his head to the side.

"Not much I can do. Can't exactly force her to do something she doesn't want to," I reply.

"I must have got it wrong then." Ozzy shrugs and stands, walking out the door to leave me with my thoughts.

Claim Cece? I have no idea what would have given him that impression. Were there times I thought about what it would be like to hold her in my arms and trail my lips over all of her smooth, silky skin? Sure. Plenty of times, if I'm honest. I may have even envisioned what her pale-blonde hair would feel like wrapped in my fist as I claim her mouth a time or two...hundred. But that doesn't mean I can act on it. She's Lucy's little sister—and she's been through hell. She needs to get her bearings, and that doesn't include a biker more than ten years older than her forcing himself into her life.

I rise from the table and head into the main room of the clubhouse, spotting Linc and Jude sitting at the bar while Barrett and Braxton are playing a game of pool. Ozzy must have headed to his office to go through the mounds of paperwork on his desk.

Waving to the brothers, I head outside to my bike just as Wyatt starts his.

"Where you headed?" I ask as he pulls up next to me.

"Maizie has work, so I'm going home to hang with Colby," he answers.

Cece used to watch Colby on the nights Maizie worked. But she hasn't been over there in weeks now.

"Alright, brother. See you later," I say, and Wyatt nods then heads toward the gate where the prospect is opening it for him.

Climbing on my bike, I start the engine with no particular destination in mind, just a need to get out on the open road for a few hours. I head out of the clubhouse parking lot and take off in the opposite direction from town. This used to be the direction I would take when

Cece would need to get out on the bike. I liked the fact that she called me to help her turn her brain off. Really liked it.

And fuck, I miss it.

The sun is beating down on my back as I wind through the country roads outside of town. These late summer days are hot as hell. Before long, I find myself at a crossroads. If I turn left, the road will take me back to the clubhouse. Right takes me to a little house I bought a few years ago.

I turn right.

When I pull onto the long drive, I slow my bike, not wanting to kick up too many rocks. Though I've owned the house for over three years, I've never moved in. Cooper and I were fixing it up after having bought it at an auction. The house sat empty for a few years, so there was a lot of work to be done. Cooper and I tackled the project together, but I was never sure if it was going to be somewhere I'd settle in. I'd planned to let Coop and his sister, Nova, live in the house when he patched in, which would've absolutely happened before he was shot trying to protect Lucy. His plan was to bring Nova up here once he started making some "real money," as he liked to call it. Not sure if she would have gone for it, but it gave him something more to look forward to.

I walk up the stairs of the two-story white farmhouse to the wraparound porch. Cooper used to talk about how great the porch would look once everything was sanded and finished. We were about halfway through before his death, and I haven't done any work on it since. I only come out here about once a month to check on things and make sure no animals have made their homes inside the house.

When I open the front door, the air is stale, so I keep it open, thankful that one of the first things we replaced in the house was the screen door. Heading into the kitchen, my gaze catches on the new appliances still sitting in the middle of the room in their packaging.

I had every intention of offering the house to Nova when Cooper died, but when I called her, she made it clear as day that she wanted no part of the Black Roses or me. For nearly two years, she blamed the club for Cooper's death. Hell, I blamed myself, so I wasn't exactly in a position to argue with her.

Walking over to the tap, I turn on the water. I've kept the utilities of the house turned on, even though I don't spend any time here. I've always had the intention of coming back and finishing the work Cooper and I started, but it's hardly been a priority. Maybe I should change that. At least get it in good enough condition to sell and buy something closer to town.

I turn the tap off and walk into the empty living room and look over the papers strewn across the card table I'd set up in here. Lists and invoices, paint swatches and carpeting, and hardwood samples for flooring. Cooper used to joke that I would have made one hell of an interior designer in another life.

A smile tips the corner of my mouth as I remember the way he loved to give me a hard time, like the little brother I considered him to be. I always got him back, though, especially after a clubhouse party. We aren't the kind of assholes who don't let prospects party with us—as long as they're taking care of the brothers and the women. But there were plenty of times Cooper would stumble into the kitchen after a night of hard drinking, and I'd immediately hand him a broom and mop with a smirk on my face. The kid never complained, though. It was part of his initiation, and he wanted to be a brother more than anything.

"Fuck," I breathe out as thoughts of the scene we rode up to after the shooting play through my head. The car was flipped over, and Cooper was lying in the driver's seat with a bullet hole through his head.

"Fuck!" I scream and swipe my arm across the table, sending papers and samples flying.

I look down and see the corner of a picture. Bending to pick it up, I see it's of me and Cooper when he first got to Shine. We're standing in front of the bike I was helping him rebuild. The kid was a wiz on a dirt bike and used to ride that around when he was younger and living in Louisiana. When I'd come back home for a visit, he'd show me some hunk of junk he'd scrounged up and gotten running. He was a natural mechanic. But this was his first "real" bike. He was so damn proud that he found it for a steal. I don't remember who took the picture, but I remember being happy that he was up here with me and my brothers. I was thrilled that I was able to help out a kid from my hometown find a place in this world.

Then it all went to shit.

And nothing has felt right—felt settled—since.

There were a few moments when the pain didn't feel like it was burning itself into my soul. That was when I spent time with Cece, but that hasn't been the case for the last several weeks. Ozzy was right when he said we found peace in being alone with each other. There was a comfort in her presence that calmed the chaos in me. The same way I hoped I did for her. But her chaos has exploded and is out of control now, and no matter what I do, I can't seem to help her through it this time.

CHAPTER FIVE
CECE

This is the first time in years that I've woken up with a sense of purpose. A sense of finally doing something that will channel all of this rage that's been festering inside me.

It's not enough for me to be happy that I got away from abusive men. It's not enough to be grateful, even though I am. I need to *do* something. I need to make a difference, even if it's not in a particularly conventional way. As soon as the thought popped into my head, I knew it was the right path for me.

No one knows. No one *can* know. My sister and everyone else will try to talk me out of it, but all these years later and this is the only thing that makes me feel like I'm finally healing. Finally able to move past the pain and into something else.

Revenge.

I want to—no, *need* to—get revenge for the women who have found themselves in similar situations to mine. Women who were brutalized over and over by violent men. I want to become the nightmare they were to the women they hurt.

Walking out of my room, I head into the kitchen and find my sister sipping coffee at the kitchen table.

She looks up with surprise written across her face. "You're up early."

Lucy and I haven't talked much since we argued the other day. We've settled back into the status quo of talking without really *talking*. I can't blame her. With everyone else, she's a ballbuster and honest to the point of almost being offensive. Basically, she's never been one to keep her mouth shut, at least since she left the cult. But with me, she tiptoes, except for the argument the morning after I showed up drunk at Elaine's.

Part of me was pissed as hell. But after sitting with it for a couple days, I'm almost glad she didn't pull any punches. I didn't ask to be treated with kid gloves, and actually, I'd prefer not to be.

Remembering the look on Colby's face still plays through my mind. The way I felt when the kid I loved so much was scared of me. I can blow off everyone else. I suppose I've done that to an extent with Colby these last few weeks, too. It was so easy hanging out with him. All he wanted was a friend, someone he could go to the park with and draw pictures with. He looked at me at Elaine's like he didn't trust me anymore—like he didn't recognize me. I think part of me was scared I'd see that expression on his face after the kidnapping. I was the one who couldn't protect him, after all. But this time it was my actions that put that look on his face. There are many reasons I called Roman last night, but remembering the way Colby's sad eyes looked at me is at the top of that list.

"I have a few things to do today and wanted to get an early start," I say while I pour myself a cup of coffee.

"About the other day..."

"I don't really want to talk about it. Things haven't been...easy. Especially after the kidnapping. I also know things have been difficult for a lot longer than that." I sip my coffee and lean against the counter.

"If you ever want to talk about it. About everything that happened—"

"I don't," I say, cutting her off, and she shuts her mouth, her lips forming a thin line. "Listen, I get that you want to help, and I get I haven't made it easy on you lately. But I'm handling it. The other night made me realize that I'm only hurting myself and the people I care about. And honestly, I'm tired of being hurt. Nothing is going to change the past, but I'm moving on. The anger isn't getting me anywhere, so I'm letting it go." And giving myself a new purpose. Finding retribution for my pain by making other assholes pay for the pain they put other people through.

"Moving on..." She looks out the window. "To where exactly?" she asks, turning her gaze back to mine.

I shrug. "Not sure exactly." Completely untrue. "But it won't involve drinking myself to death."

Lucy nods and exhales a long breath out her nose. "That's...that's good."

I can tell she's unsure, that she wants to ask questions, but doesn't want to push too hard. Which is fine by me. She wouldn't understand what I'm doing or why I need to do this, especially without asking for her help.

Actually, knowing my sister, she probably would, but she'd also try to stop me, and that isn't going to happen.

"I just want to make sure that you know you're safe. And that I'm here for you," Lucy says.

I scoff. "Safe? Are any of us ever really safe?"

"Cece—"

"I have to go," I say, cutting her off again. I don't need Lucy to worry about my *safety*. If I've learned anything, it's just an illusion that people try to comfort themselves with, at least in my experience.

I turn and pour the rest of my coffee into a travel mug. "I'll see you later," I say, then grab my purse and walk out the door.

As I'm driving to Ayre to meet Roman, I pass the park and spot Maizie and Wyatt sitting on one of the benches. I stop at the stop sign and catch Colby running around with a couple of other kids whose parents are sitting on a bench a few spots over. These are his usual park friends that he's spent many afternoons playing with at the playground while Cash and I sat on a bench like Maizie and Wyatt are. Well, maybe not *exactly* the same. Cash never had his arm around me while I cuddled into his side like they are now.

God, I miss him. Colby, not Cash. Actually, that's not entirely true, but that's a problem for another day.

Colby never failed to bring a smile to my face when I watched him for Maizie, and it breaks my heart that he thinks he did something wrong and that's why I never babysit him anymore.

I make a split-second decision, and instead of driving away, I pull into the small parking lot and get out of my car.

"Hey," I say as I walk up to Maizie and Wyatt.

"Hey, Cece," Wyatt says with a smile on his face.

Maizie greets me also, but her smile is tighter than her man's.

Colby sees me and runs over, throwing his arms around my waist.

"Cece! I missed you," he exclaims, smiling up at me with one of his front teeth missing.

I wrap my arms around his shoulders and squeeze him into my middle. "Hey, buddy. I've missed you too. I see you lost a tooth."

He opens his mouth wider to show me. "Yup. It was real loose, and Wyatt said we should tie a string around it and shoot it out of my mouth with one of my pretend guns. Mom, show her the video." He grabs my hand and pulls me to the other side of Maizie.

His mom grabs her phone and cues up the video with Colby practically vibrating next to me with excitement.

I hear Maizie's voice on the video saying, "I can't believe I'm letting you do this." There's a smile in her voice that brings one to my face.

"It's going to be awesome, Maiz," Wyatt says, smiling into the camera. "Ready, Colby?"

I watch his little head nod as he holds the toy gun, his mouth wide with a string hanging from the tooth attached to the foam bullet.

"One, two, three." Wyatt counts down, but Colby doesn't move.

"I was a little scared," Colby says, sitting next to me, his whole body nearly draped across my lap as we watch the video together.

"You don't have to do it, buddy," I hear Maizie say behind the phone.

In the video, Colby looks at her, then to Wyatt, takes a deep breath and nods. "I'm ready," he says, trying not to move his mouth and dislodge the string around the tooth.

"Okay, I'll count down again. Let her rip on three, okay?" Wyatt asks and Colby nods.

"One, two, three."

This time, Colby squeezes the trigger, and the tooth flies out of his mouth. The three of them cheer, and Colby runs to find the tooth on the ground before holding it up triumphantly.

"See. I was brave the second time. And it didn't even hurt," Colby says, looking up at me.

"You are so brave, buddy," I say, looking down into his smiling eyes. "Did the tooth fairy come?"

Colby jumps up from his seat next to me. "Yup. I got ten whole dollars." He pulls the bill out of his pocket and displays it proudly.

I look at Maizie, who has a wide smile on her face. "The tooth fairy never left me ten dollars." She shoots Wyatt a knowing grin.

He shrugs and shoots her a wink. "Inflation, baby."

I chuckle as Colby shoves the money back in his pocket.

"Okay, monkey. Why don't you go play with your friends some more before I have to go get ready for work," Maizie says.

Colby nods then turns to me. "Will you come to the park again and play with me?"

Damn if that isn't a gut punch.

I smile at him, even though his unsure expression makes me want to break down in tears.

"Of course, I will," I say around the lump in my throat. "I think I need another big hug before you go play, though."

Colby grins and practically throws himself at me, his little arms going around my neck and squeezing tightly.

"You give the best hugs," I tell him.

"I know. Mommy says the same thing," he tells me before pulling away. "See you later, Cece."

Colby runs back to the slide and climbs up the ladder, patiently waiting for his turn.

"He's really missed you," Maizie says. "You know, he blamed you not coming around on himself. He was worried he didn't protect you, and you were mad at him."

I lower my head, the lump from earlier feeling as though it's doubled in size. When I look back at Maizie, there are tears in my eyes as she holds my gaze. Her eyes soften, seeing how torn up I am about hurting her son.

"Lucy told me that. I can't tell you how sorry I am that I disappointed him or made him feel like me disappearing for a while was ever his fault. There was so much going on in my head after the kidnapping. So many memories and thoughts taking up all the space in my brain," I tell her as one tear tracks down my cheek. "It was never because of him."

Maizie reaches over and places her hand over mine that rests in my lap. "I know." She releases a humorless laugh. "Jesus, even when Nolan isn't around anymore, he can sure fuck up people's lives." Maizie squeezes my hand. "How are you doing now?"

I blow out a breath. "Not great. But I'm working on it."

Maizie lifts her brows and nods. "I get it. We all love you, Cece. We just want to help you however we can."

Hearing the same sentiment from my sister tends to grate on my nerves, but Maizie is different. I'm not sure how or why, but when she says it, I don't feel pressure to show her that I'm fine and moving past...everything.

"You know, I bet if you went and talked to Betsy, she'd still want you to sell your bread and pastries at the coffee shop. I don't know, maybe it will give you something to focus on other than..." She glances at Wyatt, unsure how to say what she really wants to.

"Getting drunk and making an ass out of yourself in public," he finishes for her.

"Wyatt," Maizie admonishes, her eyes going round as saucers.

"What?" the biker asks. "There's no point in beating around the bush. It's not like Lucy probably hasn't already handed her ass to her."

"You're right," I say. I could be offended by the way he callously described the other night, but it's the truth, and if there's one thing I appreciate about all the brothers, it's that they don't mince words. "Drinking to cover how I was feeling wasn't working. For anyone."

"Good," Wyatt says. "Maybe let Cash know, too."

My head rears back. "What does Cash have to do with anything?"

"He cares about you. Not in the same way the rest of us do, either."

Maizie smacks Wyatt in the chest and shakes her head. "Don't listen to him. He thinks he's some relationship guru now."

"I know a thing or two," he gripes.

"Anyways," she says, shooting Wyatt a look. I've seen Lucy give Jude the same look. It means there's going to be a private conversation later. "You should give Betsy a call. I really think it would be good for you, and I know it would help her out. She always says she's going to retire early just so she can sleep in."

I smile, remembering all the times I've heard Betsy make that joke. Before the kidnapping, I had every intention of calling her and talking to her about selling some of my baked goods in her shop. But after? Nope. I'm not going backward. Not anymore.

"I'll give her a call." I check the time on my phone. Though I left the house early, I need to get on the road so I can meet Roman. "Next time you come to the park, I'd love it if you gave me a call...if you want," I finish, feeling suddenly unsure that Maizie even wants me around Colby anymore. "I meant what I said. I really want to spend time with Colby again, if that's okay with you."

Maizie smiles as she stands and wraps her arms around me. "Of course it is."

I squeeze her back, and when we separate, Maizie has a much warmer smile on her face than she did when I first got here.

"I'll see you soon," she says.

I turn toward Colby, who is excitedly chatting with one of his friends. Colby has always been animated and open with the other kids at the park. To see he's still the same way, even after what we went through, fills me with a relief I didn't know I needed.

"Bye, Colby," I call to him, and he turns toward me and waves his little arm over his head before returning to his conversation.

I face Maizie and Wyatt. "I'll see you later," I say, then head to my car, my eyes filling with tears, but this time it's because I'm happy. Colby is okay, and the guilt I didn't realize I was carrying around is alleviated. He was taken while he was with me. I couldn't protect him; I wasn't strong enough. I couldn't save us.

But if I have it my way, that's all going to change.

When I walk into the diner, I stand at the front, looking around at the customers. There's a couple in a booth by the window, smiling at each other. An older man sits at the long counter, sipping his coffee, and a mom with two kids sits in another booth.

Looking toward the back of the diner, I spot a man with salt-and-pepper hair. He's sitting with his back against the wall but in full view of the front door, with his gaze trained on me. His black T-shirt stretches across his muscular shoulders and biceps. His eyes hold that certain something I see in the men in the club. It's a look of quiet confidence and a soul-deep surety that they can handle themselves in any situation. There's no doubt this is the man I'm here to meet.

Roman stands as I walk toward him. He's a giant wall of muscle, easily rivaling Braxton, the tallest of all the brothers. Under normal circumstances, I would be terrified of someone of Roman's size. Especially if we weren't meeting in a bright diner in the middle of the day. But the closer I get, the more I realize that beneath his assured gaze lies a softness I didn't see at first. His mouth isn't pressed into a firm line, but a quiet smile. A smile that says he's had this conversation with women in my situation before and knows how to make himself look...not so scary and intimidating.

"Cece," he greets and holds out his hand. I slip mine into his, and he squeezes—not with a firm, controlled shake, but with a reassuring, light pressure. A soft greeting for someone who he assumes is here after being hurt by a man. That part is true, but I'm not here for him to take care of my problem for me. Just the opposite, in fact.

"Nice to meet you," I say, and he waves his hand toward the chair in front of him, gesturing for me to have a seat.

The waitress comes over with a pot of coffee. "You want something to drink, hon?"

I flip the white mug sitting on the table and smile at her. "Coffee would be great."

She pours, and before she leaves, she asks me if I'd like something to eat. I politely decline, and Roman eyes my slender frame.

"Not much of an appetite?" he asks.

I shake my head. "Nerves, I guess."

He nods his head with a knowing look in his brown eyes. "I get that. But you're safe here."

I can't help the scoff that comes from me. "Yeah, everyone keeps telling me that. But I think we both know that's not entirely true."

At that, his eyes narrow, a question in his gaze. "Why do you say that?"

"Is anybody ever really safe? I could walk out of here right now and get mugged. Or taken somewhere and have awful things done to my body just because I look a certain way, or because I remind some psycho of his ex-girlfriend. I could be stolen right off the street and sold to the highest bidder. Or shot on that same street because I was in the way of someone who someone else wanted dead." I shake my head. "No one is safe. Not really."

Roman sits back in his seat, his eyes widened in surprise. "That's a pretty sad way to look at the world."

I shrug. "It's realistic. And honest."

He tilts his head to the side as he continues to study me. "Why do I get the feeling this isn't the meeting I was expecting?"

"What exactly were you expecting?"

"Someone who needs something. Like a message sent to an ex that he'd better leave you alone—or else. That's what I usually do."

"Fight fire with fire?" I ask.

"Something like that. But you aren't screaming *abused woman who's looking for help to make sure her abusive ex never comes back into the picture.*"

"I'm not."

Roman crosses his arms over his wide chest. "So what are you here for, Cece Thomas?"

I lean forward and cross my arms on the table. "I'm going to tell you a little about me."

He waves his hand. "Please do."

"I didn't grow up around here. I was born outside a little town in Nevada, not too far from the Arizona border. But I didn't know exactly where I lived until I was much older."

His brow arches in silent question.

"I was born on a cult compound. My father was an elder. Well, not always. He gained his elder status after marrying me off to the much older cult leader. When I was sixteen."

Now, both of Roman's eyebrows are nearly touching his hairline as he blows out a deep breath. "Yeah. Not what I was expecting."

"I don't think most people would."

"Before you keep going, I think it's only fair to tell you that I looked into you, Cecilia Thomas, resident of Shine, Massachusetts. I found your school records. Elementary, junior high and high school. And your birth certificate and driver's license."

Roman looks at me as though I'm going to react as though I've been caught in a lie. But the lie is everything he found, courtesy of Liam, Jude's older brother.

"It's all fake," I tell him.

One brow arches in skepticism. "Come again?"

"Have you ever heard of the Ashcroft Agency?"

"Any relation to the Jude Ashcroft who you live with? If your address isn't fake, that is." He's wearing a small smirk now.

"His brother, actually. My sister ran away from the cult when she was seventeen. Was on the run until she hooked up with Jude. That's who got me out."

"I'd love to hear that story."

I shake my head. "I got out along with all the women and children. That's all I'm going to say." I'm not about to implicate my family in the mass murder of every abusive piece of shit who got what they deserved.

Roman nods. "I've heard of the Ashcroft Agency. Not much, but I know they do security-for-hire work. I also know that Jude Ashcroft runs with the Black Roses MC. Is one of them the reason you called me?"

"No," I reply, shaking my head. "I don't know what you know about motorcycle clubs, but trust me when I tell you, they aren't all the same. I've dealt with horrible ones. Ones who abuse women. My husband had dealings with one from Arizona. They often came to the compound to pick up the drugs that were made there. I was one of the 'perks' they got for helping the elders distribute those drugs to the outside world."

"Jesus," Roman breathes out, his gaze now filled with compassion for the living nightmare that is my past.

"The Black Roses are nothing like those monsters. Not even close. But in a way, they are why I contacted you."

Confusion creeps into his gaze. "I'm not sure I'm following…"

"Six weeks ago, the men from the MC in Arizona came to town. They took me and were going to abuse me like they had when I lived on the compound. They didn't get that far, but it was close. Too close."

Roman's jaw tightens. "Thank fuck they didn't. But I'm still confused about this meeting."

"I've been a mess since the kidnapping," I admit. "Scared of my own shadow. Angry. Angrier than I've ever been."

"I can imagine," he says with a hint of sympathy in his tone. I really fucking hate how it sounds coming from him.

"Then I went back to my self-defense class. That's when I learned one of the women had been hurt by her boyfriend. Well, ex now. Her cousin gave me your number, assuming that I'd gone through the same thing, and that's why I hadn't been around."

"A nurse friend of mine said I should be expecting a phone call," Roman says.

"Bet you didn't expect it to be me." A small chuckle escapes me.

"I can honestly say that so far, nothing about this meeting has been what I expected. I'm still not sure why you reached out in the first place."

"When she told me what you did, something clicked into place for me. It's not enough to go to classes and learn how to fight to get away. I want to learn how to fight back for the sole purpose of fighting back. To show men like my deceased husband and those other bikers what happens when you mess with someone who you think is weaker, only to find out that you picked the wrong woman to try to hurt. Or you hurt someone and now you have a price to pay. It sounded like you were in the business of collecting on their bad deeds."

Roman chuckles. "That's an interesting way of looking at it. Yeah, that's what we do."

"I want to do it, too. I want to be the one who makes them pay."

His eyes crinkle at the corners as he shakes his head. "Cece, I don't think you know what you're asking."

"I do," I answer firmly.

He nods and looks behind me, clearly mulling over what he's going to say next. "Okay, if that's what you want, why not go to the MC you're associated with? If they are who you say they are, talk to them about your idea. We could always use some extra help."

"I can't. The brothers are...protective. Too protective sometimes. My sister is involved with Jude, which is why I live with him, too. She remembers the girl she left all those years ago. I'm far from her. If I told her about this, she would try to talk me out of it. She doesn't understand. She still thinks she can keep me safe. Like I've told you, it's an illusion."

"What my team and I do is dangerous. The guys we go after aren't afraid to hurt women. They *will* hit back. Maybe even try to kill you. And not to hurt your feelings—" He eyes me from the other side of the table. Not in any sort of off-putting way, but as though he's assessing my stature. "But just by looking at you, I can tell you it wouldn't be too hard."

"I know. Trust me. I'm well aware of how men see me. However, with your help, with your training, I could change that." I pause and take a breath. "There's an anger inside me, Roman. And it's eating me alive. I'm hurting myself and the people I care about because I can't change the way I feel. When I heard about you and what you do, I thought to myself, I want to do that, too. It's as though all that rage was focused. As though I found a purpose for everything I went through. A way to make a difference for women like me."

He listens intently and his gaze shifts from a sympathetic one to one of understanding. He's silent for several moments, his jaw flexing as he mulls over what I've presented him with. "So, let me get this straight. You want me to train you to go out and take down a man twice your size. Because that's what we do. Then we threaten to destroy their lives if they ever breathe in the direction of the woman who called us. We don't have a chat first. We don't try to convince them to do the right thing. I learned a long time ago that doesn't work. Now I start with pain and work from there."

"Some men wouldn't listen otherwise."

He shakes his head. "Some men still don't."

"What do you do if that happens?"

Roman smiles and tilts his head to the side, holding my gaze. "How about this? You come to my office next week, and I'll show you a bit of what we do. If you still want to do this, I'll train with you. Teach you how to fight. How to handle a weapon. Then, after a while, we'll reevaluate where you would fit into our little setup."

I rest my arms on the table and lean forward. "I want to do this, Roman. There hasn't been anything that's made me feel like I have a purpose in this new life I'm in now. I'm committed to this."

"All in due time, Cece. This isn't some easy little self-defense course. If you go up against a man twice your size, you need to know how to take them down quickly and how to make sure they stay down. And you don't go out until I say you're ready."

"Understood."

Roman blows out a deep breath and scrubs a hand over his face. "What am I getting myself into?"

A wide smile stretches across my face, and if I weren't trying to impress upon the man in front of me how seriously I take this, I might be jumping around in my seat.

I reach over and hold out my hand. When he takes it in his, I shake firmly. "I can't wait to work together, Roman. You won't regret this."

CHAPTER SIX
CASH

"She's still disappearing during the day, but I haven't found any liquor bottles, so that's a good sign," Lucy says as we're sitting at Thorn and Thistle with Charlie, Linc and Jude.

"Cece seemed more like her old self when we saw her at the park last week. She even stopped by when I texted her a couple days later and hung out with us," Maizie chimes in from behind the bar.

I still haven't heard from her, though.

After my visit to the house last week, I went back the next day. And the next. Slowly but surely, I've been making some progress. When I left that day and rode around for another hour before heading back to the clubhouse, it didn't sit right with me that I had left the place a mess for the last two years. Cooper and I started that project together. It's a dishonor to his memory to let it fall to ruin. So the next day, I came back with tools and a semblance of a plan. At the very least, I wanted to get the paint and the counters in the kitchen finished, and I did. It took me two days, but the creamy yellow walls and professional-grade stainless steel appliances were finally finished and set up.

"Another beer?" Maizie asks.

"Sure, thanks," I say, then turn to Lucy. "Any idea
where she goes?"

Lucy shakes her head. "No. I've always given her
the space to do what she needs to do. That first
year, she never left the house much, but then she
started spending her time somewhere. That's when
we started seeing a change in her. When I would
ask about it, it would turn into an argument like just
about every damn thing, so I stopped asking."

"And it's killing you not knowing," Charlie says.

Lucy's head tips back and she groans. "So much."

"Careful, love, you know what those noises do to
me," Jude jokes, and Lucy's head whips in his direction.

"You're a pig," she tells her man.

"Oink oink," he replies with a cocky grin.

Jesus. These two.

"What about following her?" I ask, and both Linc
and Jude chuckle while Lucy shakes her head.

"I'd rather not start a nuclear war with my sister.
If she ever found out I was doing that"—she raises her fist and makes a gesture mimicking an explosion—"there would be no hiding from that bomb
triggering." She shrugs and sips the whiskey in front
of her. "I hate this, but I can't control her. Plus, it
wouldn't be fair for me to try."

Dealing with this side of Cece has been a minefield for everyone.

"I'm just glad she isn't rage baking anymore. One more scream-metal song and I would have thrown her damn phone in the street and run it over. Repeatedly," Jude says.

And some people have been dealing with things a bit more compassionately than others.

The door opens, and Barrett and Braxton walk in, followed by Ozzy.

"Oh-ho-ho. Look who's been let off the leash tonight," Jude says with a wide smile as our prez and two other brothers have a seat at the table a few feet from the bar top we're currently occupying.

"Fuck off, arsehole," Ozzy says, raising his middle finger.

"What have I told you about that shit? Arsehole, fecking—or any derivative thereof—knackered, chuffed, and bloody are my words. You do the Queen a disservice by saying them with your American accent."

"Yes, I'm sure the Queen is rolling in her grave that a Yank is using *arsehole*," Lucy says. "Don't be a twat." Her eyes widen and she covers her mouth dramatically. "Oh, no. Am I allowed to use that word with my uncultured American accent?"

Charlie snickers beside her but tries to cover it with a cough.

"You can say anything you want, love. Speaking of twats—"

Lucy slaps her hand over his mouth and gives him a look that would scare most men. "Do not finish that sentence." She quickly jerks her hand away and wipes her palm on her jean-clad leg. "And for the love of God, stop licking my hand."

"Then stop putting it over my mouth. You should know by now that anything on my mouth gets licked."

Linc groans and shakes his head. "You set yourself up for that one, Lucy."

"So glad I left my woman at home to come hang out with you idiots," Ozzy grumbles, but the smile on his face gives away that he's happy to be out with his brothers.

"Where's Freya?" Lucy asks.

"Working on a case. She said it's a complicated one, and she's been clocking a lot of hours on it. Her client is the ex-wife of a cop, and the department has done a bang-up job at losing evidence of her reports of domestic violence. Fucking assholes."

Ozzy's woman often takes on pro bono cases for women with complex divorce or custody cases and not a lot of money.

"I have no doubt she'll nail his ass. And hopefully open an investigation into the department," Maizie chimes in as she comes around the bar before setting three beers on the table.

"Thanks, Maiz," Ozzy says and nods. "She still has a shit ton of contacts, so I'm sure someone will be looking into it."

I shake my head. There's nothing that pisses me off more than men who hurt women, then hide behind a badge and a department.

"Any word from Liam?" Ozzy asks Jude.

"They'll be back in a few weeks. Maybe sooner, maybe later. Depends on something or other. He didn't give me specifics."

"Sounds about right," Ozzy replies. "Nova and Cillian out there with them?"

Nova is Cooper's younger sister and the Monaghan family lieutenant's fiancée. She's also a retired pickpocket who has a way with disguises and relieving people of their belongings without them being any wiser. Better believe that when Liam found out, he was practically salivating at the mouth to get her to work jobs for him here and there.

"No, they're sitting this one out. Business has been busy as hell at Nova's bar."

When Nova showed up in Boston after the Monaghans and the club took care of the shitstorm with the Italians, she wanted two things: Cillian and to open a bar. We've been there a few times now. Reminds me of home with the New Orleans flair it's becoming famous for—complete with a seafood boil every weekend. I should head out there soon and check on her. Doing work at the house has given me a lot of silent hours. And a significant portion of that time has been spent remembering growing up in Louisiana with Cooper and Nova. The stupid shit Coop and I would get up to, and the way Nova used to trail behind us, wanting to be included in everything. It wasn't a perfect childhood for any of us, but the three of us made a family of our own. I was devastated when Coop died, devastated when Nova wanted nothing to do with me. Having Cece helped more than I think she realized.

The night wears on, and my brothers and I, along with Charlie, Lucy, and Maizie, share a few more beers and a lot of laughs. As the hour gets later, the other customers start to head out, leaving only our group.

"Alright, boys, time for me to head out. Freya's done with her work," Ozzy says, pocketing his phone.

"Running home to the missus, Prez?" Jude asks with a smirk.

"Fuck yeah, I am. Don't act like you wouldn't do the same," Ozzy replies.

Jude lifts his brows with a thoughtful expression. "Fair."

Ozzy strides up to the bar and throws a couple hundred on the bar top. "Thanks, Maizie."

"Ozzy, what are you doing? That's way too much," she tells him. "Plus, it's your bar. You don't have to pay for your own beers."

"That's for your tip jar," he replies.

She tilts her head. "Ozzy."

"What? You may be Wyatt's woman, but you're still my bartender. Take Wyatt out to dinner or something. Tell him I paid for it." Ozzy shoots her a sly smile. "He'll love it," he finishes.

Maizie chuckles and takes the money from the bar top. "I'm sure he will."

My prez says his goodbyes and walks out of the bar with a wave at the door.

"It's too early to go home. Let's hit up Midnight Rose," Barrett suggests.

Braxton agrees and they look at me.

"You in?" Barrett asks.

I consider my options. Go back to the clubhouse and get a good night's rest so I can head over to the house in the morning and finish installing the upstairs toilet and vanity, or finish the night with my brothers at the strip club.

Fuck it.

"Yeah, I'm in."

I instantly regret coming with Barrett and Braxton. The club is loud and busy for a weeknight, which is great for business, but not for my head.

"My man, you have been in a funk for weeks. Lighten up," Barrett says from across the table, shaking my shoulder.

"Fuck off. I've had a lot of shit going on."

"I know, I know. Working on the house. I told you I'll come help," Barrett says.

It's felt too personal to have anyone else at the house. That was Coop's and my project. None of my brothers has even seen the property. It would be like sharing my grief with Barrett, and although my brothers would be there for me with no questions asked, Cece is the only one I ever talked about Cooper with.

We were in the midst of tragedy together when we first met and came to rely on each other in unexpected ways. I guess I never reached out to my brothers because I had Cece. Maybe I should have. Maybe I should have encouraged her to talk to her sister more about the shit that was brewing inside her. We were in our own bubble. We were each other's refuge, and at times, each other's comfort when we couldn't keep the chaos out of our heads. But that's changed now. And I still don't know what to do about it.

Maybe it's time to move on and come to terms with the fact that she's shut me out.

"You know what? I actually could use your help with some stuff. It'll get done faster if I have help."

That brings a smile to Barrett's face. The man is all about helping out his brothers.

One of the dancers walks by our table and shoots Barrett a wink with a coquettish smile on her pink-painted lips. He tilts his head to get a better look at her as she walks up to the bar and leans over, saying something to one of the bartenders.

"I like the new talent Sylvie's hired," he says.

I nod in agreement. "Good-looking girls."

Sylvie, the house manager, has a knack for finding some of the most beautiful women to perform here. She runs a tight ship, too. No extracurriculars happen in this place that would bring the attention of local law enforcement.

The dancer who Barrett was eyeing returns to the table with three beers and two more girls.

"Thought you might want another round," she says, smiling at Barrett.

"Sure do, sweetheart. You're new here. How do you like it so far?" he asks her.

"It's great. No trouble, and the customers aren't hard on the eyes, either." She smiles as her gaze travels over my brother, who is casually sitting back in his chair.

His grin widens as he sips his beer. Just because Sylvie doesn't allow any funny business in the club, that doesn't mean Barrett hasn't taken a dancer or two home over the years.

"Maybe we should take this to one of the rooms. Make it a private party," the dancer closest to me says as she glides her hand over my shoulder.

When I don't answer, Barrett chimes in. "Sounds good to me. Come on, Cash."

It's not as though I haven't enjoyed my fair share of private dances, but I'm not particularly in the mood tonight.

Seeing my mood written all over my face, Barret kicks my foot and says, "Come on, brother. You need to loosen up, and what better way than to have...sorry, girls, what are your names?"

The one next to Barrett answers, "I'm Destiny and that's Angelina." She points to the blonde who is now playing with the collar of my shirt, swiping her finger between the neckline and my collarbone. "And that's Chanel," she says, pointing to the girl whispering something in Braxton's ear.

Fuck it. Maybe Barrett's right. I need a night of letting loose and having a beautiful girl shaking what the good Lord gave her over me isn't the worst way to spend an evening.

"Lead the way," I tell Destiny. The girls know which rooms are occupied and which aren't.

"Thank Christ," Barrett says with a wide grin. "There's life in you, after all."

I roll my eyes, and Angelina slides her hand down my arm and laces her fingers with mine, pulling me up. "Follow me," she says with a coy smile.

The girls walk ahead of Barrett, Braxton, and me through the low-lit hallway covered in purple-and-black wallpaper. They lead us to a door painted black and open it to reveal the VIP room. It's been a while since I've seen the inside of one of these rooms. Sylvie must have been busy redecorating. The walls are lined with velvet couches in a deep midnight blue, and there's a small stage lit from the inside in the center of the room. Ropes of blue lights outline the ceiling—making the walls and ceiling look as though they're glowing. It gives the place a sexy ambience. *Good job, Sylvie.*

And here I am paying more attention to the decor of the room than the woman leading me to the couch, lightly pushing me onto the velvet cushion.

Get it together, Cash.

Destiny grabs the remote for the sound system as Barrett settles in a few feet from me on the couch with Braxton a little farther down from him. When the deep bass begins thumping through the speakers, Angelina starts dancing in front of me. She's a gorgeous girl, but when she bends over me, her blonde hair that covers my face is the wrong shade. The hand trailing over my shirt doesn't feel right, and her fruity perfume isn't the light floral scent that I prefer.

None of this feels right.

And it hits me that I'm not the same man I was last time I was here.

Not by a long shot.

I place my hands on her shoulders, and she smiles. But the smile fades as soon as I gently push her away.

"Sorry, honey. You're great, don't get me wrong, but I have to go."

I stand and Barrett looks over at me. He must see something in my face—something it seems everyone has noticed except me—because he grins and shakes his head.

"Another one bites the dust," he says on a laugh, and I roll my eyes.

Reaching into my back pocket, I pull out my wallet and hand Angelina several bills. Though the brothers are entitled to dances, tipping better than the average customer is a must. Ozzy and Sylvie insist the girls' time is paid for, even if the house fees are waived.

Angelina looks slightly confused and more than a little worried, as though she did something wrong. But Barrett calls her over to where he is, and the girls double-team my brother, who looks as though he's having the time of his life.

"I'll catch you later," I call over the music and head out of the room and back into the main area of the club.

When I get to my bike, I head out of the parking lot and back to the clubhouse. My mind wanders to the work I plan to do tomorrow, the stain I need to order for the front porch, and the carpet samples I have for the bedrooms.

Then I picture Cece in the kitchen with her flour-covered apron. That brings a smile to my face. I wonder what she would think of the kitchen, hell, the whole house. Would she feel at home there, like I'm beginning to? Would she like the giant stove I installed that would be enough to bake for an army...or a coffee shop in town?

As soon as the idea strikes, it's as though every detail I put into the space this last week makes sense. I've been trying to figure out how to get through to her, how to get her to talk to me.

Maybe I need to bring us back to basics. Back to when she had faith that she could tell me anything or just simply be with her thoughts, but I was only ever an arm's reach away. Back before she started lumping me in the same group as everyone else and shut me out just the same.

Chapter Seven
Cash

I stopped by the house early this morning and hung some gauzy white curtains in the kitchen window that looked over the backyard. I also went over the stove and countertops with a damp cloth to clean the dust off everything. There wasn't time to hit up the home store in Ayre before I planned to stop by Cece's and take her for a ride out to the property. Plus, I don't know what the hell to buy for a kitchen, and I figured if my plan works, Cece and I will be making a trip out there soon enough to get everything she needs.

It will be the first time anyone other than Cooper or I have set foot in the house since I bought it. But as soon as the idea struck, it felt right. Cece was the calm to my chaos when we lost Copper, and it's fitting that she be in a space that always felt like ours, even though she never met him.

Thankfully, Cece's car is in the driveway when I pull up to her house on my bike. At first, I thought of calling her, but I decided maybe a surprise visit would work in my favor. I can't force her to do anything she doesn't want to, and I would never try.

But catching her before she can make excuses about why she can't come with me this morning isn't *quite* the same thing.

Knocking on the door, I wait a few moments before the sound of footsteps walking toward the front of the house reaches my ears. When Cece opens the door, she's still in her pajamas—looking adorably sleepy.

"Hey. What are you doing here?" she asks in a raspy voice as though she just woke up.

"I was thinking we could go for a ride. There's something I want to show you."

She's silent for a few moments, blinking up at me with uncertainty in her blue eyes. "Cash..."

"I know we left things on a bad note the other day. I'm not going to apologize for caring about you, but I can see your point, too. I don't want to lose you, Cece. You're important to me, and I'd like to think you feel the same way."

She chews her bottom lip and looks at her feet before meeting my gaze again. "What do you want to show me?"

There's no fighting the grin that stretches across my face. "Why don't you get dressed, and we'll take off?"

Her eyes narrow as she stares at me, but then a small chuckle escapes. "Okay, Cash. I'll go with you."

I nod and she opens the door wider for me. "Come on in and have some coffee. I'll be a few minutes."

"Sounds good, sweetheart."

Stepping into the house, I close the door behind me, feeling triumphant and hopeful. My idea might actually work.

When I'm in the kitchen pouring myself some coffee, Jude walks in.

"Morning," I say, holding up my fresh cup of coffee.

He grunts in my general direction and walks over to the cupboard, pulling two mugs down.

"What the hell are you doing here so early?" he asks. Jude has never been what one would call a morning person.

"Taking Cece for a ride out to the house."

Jude turns to face me, crossing his arms over his bare chest. He wears a stern expression on his face that's more than his usual morning grumpiness. "Surprised you're up this early after a night at Midnight Rose."

Ah, *there it is.*

"Your big-brother intimidation attempt would pack a little more punch if you weren't wearing pajama pants with Lucy's face all over them," I say, looking pointedly at the ridiculous pants.

"Feck off, arsehole. It's laundry day, and I didn't expect you in my house so damn early."

I chuckle, but his stoic expression remains.

"Left early," I say with a shrug. "It wasn't where I wanted to be."

He turns toward the coffeepot and fills both mugs. "Where you want to be better not be Cece's knickers."

"It's just a ride, brother. No need to get *your* knickers in a twist."

He sets the pot down and turns back to me. "Listen, Cash. You're my brother, and I have your back on just about everything. Key words *just about*. Fucking around with strippers, then coming over the next day to take Little Bit on a ride, doesn't sit well with me. I won't have anyone playing with her like that. Brother or not."

"Jesus Christ. I didn't fuck around with anyone, and I'm not playing anything. Cece and I are close, and things have been rocky for her lately. I'm being a friend the best way I know how, and that's taking her out on my bike and letting her clear out all the shit in her head. We've been doing it for years. She needs someone who understands that right now, not everyone trying to fix her."

"That someone is you?" he asks, his stare boring into me.

My spine straightens, becoming rigid. If having it out with Jude in his kitchen this morning is what needs to happen, then so be it.

"Yup. It is."

"Okay, I'm ready," Cece says, walking into the kitchen as Jude and I face off. "Oh, good morning. I didn't think you were up." Her eyes dart between Jude and me, probably sensing the tension in the air. She turns toward me. "Ready?"

"Let's go," I say, dumping the rest of my coffee into the sink. "See you later," I say to Jude, and he grunts his reply.

When we step outside, Cece turns to me with a question in her eyes. "Everything okay?"

"Just Jude being his charming self, sweetheart." I give her a smile, and she returns it before putting her helmet over her head.

Jude can think what he wants. I know where I stand with Cece, and I don't need his approval. This is—and always has been—between her and me.

The ride to the house is peaceful and fucking killing me inside at the same time. Having Cece behind me feels so goddamn right. The second she slid her arms around my middle and leaned against me, it felt as though my entire body exhaled. There are a million reasons why being more than her friend is a tricky situation to maneuver through. But having her wrapped around me like she's been so many times before makes me wish all those reasons didn't exist. It also makes me wonder if they're really as big and insurmountable as I've always convinced myself they were.

The instant I felt more for her than simple friendship, I shut the thoughts down. Now I'm wondering why. Maybe even kicking myself a little for it.

We pull onto the gravel road that leads to the house. When the road opens to the property and she sees the house for the first time, she cranes her neck around me. I stop the bike, and Cece hops off, removing her helmet.

"Wow, Cash. This place is beautiful. Is it yours?" she asks, spinning in a circle. The house sits on a couple of acres with trees surrounding the perimeter.

"Bought it a few years ago. Cooper was helping me remodel before...everything."

She watches me get off the bike and hands me her helmet before I set both of them on the bike.

"It's really amazing, Cash," she says with a smile.

I look around the property and the house, trying to see it through her eyes. I thought the same thing when I first bought the place, but the last couple years have changed things for me. But now, seeing Cece here and as impressed as I was when I first came out here, it's changing again. And I really like that.

"Come on," I say, grabbing her hand. "Let me show you inside."

We walk up the stairs, and she takes in the unfinished porch. "You need some rocking chairs out here. This place must be gorgeous at dusk."

I smile and unlock the door with my other hand, not willing to drop hers. If she notices, she doesn't say anything, but I don't miss the fact that she hasn't let go of my hand either.

When I swing the door open, Cece steps inside, her smile widening. "Wow. This place is great." She heads to the living room, where I've set the table that I flipped last week back to rights. "It needs work," she comments, "but that fireplace is spectacular."

"The whole house is still a mess. Except for one room," I say and she sends me a questioning look that I return with a half grin. "Come on." I hold out my hand and she takes it again.

As I lead her into the kitchen, a wide smile stretches across her face. "It's like you plucked exactly what I would have picked right out of my head."

I kind of did.

Cece and I talked about the future a few times, and she always said she wanted a light-yellow kitchen and all the gadgets to bake whatever her imagination conjured. She dreamed of a nook where she could curl up and sit in front of a window and enjoy the scent of fresh-baked anything and the breeze from a summer wind. She walks over to the stove and runs her hand along the wide eight-burner top then opens the door to one of the double ovens.

"This thing is huge," she says with a giggle before looking inside the other oven.

"Yeah, I don't know why I bought one so big, but I had the space and pretty much an unlimited budget."

Cece closes the oven door and walks over to the window as a soft breeze blows inside, causing the gauzy curtains to billow out, wrapping her in the sheer fabric.

"It's beautiful," she says, staring out the window.

"It is." I'm not looking outside, though. The sight of Cece in this space that I created for her has my chest tightening with emotion. She looks beautiful standing in front of the window where I'd planned to build a breakfast nook before I'd even met her. Now I imagine her sitting there with a coffee in her hand, looking just as serene as she does now.

This feels right. More right than anything else has in a long time.

"I was thinking you and I could head into Ayre and pick up whatever you need."

She turns toward me. "Need for what?"

"I had an idea that this could be your kitchen. Maizie said you've been thinking about doing some baking for Betsy, and this place has a huge oven without anyone to bother you. You can blast any music you want and bake double what you can at Lucy and Jude's."

Her eyes nearly bulge out of her head when she hears my offer.

"I have a lot of work to do, and I figured it might be nice if the house gets some use before I decide what to do with it." I shrug like it's no big deal, but in reality, I'm practically holding my breath waiting for her answer. "That way I can be your official taste tester again." It's one of the many things I loved about having her at the clubhouse in those early days.

"So you're really in it for the sweets?" she asks, her smile filled with humor.

"Obviously," I answer with a teasing grin. "And the company."

Her smile changes from a carefree one to a shy one as she plays with the end of her long braid. She wanders back over to the stove and glides her hand over the top again.

"How come none of the brothers come out to help and keep you company?" she asks.

I lean against the doorframe that separates the kitchen from the front hallway as Cece continues to peruse the stove, then she walks over to the huge double-door refrigerator and opens it, peering inside.

"This was Cooper's and my project before he died. I was planning to let him and his sister move in when we were finished and he was patched in, but..." I don't need to finish that sentence. We both know what happened. "It never really felt right having someone else here. Honestly, I haven't done any work on the place for far too long. But it's time for me to move on. Move forward."

Cece turns to me with understanding in her blue gaze. "I know the feeling." She inhales a deep breath, then lets it out slowly and nods. "We should probably go get your truck."

My head tilts to the side. "For what?"

"You said something about taking me to Ayre so we could get everything I'm going to need. I have the basics at home that I could bring over—"

"I want all new stuff in here," I cut in. "Fresh starts, and all that."

Cece looks surprised for a second, then a smile stretches from ear to ear as her eyes light up.

"Okay," she says on a giggle, and I light up inside, feeling how excited she is. "Let's get going then."

Once again, I'm hit with how *right* this feels. Her. Here in this space. With me.

I hold out my hand. "Let's go."

I have the radio on low, playing some classic rock in my truck. The drive to Ayre takes about thirty minutes, and Cece and I ride in a comfortable silence as she hums along to the songs playing. When she used to use the clubhouse kitchen to bake, there were many mornings she would be humming along to some song in her head. One day, I set up a wireless speaker, and when she got there, I was playing one of the old country bands I like doing mindless work to. That's when I discovered that Cece liked all kinds of different genres, but classic rock and old country are her favorites. Well, until she found scream metal apparently, but I have yet to experience that.

I park in the lot at the huge home store, and we walk in. I immediately feel out of place, but Cece seems to know exactly where she's going. She takes me to the kitchen section. There are so many different things on the shelf, and I have no idea what any of them do or what they're used for.

"Maybe we need a cart," she says as she looks over some standing mixers.

"I'll go grab one," I reply and head to the front of the store. When I get back to the aisle I left Cece on, she's talking with a woman who is a bit shorter with long curly black hair.

"She's doing okay. The surgery went well," I hear the other woman tell Cece, who looks relieved to hear the news.

"Hi," I say, walking up behind Cece. The woman looks at me with wide eyes, and Cece turns. She has a different expression on her face. It's as though she's been caught red-handed in something, but I don't have the foggiest idea why.

"Cash...uh...this is my friend Leandra."

"Hi, nice to meet you," I say and hold out my hand. Leandra takes it and tentatively shakes it a few times before dropping it.

"Nice to meet you, too. I'll let you guys get back to it. It was good seeing you, Cece."

"You too. Please tell Thea I've been thinking of her."

Leandra nods. "Will do," she says before she offers Cece a warm smile and me a tight one, then turns to leave.

"She seems nice. Where do you know her from?" I ask Cece, who has turned her attention back to the mixer.

"Around," she answers without sparing me a glance.

"Around where?"

Jude has often complained that Cece disappears and never says where she's been. Now I'm wondering if it could have something to do with Leandra and some other woman named Thea.

Cece blows out a breath and turns to me. "I've been taking self-defense classes a few blocks from here. That's where I met Leandra and Thea," she answers in a low voice.

My eyes widen in surprise, and Cece shakes her head.

"Please don't tell Lucy. It's kind of my own thing, and I know Lucy would want to somehow involve herself or insist that I train with her."

"That sounds about right," I say with a laugh. "No worries, sweetheart. Your secret is safe with me."

The relieved smile on Cece's face breaks my heart a bit. It means she doesn't feel like she can trust me to keep her confidence like she once did.

"I think it's great that you signed up for a class like that. You're taking steps to be better prepared..." I let the statement trail off. Better prepared for what exactly? If someone tried to kidnap her again? I don't want my mind to give that thought any life, considering the relaxing day we've had so far.

"I know what you mean," she says with a small smile. "Now what's our budget?" she asks, looking over the other items on the shelf.

A grin tips up the corner of my mouth. "Unlimited."

It takes about thirty minutes for Cece to fill up the first cart—and then the second one I grabbed. She protested a bit, saying she had a lot of this stuff at home, but I wouldn't budge. I want the kitchen to be completely hers. We take the truck back to the house so I can unload everything and she can set it up how she wants. She's humming the song that was playing on the radio as I open box after box while she arranges things how she wants them.

After breaking down the boxes and throwing them into the giant dumpster I have for the construction waste, I walk back into the house.

"You ready to head back, sweetheart?"

I look at my phone to check the time. Ozzy and I have a meeting to go over some financials before he takes off for the day.

Cece readjusts the ponytail she threw her hair up in while we were working on the kitchen and smiles. "Yup, I think I'm all set here."

That smile remains on her face the entire way back to her place.

When I park in front of the house, I reach into my pocket and pull out a set of keys. I don't know why the nerves in my stomach have flared to life all of a sudden. Cece may not realize it, but having her in the space I'd only shared with Cooper up until today is a big deal for me. This is a small step toward letting go of some of the grief that has been my constant companion for the last two years. The grief that only seems to be muted when I'm around the girl sitting next to me.

"Here," I say, handing the keys over. "Now you can head to the house whenever inspiration strikes, or when you just need some breathing room."

That's what Cece is for me, my breathing room.

She looks at the keys then back to me. "Are you sure? I don't want to impose or..."

"Or what? It's your kitchen. As long as you save me a few desserts, I have no problem with you being there whenever you want." I shoot her a wink, and the pretty blush that runs up her exposed neck to her cheeks doesn't go unnoticed.

"Alright, then," she says with a small tilt of her lips. "I'll go to the grocery store tomorrow and pick some stuff up. Any requests?"

"Do your magic. I can guarantee I'll love anything you make." There's no doubt about that.

Cece bites her bottom lip, trying to contain her smile as she opens the truck door. "Okay. See you tomorrow."

I nod, the corner of my mouth tipping up as she gets out of the truck. "Sounds good, sweetheart."

The truck idles in front of the house as I wait for her to unlock the front door. Once she opens it, she turns and gives me a small wave before closing it behind her. I blow out a breath and head back to the clubhouse, feeling a little lighter than I have in a really long fucking time.

CHAPTER EIGHT
CECE

When I walk into the grocery store the day after Cash and I went to Ayre to buy every gadget and appliance I could possibly need to fill the kitchen and have it ready to go, I'm giddy with excitement. When was the last time I felt giddy? Actually, I don't think that's ever happened. Well, maybe when Cash would moan after tasting one of my desserts, I don't think giddy is quite the right word to describe it, though. That sound would send flutters through my belly. It was a foreign feeling, but I soon came to realize it was an attraction I didn't think I had the capacity to feel. Not after everything I'd been through. But Cash was the complete opposite of anyone I'd ever experienced. And the more time I spent with him, the easier it was to separate the two.

My shopping excursion doesn't take long at all. I'm going to experiment with a couple new recipes and some old favorites. As soon as I have the new ones perfected, I plan on giving Betsy at Cool Beans a call. Baking has always been a passion of mine, even more so since coming to Shine, since I could experiment with all kinds of different things. Cash was right, it's time to move on and move forward. That means eventually earning enough to get out of Jude and Lucy's place and into one of my own.

After loading up my car with everything, I head to the house. Cash gave me a set of keys and said I'm more than welcome anytime. He wants the kitchen to be my space—as long as I save him a few desserts. The wink he shot me when he said that had a riot of butterflies exploding in my belly. It was almost as though we were back to normal. Just Cash and Cece without all the noise of the last few months. Before the all-consuming rage infiltrated every cell of my being after the kidnapping.

I pull up to the house and pop my trunk open, grab the bags, and carry them up the front steps. I take a look around the porch and think the place could do with some hanging plants as well as the rocking chairs I suggested. It's easy to see myself coming here and sipping on an iced tea, rocking away on the porch, surrounded by colorful hanging pots with flowers of all shades blooming in them.

Okay, reel it in.

This isn't my house, and Cash might not even want flowers on his porch...but they would look good when all is said and done if he decided to sell the place. Plus, I could enjoy them in the meantime. And I'd be the one to take care of them since baking does have some downtime when everything is in the oven.

"Get it together, girl," I mumble to myself. Cash offered me the kitchen for baking; he didn't ask for my decorating tips.

The house is a bit stuffy, so I decide to leave the front door open. There's a nice breeze coming through, and the screen door will keep any unwanted bugs outside.

Setting the bags on the counter, I walk into the middle of the kitchen and let out a very girlish squeal as I spin around, still in slight disbelief that Cash thought to offer me this amazing space. When I saw the oven yesterday, it was as though I could smell all the delicious things that I could bake in it. I've daydreamed about having something like this—a place like this to call my own. Though it isn't *technically* mine, no matter what he says, I'm going to imagine it is all the same.

I go about unloading all of the bags and pulling my new mixing bowls out of the cabinet, opting for the most colorful ones we could find at the store. The kind I never would have been allowed in my previous life. Not that there was much use for anything other than the giant clay bread bowl I used on a regular basis.

Stop thinking about that time, Cece. It has no place here.

Giving my head a little shake, I shut out those thoughts and organize things between what I need immediately and what I'll use later. For the oven's maiden run, I've decided to start with pain au chocolat. There are several complex steps that go into making the delicious dessert, but I've always wanted to try.

As I'm measuring out the flour, my phone dings. When I see Cash's name, a smile immediately spreads across my face. The same smile I used to get before...well, everything.

Cash: *Hey, sweetheart. You at the house?*

Me: *Just got here. Getting ready to make something new.*

Cash: *Can't wait to try it. I'll be over in a little while. It was a late night, so I'm running behind. Need anything?*

I frown at my phone. *Late night?*

Me: *I think I have everything. We did buy out that little store in Ayre yesterday. I don't know what I could possibly need.*

What does he mean by late night?

Cash: *Okay. See you soon.*

Cash doesn't owe me any explanations, but when he left me yesterday, he said he had some work to take care of. I know from overhearing Jude and Lucy's conversations, the guys put one of the brothers at the strip club for extra security before the kidnapping. Were they still doing that? Was last night Cash's turn? Maybe he took one of the girls home with him and didn't get any sleep at all. Cash has always been a morning person, but I know he sleeps in after club parties—and from what I've seen at those parties, the girls make it perfectly obvious that they want in his bed. I've never seen him take one to his room, but I usually leave before things get too out of control. I've certainly never asked him about it.

What else could *late night* mean?

A million things, Cece. Knock it off.

Blowing out a breath, I try to recenter myself and get back to the task at hand. But now that the thoughts have invaded my brain, it's becoming more and more difficult to concentrate. Or to be as excited as I was when I first walked through the door.

Cash and I have always had something different between us than I ever had with anyone. There was a connection that came from shared pain, but it turned into something else. At least for me. Until I pushed him and everyone else away. It's not as though anything ever happened between us to make me think there was a chance of us being more than friends. It was just my girlish imagination running away with itself a few times. Okay, more than a few, if I'm being honest.

Cash is sweet and flirty, at least toward me. But he's never outright made it known that he intended anything more than friendship between us. That didn't stop me from developing a crush, though.

And this feeling in my chest right now makes me realize exactly why it's called a *crush.*

The thought of him spending the night with a woman sends bitter jealousy coursing through me. The idea that Cash would see me as anything more than Lucy's fucked-up little sister is almost laughable. Isn't that how everyone else looks at me? As someone who is as fragile as a baby bird that fell out of the nest? I've certainly felt that way a few times over the last couple years. Why would he be any different?

I grab my phone from the counter and pull up one of my playlists. Jude likes to call it my rage-baking music, but it matches the mood I've suddenly spiraled into. Sometimes a girl just needs to scream along with some metal to get it all out.

Pushing the ingredients for the pain au chocolat to the side, I grab what I need to make some blackberry turnovers. It's an easy enough recipe, and something I can do mindlessly. I don't have the patience for anything complicated at the moment, but I need to keep my hands busy.

After an hour, I have two sheet pans in the oven with the turnovers baking. I'm mashing fruit for my second batch of blackberry compote and screaming out the lyrics to the song playing through the small portable speaker I brought with me. This feels good. Keeping my hands busy and being as loud as I want without anyone around to grumble about it. So many times in the past, I would've reached for a bottle when these feelings bubbled up, but not this time. I swore to myself that I would no longer numb the pain with alcohol, so crushing berries to within an inch of their lives and belting out some scream metal will have to do.

The last drink I had was at Lottie's. It wasn't even something that I liked. I was trying to convince myself if I drank beer and didn't enjoy it, I wouldn't be tempted to have another, then another. Imagining that beer causes my mouth to water. I don't like beer, but a craving for it overwhelms me. I can practically taste the malty flavor on my tongue. Feel the bubbles tickle my mouth and throat as I swallow. One beer wouldn't hurt anything, right? As long as I stay away from wine or anything hard, I shouldn't have any problems stopping at one beer. Or two. I could put the turnovers in the oven and run out to the store.

The music turns off suddenly, and I spin around to see Cash with my phone in his hand after he's paused the music.

"Jesus, you scared me," I say, then turn back around and set the bowl on the counter so I can really get in there and give the damn berries a good crushing.

Now that Cash is here, my daydreams of that beer are shattered and the cravings have disappeared. The only thing I feel now is irritation over his *late night*.

"Sorry. I called your name a few times, but you didn't hear me. Guess now I know what Jude was talking about with your rage baking." There's a lightness in his tone, and I know it's meant as a joke, but my hackles rise.

I set the bowl on the counter and turn back around. "You said I could use this space as my own. This is what I do when I bake."

"I've seen you in the kitchen a million times, Cece. This was never your norm before. What's going on?" Damn him and his uncanny ability to read me better than anyone else.

"Nothing," I say and cross my arms over my chest. "Guess I'm a little grumpy. Late night."

My gaze holds his, but he doesn't pick up on the reference to his excuse for why he's getting a late start.

"Okay...I'm going to get to work upstairs. Holler if you need anything." He offers me a tight smile and turns, walking out of the kitchen.

And I'm left feeling like the biggest brat.

Not even a day after Cash and I called a truce, I'm acting like a complete bitch to him. And for what? Getting jealous over a woman who may not even exist about a night this fictitious woman and Cash probably didn't spend together. If people didn't think I was already a little off my rocker, the scenario that just played out in my head would be enough to tip things over the edge into straight loony town.

I take a deep breath and think about where my mind went. The bar, the beer, the anger. It was too much. It was too easy to get wrapped up in all of it. So I play the tape through. What if I'd had that beer, then what? How long would it have taken me to be back at the quarry? Lying to everyone around me about what I'm doing and where I'm going. A week? A month? How long until I show up drunk and pissed off at another family event? Those are all questions I can't answer, and that scares me. That's not who I want to be. I also don't want to be a jealous asshole that lashes out at someone over some fictional situation that probably didn't happen the way I was picturing.

Or at all.

I'm not great at apologizing with words, but thirty minutes later, when the turnovers are cooling on a rack, I head upstairs and find Cash in the hallway bathroom. It's several degrees warmer up here than downstairs, and he's taken his shirt off, kneeling as he bends over to tape off the baseboards. This is the first time I've seen the man without a shirt. The muscles of his tanned back and shoulders flex with his movements, sending chills racing down my arms.

"Hey," I say, and he turns his head. "I made a batch of blackberry turnovers. They're still warm if you want to take a break." I look down at my hands and pick at a bit of dried flour on my wrist. "You know, since you're my official taste tester and all."

When I look back at Cash, he's wearing a smile as he stands, turning to face me.

And holy shit, I was not prepared for this rush of desire to careen through me.

His chest is toned and glistening with a light sheen of sweat. My gaze travels down his pecs and over every inch of his perfect six-pack to where the muscles form a V before it's cut off by the waist of his jeans. The breath stalls in my chest, and I almost feel lightheaded from the sudden burst of lust racing through me at the sight.

Cash grabs his shirt that's sitting on what looks to be a new vanity and puts it on, covering himself. *Unfortunately.* Actually, it's probably better for my sake if he's fully clothed. That was the first time I've had such a visceral reaction to seeing him, and I need a second to catch my breath before I really do pass out.

Is that a thing that could happen? It feels like it could. How would I even explain it? *Sorry, seeing you half-naked made me have a mini stroke, and I lost consciousness for a second. Don't worry, everything's fine now. Just please keep your shirt on.*

That's not ridiculous at all.

"You good?" he asks, eyeing me with concern. "You're a little flushed."

"Oh, uh... yeah. It's hot up here, huh?" I stammer out, fanning my heated face.

"Yeah. Heat rises. Especially in old houses like these."

It sure does.

I stand in the doorway, still a little afraid that my jelly-filled legs are going to give out on me.

"Come on. I'm dying for a taste. It's been forever," he says, taking a step toward me.

"Huh?" I ask, raising my head to his when he's right in front of me.

"The turnovers? I haven't had one in ages."

"Oh, right. The turnovers," I answer, but don't move.

"Okay, sweetheart, I'm starting to get a little worried. You sure you're okay? Do you need some water or something?"

I giggle—fucking giggle—before I move out of the way. "Sorry, I'm a little tired."

Turning around, I head back down the stairs and feel Cash's gaze on me as we walk down the narrow staircase. This man probably thinks I'm a complete nutcase right about now.

When I get into the kitchen, I pull down a paper plate from the cabinet and place one of the warm pastries on it, handing it over to him. He takes a bite and lets out the familiar moan that I've heard plenty of times in the past. I turn and busy myself with the compote mixture so he doesn't see the blush that I'm sure is making me red as the strawberries I have sitting on the counter.

"Damn, sweetheart, this is the best one yet," he compliments around a mouthful.

"Thanks. The blackberries they had are so sweet," I say as I turn around with the mixing bowl in my hands. Cash is standing right behind me, and it startles me. I drop the bowl between us.

"Damn it," I say and spin to grab the paper towels. When I turn back around, Cash is kneeling on the floor, trying to scoop everything back into the bowl.

"It's such a mess," I say, noticing the berry splatter on his jeans. I wipe a paper towel on his leg, but all it manages to do is spread the stain. "I hope you aren't attached to these pants. Pretty sure I ruined them."

Cash looks down and chuckles. "It's no big deal, sweetheart."

I look into his smiling eyes and we fall silent. His gaze is traveling over my worried face. I still get a little anxious when I make a mess. That never ended well for me in my old life. But the smile on Cash's face puts all those old anxieties to rest.

"You have blackberry on your face," he says.

"How on earth did that—"

I'm struck speechless when his thumb grazes the apple of my cheek, and it comes away with a bit of berry.

He puts his thumb in his mouth and sucks the compote off. "Delicious," he whispers, and both of us hold our breaths, staring into each other's eyes. We're so close, yet a million miles apart at the same time. His head slowly moves toward me as though he's about to—

And my phone chimes loudly with a text.

He leans back on his haunches, his head dropping to his chest as he blows out a breath.

When he lifts himself from the floor, he holds out his hand, and I give him the soiled paper towels before I finish wiping up the remnants of the compote from the floor.

"Well, at least I got a couple batches done," I say, throwing the rest of the paper towels in the trash.

Grabbing my phone, I see there's a text from Roman.

Roman: *Sorry, it's been a little busy here this week. If you're still interested in working together, come by in an hour or so, and I'll show you around.*

This last week I've been spending time in my self-defense class, but still haven't managed to catch Roman at a good time. Then yesterday, with my surprise, and today with the baking and mini mental breakdowns, I haven't even thought about it.

Me: *I'll be there.*

Cash has been wonderful—giving me a place to have some freedom and an amazing, fully stocked kitchen to make all my creations in. It's more than I could've ever asked for. But that doesn't mean it's going to fix everything for me.

It strikes me that I feel so at odds with the life I always thought I wanted. The one where I'm happy and in a kitchen and creating—which is something I love.

I could tell Roman to forget it and come to terms with making pastries for Betsy and living a quiet, peaceful life. Or I can take this new path that I never envisioned for myself but feel, down to the very marrow of my bones, that this is what I need to do. Not just for myself, but for all the other women who have found themselves in the same situation I was and need to get out. The ones who need to know that those who threatened them will finally leave them alone.

"I have to get going," I say to Cash, who is still standing behind me.

"What? Why?" The tone of his voice is almost pleading.

"I have some things to take care of," I say as I grab a couple of containers and begin packing the turnovers away.

"Is this about what happened a second ago? I'm sor—"

"No, not at all." The pitch of my voice is a little higher than I meant for it to be. "I just have to be somewhere." Not a lie.

"Oh, are you going to your self-defense class?"

"Yeah. Time got away from me." That one is a lie.

"I get it. Here," he says as he grabs the sponge I was reaching for. "I'll clean up."

"You don't have to," I say, shaking my head.

"It's important for you to go to those. I don't mind at all." He shoots me a smile, and I feel like shit for lying to him. But I really do have to get going since Cash's place adds about fifteen minutes to my drive to Ayre. This meeting is important to me. To who I want to be.

I grab my bag from the counter. "Thanks, Cash. For everything."

"Drive safe," he tells me.

"I will. Promise."

He gives me one last smile before I head out the front door and get in my car, hating the bitterness the lies have left in my mouth.

When I pull up to the address that Roman sent me, it's a four-story brick apartment building. I don't know what I was expecting. Maybe some offices or something, but this quiet, tree-lined street wasn't it. I park across the street and walk up to the door. Before I get there, Roman opens it.

"Hey," he greets. "Glad you could make it."

"Hi. Were you about to head out?" I'm going to be utterly disappointed if I've left Cash's for a meeting that isn't going to happen.

"Nope. Saw you on the camera," he says, pointing to the discreet dome-looking device attached to the wall facing the street.

"Afraid someone could sneak up on you?" I ask, only half joking.

"Something like that." He opens the door wider so I can step through. "Come meet everyone."

We walk up the staircase, and he opens one of the apartment doors. It's laid out like a regular apartment with a hallway to the left that probably leads to bedrooms and a large open kitchen to the right. There are a couple couches with a low coffee table between them, but what sets it apart from looking like a homey little apartment is the three desks with at least two computer screens on each and the surveillance monitors covering one of the walls.

"This is Cyn," Roman says, pointing to a young woman who can't be much older than me with bright-purple and pink hair. Her nose piercing glistens in the light when she lifts her head from her computer screen, giving me a warm smile and a wave.

"She works background checks and various other inquiries I have," Roman says.

The vagueness of his statement hints that they aren't all of the legal variety. Having spent time around the

Black Roses and Liam has made me adept at hearing what *isn't* being said.

"This is Carter. He works surveillance," Roman says.

Carter gets up from the couch and strolls over to me, holding out his hand for me to shake. "Nice to meet you."

Looking at Carter, I can tell why he would be good for surveillance. He has an unassuming way about him and looks like any regular guy. Not too tall or packed with muscle. He's got short brown hair and an easy smile. You would pass him on the street and not take note of anything in particular standing out.

"James and Billy are downstairs working out," Roman tells me.

"You have an entire organization set up here," I comment.

Cyn groans. "That term is too...organized. We're just a group of people who help out other people who find themselves in shitty situations on occasion. Nothing fancy."

"Cyn isn't partial to establishment terms. She's a free spirit and all that," Roman teases. In turn, Cyn replies by sticking her tongue out at him.

Roman opens the front door of the apartment. "Come on, I'll introduce you to the other two."

"See you later," I say, waving to Cyn and Carter.

Walking back down the stairs, Roman opens a door on the first floor. Though the other apartment looked like it could be an actual living space, this apartment is set up as a gym. The walls have been knocked down, leaving a small open kitchen to the right and a bathroom to the left. The rest of the space is one huge room with brick walls, where all sorts of workout equipment and punching dummies are set up. Two men are currently grappling on a mat in the center of the room.

"James, Billy, come meet Cece," Roman calls over the rock music playing in the background.

The two men pause their fight and walk over to us, one turning the stereo down on his way. Both are big. But neither looks particularly intimidating as they head toward us with smiles on their sweaty faces.

"James," the first man says, holding out his tattooed hand for me to shake. "Roman said you wanted to train with us."

I slide my palm into his, and his grip is light. "I want to do more than that."

The man next to him chuckles, and James releases my hand before Billy holds his out. "We'll see about that. Let's take it one step at a time."

Roman said something similar when I met him at the diner last week, but I'm just as determined now as I was then to follow my plan through.

"You guys get back to it. Cece and I are going to have a chat," Roman says.

The men nod and walk back over to the mat, resuming their sparring.

Roman tips his head to the door. "Let's take a walk."

He leads me from the building, and we step out into the humid summer afternoon.

"This is going to be a big commitment. Knowing a little about your past, are you sure you're up for it?" he says as we walk side by side down the sidewalk.

"I'm here, aren't I?"

Roman nods. "You'll be training floor technique with the three of us. I'll be honest, this isn't something any of us has ever done, but we won't go easy on you. It means you might get hurt. Scratch that, you'll definitely get hurt. If you want this, you're going to have to know how to take a punch and not crumble to the ground. I still go home with bruises. When you're out there against some guy who doesn't give a shit about hurting women, they aren't going to stop if you cry. Shit, they get off on it."

"I'm aware." More than he could possibly know. "Can I ask you something?"

"Shoot."

"Why do you do this? I can't imagine that it pays anything, considering you're doing this for women who probably don't have much to begin with, and all of you could land yourselves in jail any time you go out and *take care* of someone."

"You're right. We don't take money for what we do. Each one of us has our own reasons. But it all boils down to the fact that at one time or another, the system failed us or someone we love. This is our way of making sure the women who reach out have a shot at a life free from the men who hurt them. Some of them are scared to go to the cops, and some have tried but didn't get anywhere. We bridge the gap for them."

We walk in silence as I consider what he said. *Bridge the gap.* I like the way he looks at what they do.

"So it's not about revenge?" I ask.

Roman chuckles. "Oh, that's part of it, too. But that's not all of it. You'd burn out pretty quick if it was." He stops and turns to me. "How are you with handling a gun?"

I shrug. "I learned on the compound, but it's been a while."

"What about disarming a man twice your size?"

"Never tried."

Roman smiles. "We'll fix that."

I return his smile, feeling like I'm finally getting somewhere with Roman, other than having him give me all the reasons why this could go horribly wrong for me. "I can't wait to get started."

Chapter Nine
Cash

"Fuck, I'm beat," Braxton says as he gets off his bike at the clubhouse.

We just got back from another run, this one taking us down to New Orleans, then up to Michigan to drop off some inventory to the Iron Disciples for the Monaghans. It's been a week on the road, and we're all fucking tired. Linc and Jude opted to go home to their women, while Braxton, Barrett, and I came back to the clubhouse.

"Good thing the Monaghans don't use the NOLA port much anymore. I think it's going to be a while before we have to go back down," Barrett says, hopping out of the van we take with us. "Help me unload my bike, and we'll have a few beers. I need it after today."

"I sure as fuck hope they don't need us down there again before November. I don't think I've sweated so much in my goddamn life," Braxton says, opening the back of the van and pulling the ramp out.

Barrett and Braxton hop up into the back, and Barrett undoes the straps holding his bike down as Braxton keeps it steady from behind.

"Then you're doing something wrong, brother. Nothing like a good, sweaty workout with a beautiful woman," Barrett quips.

"Shut the hell up, and make sure the bike doesn't fall over," Braxton replies.

"Cranky," Barrett teases.

If looks could kill, the man would be dying a very painful death right about now from the knives shooting out of Braxton's eyes.

I shake my head and grab my saddlebags before walking into the clubhouse.

One of our prospects, Gabe, hops up from the couch as soon as he sees me. "You need some help out there?"

"Nah, they got it. You can set us up with some beers, though."

"On it." He heads to the bar and pops the cap off three longnecks just as Barret and Braxton make their way inside.

"All I'm saying is that girl in New Orleans was absolutely giving you the eye. Shit, any of the girls at the Disciples' clubhouse would've been more than willing to drop to their knees for you," Barrett says to Braxton as they walk into the clubhouse.

"Why are you so fucking obsessed with my sex life? You had your hands full everywhere we stopped. Don't worry about where I get mine."

"But are you getting it?" Barrett asks our very annoyed-looking sergeant at arms. "It's not healthy to not unload, if you know what I mean. That shit could cause cancer."

"Where the hell did you hear that?" Braxton asks.

Barrett shrugs as he comes to sit next to me at the bar. "I don't know. It's one of those things everyone knows, though."

"You're an idiot," Braxton replies.

"Tell him, Cash." Barrett waves from me to Braxton. "You need to empty your balls, otherwise that shit backs up."

"I don't want to talk about another man's balls," I reply. "But I do find it odd you're so concerned with Braxton's."

"Whatever, man. I'm just trying to look out for my brother's health," Barrett says before sipping his beer. "Speaking of, that redhead in NOLA had a mouth like a fucking Hoover. Goddamn, some of the best head I've ever had. I should have gotten her phone number."

"I wish you would have, then she could listen to your bullshit instead of me," Braxton says.

Yeah, I think Barrett was right. Our sergeant at arms is one cranky asshole tonight.

"I've had enough of you fuckers for the week. I'm going to bed," I say, grabbing my beer and my bags before heading down the hall to my room.

I toss my saddlebags in the corner and strip out of my dusty clothes, then go into the bathroom and turn on the shower as hot as I can stand it. It was fucking sweltering riding down to New Orleans, up to Michigan, then back to Shine, and I desperately need to wash the road dirt off me and soothe my aching muscles.

As rough as the trip was at certain times, I wouldn't change it for the world. I fucking love my brothers and the life I've built in Shine—even when I want to knock their skulls together.

I step under the steaming-hot water and exhale a deep breath. It's good to be home. That thought brings me to the house, and straight to Cece. We had a moment the other day. I was so close to crossing the few inches of space between us and taking her mouth in a kiss. And there was no doubt that she would have let me. There are plenty of reasons why starting something with her is a bad idea, but fuck, they were the furthest thing from my mind in that moment. Then she ran out, and I left for a run the next morning.

We've texted a couple times since I've been gone, but neither of us has brought up the *almost* kiss. I sent her a picture of the sunset over the Mississippi River, and she sent me a picture of some chocolaty dessert that she made. It made me feel fucking good that she was in my kitchen when I wasn't there. Knowing she's in the space that I created for her, doing something she loves...I don't know. It fills me with pride.

When I get out of the shower, I pull on a pair of shorts and collapse onto my bed, sipping the beer I brought in here earlier. My phone dings, and Cece's name flashes on the notification.

Cece: *Hey, happy you made it home safe.*

Me: *Fucking relieved to be back without murdering one of my brothers.*

Cece: *Was the road wearing you thin?*

Me: *It was wearing all of us thin. Maybe except Barrett. Hopefully I'm not digging a grave for him in the morning.*

Cece: *I was going to ask, as long as you're not burying any bodies, if you had plans tomorrow?*

That piques my interest.

Me: *I'm free.*

Cece: *Remember when I said I was thinking about talking to Betsy? Well...I did and I'm supposed to bring her my first delivery tomorrow.*

Me: *That's amazing, sweetheart. I'm so fucking proud of you.*

A wide smile stretches across my face at her news. This is more than just baking for me and my brothers on occasion. This is a step that is going to get her somewhere.

Cece: *I was hoping you could meet me at the house and take me over there. I can do it myself if you can't make it, but it feels right having you with me.*

Me: *Cece, I wouldn't miss it. I'll see you in the morning.*

Cece: *Is seven too early? I know you just got back, so it's really okay if you can't.*

Me: *Will you have something warm ready for me when I get there?*

It strikes me how suggestive that sounds, but it's also not like I wouldn't be open to it.

Cece: *I'll have a fresh batch of scones and danishes. I'll let you have the first pick.*

Me: *Then seven is perfect. Good night, sweetheart.*

Cece: *Goodnight, Cash.*

I set my alarm and put the phone on the charger next to my bed. Fuck, I've never been this damn excited to wake up early in the morning.

When I open the door to the house, the smell that greets me instantly makes my mouth water.

"Hi, honey, I'm home," I call.

There's some soft country music playing from inside the kitchen. I don't want to scare her like I did the first time I came here when she was baking. Though that time she was blaring her metal and wouldn't have been able to hear me over the music.

Walking into the kitchen, I spot Cece placing a couple more Danish into containers. She looks up at me with a wide grin.

"Hi. You're just in time," she says, nodding to the cooling rack on the counter behind her. "I tried a new recipe. Strawberry and clotted-cream turnovers. They should be cool enough to eat now."

The sight of her loosens the knot in my chest that I didn't even know was there. Fuck, she is so damn pretty standing in the kitchen in a baby-blue sundress with her hair pulled up in a messy ponytail. The urge to walk over to her and find out exactly what her smile tastes like is strong. But I hold myself back.

Instead, I walk to the counter and pick up one of the turnovers, taking a giant bite. The creaminess mixed with the strawberry electrifies my taste buds, and I moan.

"So good," I say and take another bite.

When Cece turns, her cheeks are a rosy-pink color. "I'm glad you like it."

Finishing the pastry, I head over to the sink to rinse my hands. Cece's light jasmine perfume tickles my nose, and I take a deep breath, inhaling her intoxicating scent. We've gone longer than a week without seeing each other, but for some reason, being in her presence again is sensory overload. The way she looks, the way she smells, the way I want to reach out and take her in my arms and feel her body pressed against mine, it's affecting me in a way it never has before. But I don't hate it.

"What can I help with?" I ask, wiping my hands on a towel.

"If you want to start taking these out to the truck"—she points to three giant bags on the counter—"I'll finish packing up what's left, and we can head over."

"Sounds good, sweetheart."

When we get to Cool Beans, the street is quiet. It's still early, just after seven, but Cece wanted everything set up for when Betsy opens at eight.

She knocks on the front door, and Betsy walks over from behind the counter with a grin stretching across her face.

"I can't tell you how excited I am to finally have your pastries in here, Cece," she says when she opens the door. "I made plenty of room in the case because I know I'm going to sell out before the day is through."

Cece and I walk in carrying a huge travel bag in each hand, packed to the brim with containers.

Betsy leads us behind the counter, and Cece begins loading all of her creations inside the large glass case.

"Do you guys want a coffee?" Betsy offers.

"I'd love an Americano with an extra shot. Thanks, Betsy." I sure as shit need one this morning.

"I'll have the same," Cece replies. "I couldn't sleep last night. Too excited."

Betsy goes about making the drinks, and when they're done, she hands me mine and Cece hers. "I put a little sprinkle of cinnamon on yours. Just how you like," she tells Cece.

"Thank you." Cece smiles and sips the coffee. "Perfect."

"I left my checkbook in the office. I'll be right back," Betsy says before she heads down the hallway.

As Cece finishes loading the pastries into the case, I notice a line of bruises on her inner arm.

"What happened to you?" I ask, nodding toward her outstretched arm.

"Oh," she says, looking at the bruise. "Not sure. I bruise pretty easily." There's a lightness to her answer, but it seems a bit forced.

"Okay, Cece. Here you go." Betsy comes from her office and waves the check.

Cece stands, grinning from ear to ear. "Thank you so much. I hope everyone enjoys them."

"That's not something I think you're going to have to worry about. Let's see what the crowd favorites are, and I'll text you with another order later."

"Betsy, I would like to buy two of each, please," I say.

"You got it," she replies and grabs a paper bag and the tongs sitting next to the case.

"What are you doing?" Cece asks. "I'll bake you whatever you want."

I shoot her a grin. "I know, sweetheart, but I want to be your first customer."

She shakes her head, but the smile is bright on her face.

Betsy hands me the bag and tells me the total. After I hand her the money, I grab the pastries and my coffee in one hand, loop the handles of the bags we came in with over my arm, and hold my other hand out to Cece.

"Come on. I want to take you somewhere," I tell her.

She nods and slides her palm into mine.

"Bye, Betsy. Thank you for the coffee," she says as I lead Cece to my truck, dropping her hand so I can open the door for her.

When I get in the driver's side, Cece is buckling her seat belt. "Where to?"

I turn the truck ignition over and face her. "Somewhere I think you'll enjoy as much as I do."

Twenty minutes later, we pull into the parking lot of an animal rescue.

"You want to get a dog?" she asks, reading the sign.

"I volunteer here a few times a month. It's been a while since I've had time to stop by, and I know the ladies would love to meet the woman who bakes the best damn pastries and bread they've ever tried."

Over the last two years, I've brought Cece's baked goods out here for the women who run the shelter. Now, if I show up empty-handed, they threaten me with doo-doo duty.

I exit the truck and hurry over to the passenger side, opening Cece's door before she has a chance to do it herself.

"Such a gentleman," she remarks.

I give her a devilish grin. "Not always."

Cece hums and allows me to take her hand to help her out of the truck.

We stroll into the center, the workers having just gotten here since it's not quite eight in the morning.

"I brought breakfast," I say, holding up the bag. "And your favorite baker."

Cece waves, and the two women greet us with wide smiles.

"Girl, I don't know what you put in those turnovers, but it's magic. My taste buds thank you, even if my waistline doesn't," Karen, the owner of the shelter, says.

"And you can now purchase these delectable treats at Cool Beans," I inform them.

"I did not need to know that, but I'm so happy I do," one of the employees says before I hand her the bag. "Is this a lemon-and-blueberry scone? Girl, that one is my favorite."

"I'll take those," Karen says, grabbing the bag. "Oh, apple turnovers."

I laugh as the women fight over Cece's treats.

"We're going to head back," I say, pointing to the double doors.

Karen waves me on. "It's breakfast time. Be a doll and handle that while I enjoy your girl's delicious baked goods."

I don't bother correcting her and nod toward the door. "Come on. Let's go play with some dogs."

When we get to the back, most of the kennels are empty, which is always a nice thing to see at a shelter. There are four kennels currently occupied, and the dogs are beyond excited when they see us enter.

"Oh my gosh! They're so cute," Cece says as she holds her hand to one of the gates to let the giant brindle pitty lick her fingers.

"That's Big Momma. She's going to be giving birth any day now," I tell her. "We'll feed her first."

I open her gate, and Cece gives her lots of head and butt scratches.

The dog waddles over to me and looks up expectantly. "Yeah, you know what time it is." I take her into the feeding area outside and put extra in her bowl since she's eating for more than just her now.

"What's going to happen to her puppies?" Cece asks as I set the bowl in front of the dog.

"After six weeks, they'll start advertising the pups for adoption. Karen never has a problem placing puppies. Sometimes the older dogs take a little longer, but they're well loved while they're here."

"I'm surprised Ozzy didn't make Wyatt bring Pepper here when he brought him back to the clubhouse," Cece comments.

"Please, that dog was Wyatt's at first lick. Plus, I don't care what Ozzy says, he fucking loves that dog."

It takes no time at all for Big Momma to finish her food, and we let her out into the grassy yard so she can sniff around and do her business.

I hold out my hand for Cece. "Come on, let's go get another one."

After a couple hours, all the dogs have been fed and loved on by me and Cece. Karen comes out and keeps Cece company while I help the other volunteer clean out the kennels. When we get back in the truck, Cece is still wearing the smile she's had for the last two hours.

"This is sort of an odd thing for a biker to spend his off days doing. How'd you end up volunteering here?"

"Tanya."

Cece barks out a loud laugh. "Yeah, I could see her roping one of you guys into something like this."

"To be fair, all she did was organize a fundraiser for some local shelters. I met Karen, and I don't know...I just liked what she was doing here. I came by a few days later to drop off the check from the fundraiser, and she showed me around. They had a few more dogs here at the time and not enough volunteers, so I pitched in. I liked the dogs, and they liked me, so I came back a couple weeks later and did it again."

"And the rest is history?"

"Pretty much," I say with a chuckle.

Cece lets out a small sigh. "I don't know how you don't take them all home with you."

That pulls another laugh from me. "Guess I'm not as brave as Wyatt."

"I doubt that. You're one of the best men I've ever met." Cece gives me a soft smile, and I return it. Then I hear her stomach growl loudly.

"You hungry, sweetheart?"

Her light giggle fills the cab of my truck. "Yeah. I was too excited to eat this morning."

"Let's grab some breakfast."

"Please. Then I want to take you somewhere, too," she says with a small grin on her face.

"Where's that?"

"A place I think you're going to enjoy as much as I do," she replies, using my answer from earlier.

I shake my head, chuckling along with her. "Sounds good, sweetheart."

We grab some breakfast sandwiches from Cool Beans, and I'm impressed to see that half of what Cece brought in is already gone.

"It's been a busy morning. As soon as I told my customers these were baked by the girl who usually sells at the farmers' market, they grabbed one."

Cece tries to temper her delighted smile, but I feel the excitement radiating from her. She did it. She was scared and anxious, but she set her fears aside and took the leap. And judging by the half-empty display, it's working out better than she thought. It's been a while since she had a booth at the weekly market, and it seems that everyone was missing her delicious baked treats.

We get back into my truck, and Cece directs me out of town. About fifteen minutes later, she instructs me to turn down an old gravel road. When we come to the clearing, I look over and catch Cece with her lips stretched into a wide smile. It's a good look on her, and for the millionth time today, I want to reach over and taste that smile.

We get out of the truck, and Cece leads me to the edge.

"After I got my license, I used to drive by this road and would see the sign for the quarry. One day, after

I bought my first bottle of wine, I came out here and drank it. It felt so good to be alone without anyone asking if I was okay or giving me their sad, worried looks like I was going to break any second."

"Lucy used to complain about you disappearing all the time and not telling anyone where you were. Is this where you came?" I ask in a quiet voice that seems fitting for this place.

She huffs out a humorless laugh. "Yeah. Or I'd go to my self-defense class. But during those first few months, this is where I was."

"It's beautiful," I say, looking around. "And peaceful. I can see why you like it."

She sits down and dangles her legs off the edge. "No one knows about it. Or at least, I've never heard anyone talking about it. It's always been a place where I can come to do whatever I want without people judging me."

"What would you do?" I ask, taking a seat next to her and handing over her breakfast.

She shrugs as she bites into her bacon-and-egg sandwich. "Blast music, cry, dance around. Drink."

A small flare of anger ignites inside me. "Then you would drive home?"

She nods.

"Cece, you're lucky you didn't drive into the quarry. And no one would have known where to look for you. That's so fucking dangerous."

"I know. It was stupid, but honestly…" She looks out over the quarry. "At the time, that wasn't a deterrent."

My heart breaks for the girl sitting next to me. "Cece…"

"It's not like that anymore. I haven't had a drop of alcohol since two days after Elaine's. That's when I decided I needed to stop hurting myself, thinking it would solve the problem of being in pain."

"Nothing since then?" I knew Lucy wasn't finding any empty bottles, but that doesn't mean she wasn't hiding them since she's been called out.

"Nope. Sober as a judge. The temptation has been there a couple times, but I've stayed true to the promise I made myself."

My eyebrow arches. "I've met a few judges. They're hardly sober," I quip.

Cece laughs again and rolls her eyes. "You know what I mean."

We sit in silence and finish our sandwiches.

"Alright. I want to see what makes this place special. Let me hear it," I say, crumbling the wrapper in my hand.

She tilts her head in confusion. "Hear what?"

"The screaming. Give me the best, loudest scream you can muster."

Cece narrows her eyes at me for a moment, then opens her mouth and yells into the void of the pit.

"That's it?" I ask, shaking my head. "I barely heard you."

"You do it, then."

I open my mouth and yell loud and long.

"What were you thinking about?" she asks.

"I didn't know that was part of the assignment."

Cecc shrugs. "It doesn't necessarily have to be, but I think there might be something therapeutic about screaming out whatever's bottled up inside you."

My gaze travels to the sky. God, there's so much. Loss, grief, shame. Feeling the burden of not being able to protect Cooper, of being the one who brought him into the club. Of being the one who couldn't protect Nova from the pain of losing her brother. I swallow around the lump in my throat.

When I open my mouth again, I let out a frightening roar. Then, when I'm out of breath, I inhale deeply and do it again. I roar for the life that was cut short, for the loss I won't ever *not* feel, but somehow have to find a way to live with. I scream until my throat is raw, and when I finally stop, I'm out of breath.

A memory of Cooper pops into my head. His whooping laughter when he started his bike for the first time. He was so proud of that damn thing. He said it meant he was one step closer to being a brother.

I look toward the sky, not sure if I believe in any sort of heaven, but knowing if there is one, my brother is up there right now, probably laughing his ass off at what a little bitch I've been. He died doing what he knew needed to be done—protecting our family. And I know without a shadow of a doubt he wouldn't have had it any other way. The brotherhood meant the world to him, like it does for the rest of us, and his sacrifice will never be in vain.

I look at Cece, and she has another beautiful smile on her face. This time her eyes hold a bit of wonder, as though she can't believe I did that.

"How do you feel now?"

I release a deep exhale and smile at Cece. "Lighter."

"What were you thinking about? You don't have to tell me or anything," she says with a shrug.

"Cooper. I remembered him laughing. That kid was so damn full of life. I don't know...but thinking about him right now doesn't hurt like it usually does." I tilt my head toward Cece. "Alright. You're up."

She shakes her head. "I already went."

"And I told you, you can do better."

She shoots me a narrow-eyed glare and closes her eyes for a few silent moments. When she opens her mouth again, she screams with everything she has in her. It breaks me apart and puts me back together at the same time. To know that she used to come out here and do this alone. Release all her pain by herself. But now she brought me here, and she's letting me witness it and share her place with her. Her vulnerability that she doesn't show anyone else.

"There you go," I say with pride in my voice.

Her breaths are coming out in hard pants as she laughs. "Why does that feel so good? It's like everything just explodes out of me every time I do that."

I shake my head. "No idea, but I'm happy it helps. Okay, one more time."

Cece nods, and her smile is beaming as she opens her mouth again and lets a scream rip from her throat. This time, I yell along with her, which quickly turns into both of us laughing.

"Right? It's like it all"—she wiggles her fingers toward the sky—"floats away. It's a thing of beauty, if you think about it."

I stare at her bright yet calm smile while she looks toward the sky, as though she sees all her worries and fears drift into the ether. I'm so damn tired of fighting against myself. So tired of talking myself out of this attraction I feel toward her. This connection.

When she looks at me again, I can't help myself. I lean over and press my lips to hers. All the worries about me being too old for her, being part of a dangerous life that she shouldn't want any part of, what her sister and everyone else is going to have to say about it—it all floats away, just like Cece said. I don't deepen it, don't do anything more than press my mouth to hers, tasting the smile I've been dying for all morning. Shit, for a hell of a lot longer than that. Her lips move against mine, soft and tentative and so damn sweet.

When I pull away, I press my forehead against hers. "Absolutely beautiful."

CHAPTER TEN
CECE

The last three weeks are out of a dream I never allowed myself to have. After the morning at the quarry, Cash and I have seen each other nearly every day. He texts me in the morning to find out my plans, which usually involve baking while the sun rises to fill Betsy's order, then a bike ride or a drive with Cash out to what's become our spot. And I always get a goodnight text. Last week, instead of going to the quarry or for a ride, he took me to a furniture store.

"What are we doing here?" I'd asked and his grin made my chest tighten.

"I'm still not sure what I'm going to do with the house once it's finished, but I figured in the meantime, it needs a couch and a kitchen table. Somewhere comfortable for us to sit. Maybe we'll even find a couple rocking chairs for the porch."

"And I'm here because..." I asked, looking around the giant showroom.

"You spend just about as much time there as I do. I want you to be comfortable. Plus, picking out furniture and shit isn't my strong suit."

I chuckle and look around the sea of couches we're standing in front of. "And you think it's mine?"

"Sweetheart, between the two of us, I think we have a good shot at finding something nice."

So we did, and the pieces were delivered yesterday. Now the living room has an oversized plush leather couch with a couple fancy throw pillows, and the kitchen contains a light oak dining table and chairs. We found a set of two cushioned rocking chairs. I was right. Dusk is a beautiful time of day on his front porch, especially in the most comfortable rocking chairs I've ever sat in.

He hasn't tried for anything other than a few sweet kisses. He never pushes for more, saying we have all the time in the world, and I've never been wooed. The man *actually* used that word.

Cash has no idea that the day he kissed me at the quarry was my first real kiss. I've had men smash their mouths against mine, but none were ever gentle like Cash, and none were ever consensual. The way he lights me up to my very core is something I didn't know I could feel. There's a perfect intimacy in the way his lips move against mine, and for the first time, I want to take things further, want to know what it feels like to let someone in my body on my terms. The thought of taking things to a new level with Cash doesn't scare me in the least. It never could.

A few times, he's shown up at the house after I've already been there for a couple hours. He sets a vase of flowers on the kitchen table he purchased, gives me a sweet kiss, then we pack up his truck and take the pastries to Cool Beans.

I like that Cash wants to take it slowly. He's building trust between us, and that makes me feel important. Not that I thought I wasn't, but this is an entirely new layer to our relationship, and I'm not exactly well versed in starting something with someone who I actually care about. My marriage, if you can even call it that, certainly wasn't in the realm of consensual. But those thoughts have no place in what's developing between me and Cash.

I save all of that anger for when I'm training with Roman. He wasn't kidding when he said they weren't going to take it easy on me. I've come home with a lot more bruises than the one Cash saw the first day we delivered to Cool Beans.

I didn't know how to answer him when he asked me about the bruises since I haven't yet clued him in that I've taken the self-defense thing to an entirely new level. I know it's a lie. I'm not stupid. Maybe not outright, but a lie by omission is still a lie.

When I leave the house in the evenings, he thinks I'm going to self-defense class, and I let him. I'm still not ready to tell him. Maybe I'm afraid he'll try to talk me out of it. Maybe I'm afraid he'll think I'm crazy for even attempting it. Or maybe I still don't one-hundred-percent trust that he won't run to Lucy and Jude with the information. Trust takes time to build. I just hope it doesn't blow up in my face before I'm ready for that conversation. But even that thought isn't enough to stop me from making the drive into Ayre every night.

"It's really something," Roman says after we've finished a round of sparring at his makeshift apartment gym. We're sitting on the mats, and I'm guzzling water like I've been deprived for days. "How far you've come. I don't think I ever worked with someone who was so attuned to their own body and aware of where the other person is, as well as being able to anticipate nearly every move."

"I've had plenty of practice. I had to get good at it. If I wasn't aware of Otto at every moment, I never would have been able to brace myself and probably would've been hurt much worse."

"Your weapons knowledge isn't too shabby either," he says with a tilt to his lips.

I may have let him think I wasn't as handy with a pistol as I actually am. The first time he took me to a range, the way his eyes widened was comical. Thank God he had a good sense of humor as he mumbled, "Been awhile, huh?"

"I'm not quite as good as my sister, but I can hold my own," I admitted to him.

"I can see that," he'd said when he looked at the paper target with the outline of a body that had two shots to the chest and one to the head.

I smile at the memory and set my water bottle to the side. "When do you think I'll be ready?"

"You have some more work to do, but it'll be soon. Don't rush it," he answers.

"Yeah, yeah, yeah. I need to be *patient*." His entire team has been pounding that into my head since the start.

"It's important you understand that, Cece. I don't want you getting hurt. You still struggle with disarming someone, and Jimmy can incapacitate you too easily if you're not focused enough."

"Only if I'm not focused, though."

"What do you think it's like out there?" Roman pins me with his stare. "There is no controlled setting where you're going to be able to call it quits, or the guy stops at simply getting you on the ground. So yeah, I'm going to make damn sure that when you go after someone, they won't get the upper hand. The fact that you're a woman taking on a man possibly twice your size will stun them, sure. But only for a few seconds at most. Then they won't care. And that's when they become unpredictable."

I have plenty of experience dealing with unpredictable men. Actually, they've all been pretty damn predictable. They enjoy hurting women. All of them.

Now it's finally my turn to hurt them back.

Grabbing my phone, I check the time. "I should go. I have to be up early," I say, noting the late hour.

Roman shakes his head and releases a light chuckle. "Baker by day, vigilante-in-training by night."

"What can I say?" My lips curl up at the corners. "I'm a multifaceted woman."

"That you are."

Roman hops up and offers me his hand, pulling me from the mat.

I walk over to the kitchen counter and grab my bag. "See you later," I say, waving at him on my way out the door.

Instead of going to Roman's the next evening, I head to my self-defense class. The training I get with Roman is a far cry above what we learn here, but I've become attached to these women. Maybe even close to being friends. That's not something I've ever had outside of my sister and her friends.

Leandra is here tonight, but I still haven't seen Thea. It's been a few weeks since her surgery, so I'd imagine she needs more time to heal.

"Hey," I say, having a seat on the mat next to Leandra.

"Hey, girl. It's been a minute since I've seen you. Your man keeping you busy?" she says with a knowing grin.

I return her smile and feel the blush creeping up my neck. "A little."

"I have to say, he wasn't what I was expecting. Not that I expected anything, since you've never talked about him." Leandra quirks her brow.

"It's still new. And we're taking things slow."

"Slow is good," she says, nodding.

"It is. But sometimes I want to…" I try to think about how to describe exactly how I'm feeling about the place our relationship is in.

"Climb him like a tree?"

I bark out a laugh. "Yeah, something like that."

"I don't blame you," she says, laughing along with me.

"How is Thea doing, by the way? You haven't said much since letting me know her surgery went well."

Leandra blows out a long breath as she stretches her arms over her head. "Physically, she's much better. Mentally, she's afraid of her own shadow. She's been staying with me since she got out of the hospital, and every time she hears someone walking up the staircase outside of my apartment, she freezes and listens to make sure they keep walking. She's terrified he's going to find her. I don't necessarily want her to, but I think she should move home with her parents. He's a lot less likely to show up out of state than he is to see her again when I live so close."

"I thought that was the plan. Did she change her mind?"

"She's still embarrassed. It's crazy that her asshole ex is running around town without a care in the world, and she feels shame for what he did to her." Leandra shakes her head. "It fucking pisses me off. Danny's still out there living his life as though he didn't nearly destroy hers."

"That's her ex's name?"

"Yup, Danny Crispin. Upstanding correctional officer for the state of Massachusetts." Her nose scrunches with a look of disgust covering her face. "God, I wish she would have called that guy."

Leandra is referring to Roman. Honestly, I wish she would have called him, too. Sounds like Danny could use a taste of his own foul medicine.

"A girlfriend of ours says she sees him out at that bar a few blocks from here. Lottie's something or other."

"Lottie's Tavern?" I ask.

"Yup. That's the one. It's his local hangout. I can't tell you how badly I want to go in there and give him a piece of my mind, but I know it wouldn't do any good." Leandra jumps off the ground. "Come on. Let's go hit some shit. That always makes me feel better."

About an hour later, I'm pulling out of the parking lot of the gym. When I came to Shine, I hated waking up early. It was something I had to do at the compound. Be up before Otto so I could have breakfast ready for him and my father. Sleeping in was one of my little rebellions, even though there was no one to rebel against anymore. But now I love it. Probably because I'm doing something I love. Something creative that I pour myself into.

I stop at a red light and look to my right. The neon sign of Lottie's Tavern blinks at me. I remember it well. I ran out like my hair was on fire just over a month ago. That's the night I decided I was done being a victim of my past and needed to do something more than survive and move on.

It sounds like Thea is still firmly in the just trying to survive every day headspace. And I hate that.

I turn right onto the street of the corner the bar sits on, parking my car and getting out. Thoughts of what that man put the woman he was supposed to care for run through my head, as well as Leandra's voice saying that she wishes her cousin would have called Roman. She didn't, but that doesn't mean I can't stand up to him for her.

This is what I've been training for.

Roman thinks I'm close to being ready.

Tonight, I'm going to prove that I am.

I walk in and realize I don't know what the guy looks like or if he's even here. But if this is his watering hole, then chances aren't too bad that I'll run into him.

Walking up to the bar, I take a seat. There are more people here than last time, but it's later in the evening. It's a different bartender—thank God, because that would have been embarrassing, considering how I ran out last time.

"What can I get you?" the young woman asks.

"I'll take a bottle of light beer."

She nods and turns to get my drink. I have no intention of drinking it, but it would look odd sitting at a bar without something in my hand.

A group of guys enters the bar. They are all wearing uniform pants and black boots, but they all have on white T-shirts—as though they took their uniform shirts off to go get a drink after a shift. Like, say, a prison guard shift.

When the bartender returns and hands me my beer, I slide a ten-dollar bill across the bar.

"Is there a base around here or something? Those guys look like military," I say.

She looks over to the group who are taking up a table in the back.

"Prison guards. They come in practically every night," she answers.

"Oh, that makes more sense," I say with a little giggle.

"Hey, Danny, it's your turn to buy," one of the guys calls.

"Yeah, and none of that cheap shit either, Crispin," another jokes.

"Whatever, assholes, it goes down just as easy either way," one of the men answers as he walks toward the bar.

This must be Danny.

I didn't think to change, not that I had anything to change into, but my hair isn't a complete mess, seeing as I took it out of the ponytail and brushed my long blonde locks before getting in my car. I'm still in my gym clothes, but tonight that consists of a tight blue tank top and black yoga pants. The loose clothing was getting in the way when I was training with Roman, so I've gotten used to more formfitting workout attire.

When Danny walks up to the bar, I sit a little straighter, pushing out my chest a bit. My head turns to him slightly so I can watch him from the corner of my eye. He's standing two seats down from me, but no one is sitting between us. After he orders, he turns his entire body toward me, and he isn't subtle about scanning me from head to toe.

"Haven't seen you here before," he says.

I look around, faking confusion, as if I'm not sure he's talking to me. "Oh. This is my first time here. I just got out of the gym and decided I wasn't ready to go home quite yet."

He gives me what I'm sure is supposed to be a charming smile, but he looks more like a shark showing all of his teeth.

"This might sound forward, but what if I drop this off to my friends"—he points to the pitcher of beer the bartender set in front of him—"and come back and have a drink with you?"

A deceptively coy smile tugs on the corner of my mouth. "Sure."

"Be right back."

He takes the beer to his friends and says a few words to them. One of the three guys looks over at me and doesn't even try to contain his wolfish grin. They think he has me in the bag.

They're wrong.

Danny comes back over with his beer and sits next to me, holding out a hand. "I'm Danny," he introduces.

I slide my palm into his with a shy grin. "Cecilia."

"Beautiful name," he says, holding my hand a touch longer than necessary. "So you like to work out?"

"Yeah. I got into it a few months ago. I try to get in a workout a few times a week. There's nothing like the endorphin rush from pushing your body."

Once again, his gaze travels the length of me, and I have to control the shiver of disgust that rolls through me. Men like him only see one thing when they look at a woman, and judging by the way his eyes have a certain glint in them, I know exactly what that is.

"I hit the gym and do some lifting every now and then. Work keeps me pretty busy," he says.

"Oh yeah? What is it you do?"

"I'm a prison guard. Work a lot of twelve-hour shifts." He puffs out his chest a bit, like that's supposed to be impressive.

"That must be interesting. And scary sometimes. I can't imagine being around all those dangerous men."

He gets a cocky smile that I want to slap off his face. "Nah. They know who's boss in there. What about you? What do you do for a living?"

"Oh, I work for a food magazine. It's just online right now. It's mostly restaurant hotspots and up-and-coming places. That's one of the reasons I got into working out. Eating out all of the time can really pack it on." I let out a girlish giggle, and he eats it up.

"Maybe one of these days you can let me take you out to dinner. You must know the best places to go."

"We'll see," I say with a suggestive smile.

Danny hums and takes a sip of his beer. He looks behind him at the two pool tables. "Do you play pool?"

"I have a couple of times. I'm not very good, though."

"Well, you happen to be in the company of a pool expert. Come on, let's grab a table." He nods toward the back. "I can help you tighten up your game."

Letting out another stupid, flirty giggle, I nod. "Why not?"

He gets up from his seat and holds out his arm, signaling for me to walk in front of him. When we get to the pool table, he racks the balls and grabs two pool cues from the wall, handing one to me.

"I'll break and show you what to look for, okay?"

I nod and set my untouched beer on the table, pretending that I'm going to concentrate on what he's doing. "Okay."

Danny breaks, and nothing goes in. He points to a ball and shows me how to line it up and takes the shot. Again, he misses.

"I'm a little off my game tonight. You must have me nervous or something."

Smiling sweetly, I have to stop myself from rolling my eyes.

I take my turn and miss. Not surprising, considering I really am terrible at this game. My sister is the pool shark of the family, but having watched her play a few times, I know that Danny isn't nearly as good as he tries to boast when he takes his next shot and misses again.

He laughs it off, but I can tell he's getting frustrated that he isn't impressing me the way he'd hoped.

When it's my turn again, I take the shot and it goes in. I jump up and down like an excited teenager.

"Good job. Now let's see if you can do it again," Danny says with a tight smile.

Might have hit a nerve with that shot.

I purposely miss the next. "Darn," I say with a little frown.

Danny sends me a wink and walks around the table, studying the balls. He's making a big show of trying to find the perfect shot, and again, I have to stop myself from rolling my eyes. Instead, I walk over to the tall table where my beer is sitting and wrap my hand around the bottle, squeezing it to release some of the pressure building inside me. Pretending to give a shit about this guy and the stupid way he's trying to impress me is grating on my last nerve.

Before Danny takes his shot, something behind me catches his attention. I turn around, and standing only a few feet from us is Cash.

And he looks fucking pissed.

"What the hell are you doing?" Cash asks, looking at the beer in my hand and then over to Danny before his ice-cold gaze finds mine again.

"You know this guy, Cecilia?" Danny asks.

Cash's stare shoots to Danny. "Yeah, asshole, she does," Cash answers before he turns his frigid blue eyes back to me. "And I thought I knew her, too."

I'm speechless. I have no idea what to say or do at this moment. All the scenarios that ran through my head when I imagined how I would play this kind of thing never accounted for Cash showing up.

"Let's go," Cash says.

"I don't think she wants to go with you, buddy," Danny says.

"I didn't ask for your opinion, *buddy*," Cash replies.

"It's fine," I finally choke out, standing from my chair and looking at Danny. "It was nice meeting you." I grab my bag, and Cash turns, expecting me to follow—and I do.

When we get outside, I hurry my steps behind Cash's long, angry strides to his bike that's parked right behind my car.

"How did you know where I was?" I ask.

He whirls on me, anger flashing in his eyes. "That's seriously what you want to know right now?"

"Are you tracking me?"

He scoffs and shakes his head. "Unbelievable. No, Cece, I'm not tracking you. I never thought I'd have a reason to. I was picking up a part for the bike shop and saw your car parked next to a bar. A fucking *bar*. You told me you stopped drinking."

"Look, I can explain. I—"

"Are you drunk?" he asks, cutting me off.

"No. No, I didn't have one sip. I swear."

He releases another huff that tells me he doesn't believe me.

"I swear to you, I didn't drink anything. If you would just let me explain why—"

"Get in the car," he demands, shutting me down again. "I'll follow you home."

The fact that he thinks he can demand anything from me without hearing what I have to say pisses me right off. I know exactly what it looked like, but Cash is refusing to let me explain—to hear my side.

I shake my head. "You know what? Don't bother."

Grabbing my keys from my purse, I unlock my door. Cash gets on his bike, and as soon as my car starts, I throw it in drive and take off down the street. If he won't listen to me, then I'm not going to wait for him.

It doesn't take long for him to catch up to me on the road. There's only one highway between Shine and Ayre. When we get to my house, he pulls up behind me. I know Lucy is working tonight, which means Jude is probably at the bar with her.

I get out of my car and stand next to it with my arms crossed while he dismounts his bike.

"Are you going to let me explain now, or are you going to keep cutting me off?" I ask with a very obvious bite to my tone.

"You know," he starts with a caustic chuckle as he stalks toward me. "Imagine my surprise when what I thought was going to be a simple errand turns into me catching you out at a bar, flirting with another man. What the fuck are you doing?" he asks through a clenched jaw. "Because to me it looks like you're burning your life down and taking me with you. You finally have something good, Cece, and you can't deal with that, I guess."

"That's not what was happening."

"I saw you with my own two eyes. You were holding a beer and hanging out with that guy in a bar, for Chrissake. I'm not a fucking moron."

"Could have fooled me," I mumble under my breath, but he catches it, nonetheless.

"You know what? Fuck this." He spins on his heel, and in four long strides, is back to his bike.

"Wait," I call. I'm pissed, and he's definitely not happy with me right now, but I have to make him hear me out. Because he's right. My life is good. And I've worked hard to get it here.

"I wasn't flirting to flirt. I..." *Shit, how do I explain this?* "I met this guy—"

"Are you serious right now? You're running after me to tell me you met someone else?"

Immediately my head starts shaking back and forth before he finishes his sentence. "No. Please let me get it all out." He stares at me for a beat, then nods once. "I got the number for a guy who makes men who hurt women pay. I guess you would call him a vigilante of sorts. You know how you met my friend Leandra in the store a few weeks ago?" He nods again, but his jaw is still set hard enough to cut glass. "Okay. Her cousin's boyfriend beat her to hell. When Thea was at the hospital, one of the nurses gave Leandra a phone number for a guy who helps women out of those kinds of situations. He sends a message, and if they don't listen, he basically burns their life down. When I didn't show up at my self-defense classes for a few weeks after the kidnapping, Leandra thought maybe I'd found myself in the same situation as her cousin and gave me the number."

"What the hell does this have to do with you going to a bar?"

"I'm getting there." I inhale a deep breath. "That guy you saw me with was the man who put Leandra's cousin in the hospital."

"What the hell, Cece?" he asks in a booming voice. "Why on earth would you put yourself in a situation like that?"

"I called the number Leandra gave me. Not because I needed his help, but because I want to do what he does. I met with him and asked him to train me. To make me a fighter. I don't just want to be able to get away. I want to be able to do some damage. Real damage. Damage that makes them never hurt another woman again."

"Wait. So you've been training with a vigilante...to become a vigilante? And what? You were going to take that guy on?"

I nod. "Yes. And I still plan to."

CHAPTER ELEVEN
CASH

What in the actual hell?

"I know it sounds crazy," Cece says, holding her hands in front of her. "But listen. Guys like that don't see women as a threat. It's kind of perfect. Roman has been training me, and I'm a good fighter, Cash. He thinks I'm almost ready to go in the field."

"*Almost?* Then what the hell were you doing there tonight?"

"I went to my self-defense class. I missed the girls since I haven't been going as much. Leandra was there talking about how Danny is out there living his life, and her cousin is scared of every little noise. I remember that feeling, Cash. She mentioned the bar he hangs out in, and I don't know, I was pissed, and the bar is on my way home. Thought I would go in and check it out, see if he was there."

"And then what? Take him out back and beat the shit out of him?"

"Yeah, that was the plan I was going to go with," she replies with a shrug. *A fucking shrug.*

"So many things could have gone wrong with that, Cece. What if he had a weapon? What if his friends would have come out there? You could have been arrested, or hurt worse than anything you did to him."

"I've been hurt, Cash. I've been nearly broken, but I survived. And now I know how to fight back. I know how to hurt back."

"You're not doing it. I won't let you."

Her head rears back and the look on her face is eerily similar to the one I've seen on her sister's face. And we all know how well that tends to turn out.

"You aren't going to stop me."

Cece whirls around and stomps down the walkway to her house and up her stairs before punching the key in the lock and slamming the door behind her. Before she has a chance to relock the door, I open it and step inside, coming face to face with a very pissed-off woman.

"I'm trying to keep you safe. Why in the ever-loving hell would you want to put yourself in that situation again?"

She marches into the kitchen and grabs a glass from the cupboard, then fills it with water before taking a drink. When she slams the glass on said counter, she pins me with her glare.

"Because I have to. The only thing that has made me feel right in my skin—right in my head—has been focusing all the rage into something else. This is that something. I can't explain it to you since you've never been through what I went through, but having this goal, learning how to use my body to hurt someone who hurts women, has given me a purpose. I won't let you or anyone else take that away from me."

We're both breathing hard as we stare at each other over the counter separating us. Neither of us says anything for several moments as what she's telling me sinks in. It's the determination—the passion—in her voice that gives me pause. But it's more than that I hear from her lips. She lost her power being on that compound. It was stolen from her again when she was kidnapped and that disgusting asshole was on top of her. She's fighting tooth and nail to get it back. To take her pain and bend it into something else, something that gives her back what was taken from her over and over.

I inhale a deep breath and blow it out, trying to make sense of all of my thoughts. There's no way I can let her do this. She's alone, and I don't care what this Roman guy says, she's not going out by herself—no matter how ready he thinks she is.

But I also understand her need to do something. The drinking didn't help, the rage baking didn't help, and the constant pressure she feels to move past years of hurt and abuse definitely doesn't help.

"Here's the deal, Cece. I can't let you do this alone. I don't know what Roman's protocol usually is, but if this is something you need to do, you have to do it with me."

"I don't know if that's allowed. Roman doesn't know you and—"

"I don't give a shit about Roman and what he does or doesn't know. I know you, and I know that me telling you outright not to do this isn't going to work. What I'm asking you is, please, if this is the path you choose to go down, let me go down it with you."

"What do you mean exactly? You're going to help me? Not try to stop me?" She eyes me suspiciously.

"That's what I'm saying."

"What if I tell you I don't want your help?"

I splay my hands on the countertop and lean forward. "Then I'm going to tell your sister what you've been doing, and you'll have to deal with her without any help from me."

"That's low, Cash."

"That's the deal, Cece."

Her eyes narrow, but I don't waver. Honestly, I can't believe I'm even suggesting going along with this crazy agenda she has, but I know I can't let her do this alone. Even with me, this could go wrong in a million different ways, but at least I'll be there to protect her.

She nods decisively. "Okay. I can live with that."

"That means no running off half-cocked. You can't be pissed and try to confront this Danny guy—or any guy—on your own. We have to be methodical and levelheaded, yeah?"

"It's a deal," she says, holding out her hand. I grip it in mine and then pull her over the counter, placing a kiss on her pink lips.

When I pull away, she has a slightly dazed look on her face. "What was that for?"

"Our make-up kiss," I tell her. I bend over the counter and take her lips again, letting mine linger. The last thing I want to do is fight with her. We've spent enough time doing that tonight. "Come walk me out. It's late, and we both have an early start."

She walks around the counter and to her front door. When she opens it for me, I bend and kiss her again.

"And you won't tell Lucy, right?" she asks.

"As long as you stick to our agreement." Telling Lucy would have only been a last resort to begin with. Cece trusts me to keep her confidence. If I couldn't have convinced her to either stop with this insane plan or to at least let me help her, then I would have *maybe* considered it. But I would've probably put some sort of tracking device on her car or phone, like she accused me of earlier, rather than run to her sister. I know Cece well enough that it wouldn't have stopped her anyways. It would have only given her a reason to shut me out. This time, probably for good.

"I'll see you in the morning, sweetheart. Lock up behind me."

Walking to my bike, I get on and start it, watching as Cece closes the door before pulling out of her driveway.

On the way back to the clubhouse, one question keeps tumbling through my mind over and over.

What the hell have I gotten into?

Two days later, while working at the house, Cece came upstairs. I've finished the hallway bathroom and have been working on pulling the flooring and making sure the boards are secure before I have someone come lay new carpet. I opted to have hardwood downstairs, but I want the bedrooms to have a plush, warm feel. Seeing as the house is old, it's a good idea to double-check all the subflooring to make sure it's sound. I turned and Cece was standing awkwardly in the doorway of the bedroom I'm working in.

"So, I want to go back to the bar tonight," she told me.

It's not as though I'd thought she'd forgotten about anything. I'd never be so lucky. Honestly, as determined as she was the other night, I was surprised she didn't tell me this yesterday.

"Okay," I said, and she looked at me with a hint of surprise in her eyes.

"Okay? That's it?"

I stopped trying to tear up a stubborn piece of padding that they must have used a gallon of glue on and stood up.

"I knew it was coming, sweetheart. I told you I was in whenever you needed me, and I meant it."

"I don't even know if he's going to be there," she said.

"Only one way to find out."

And that's how we ended up sitting in my truck across the street from the bar, keeping an eye on the front. I'd come by earlier and checked for cameras in the alley behind the building. Since there were none to be found, Ccce decided she was going to somehow lure him out there. I have an idea how she's going to do it, and I am not thrilled with any man thinking he's got a shot at getting in my girl's pants in the back of a dirty alley. Even if it's only because she's playing the part. But she's right about it being the fastest and least complicated way to get him where she wants him. Still doesn't sit right with me, though. Not that any of this does. But it beats the alternative of having her sneak away and potentially getting herself into a situation she can't get out of.

"I think that's him," she says, dipping down in her seat.

Looking over, I see the asshole from the other night walking toward the entrance with a couple of his friends. They aren't all dressed in the same pants and white T-shirts this time. Instead of coming from work, they're obviously on the prowl, wearing their finest jeans and fitted tees with about twenty pounds of gel in their hair between the three of them. Fuck, I can practically smell their body spray from here.

Fortunately—or unfortunately, depending on how you look at it—this works in our favor.

"Okay, let's go over the plan," I say.

"I'm going to go in there and flirt up a storm. Tell him you were my ex, and I just wanted to get rid of you quickly. I'll tell him how I couldn't stop thinking about him, blah, blah, blah. I'll be out in forty-five minutes. Tops."

"I fucking hate this," I murmur, and Cece shoots me a sympathetic look.

"Thank you," she says, and I look at her in confusion. "I know this is hard for you. That being here while I put myself in this situation goes against everything you stand for. And I know you're doing it for me."

My hand cups the side of her face, and I brush my thumb along the warm skin of her cheek. "Cece, I'm here for me as much as you. There is nothing in this world I wouldn't do to help you feel like you have your life—your power—back. Yes, I hate that you're walking in there, but men like him deserve to feel even a fraction of what you felt so many times over. If this helps *you*, then that's all I really care about."

She looks at me with so much appreciation in her soft blue gaze. I'd rather take her out of here and to our spot, where I would be content holding her and kissing her, hearing the little gasps she lets out when I trail my lips across hers. I haven't even had her in my bed yet, but I'm completely addicted to her. That wouldn't be enough for her though, and so I'm going to help her find what she needs here.

"Okay," she says, blowing out a long breath. "I'm going in."

"If at any point you feel unsafe, text me immediately," I tell her for the twentieth time since we left the house.

"I won't. Knowing you're out here, I've never felt safer."

She smiles and opens the truck door, crossing the street and heading into the bar and out of my sight.

Forty minutes pass, and if anyone noticed me here, they'd probably have called the cops by now. I don't think I've moved an inch since she walked into that bar. Shit, I don't think I've blinked. The only movement I've made is my eyes checking the clock on the dash for half a second before staring at the door again.

Finally, it opens, and that asshole walks out, holding Cece's hand. He leans down and whispers something in her ear, and she tosses her head back in laughter.

Fuck, I really hate this.

When they disappear around the corner, I get out of my truck and follow. Just as I turn the corner, they dip behind the building into the alleyway I checked earlier today. I reach the edge of the building and see Cece leaning against the wall with that asshole pressed against her. My body tenses, but Cece turns her head and gives me a small nod, telling me that she's okay. This is part of the plan—my least favorite part—but she's still in control.

"A friend of mine told me that she knew you when I talked to her yesterday," Cece says as the asshole kisses her shoulder, his hand grabbing her waist.

"I'm not really interested in talking about your friends right now, baby."

How a punk like this would think Cece could ever really be interested in him is beyond me. I suppose this proves that she really is a good little actress.

She lets out a deceptively light giggle. "I'm sure, but she had a lot to say."

"Still don't care," he mumbles.

"No? What if I told you her name was Leandra? Said you used to date her cousin, Thea."

Danny stops pawing at her and stands straight. "What?"

"You remember Thea, right? You are the one who put her in the hospital a few weeks ago. The surgery to fix her orbital bone went well, by the way."

He takes a step back. "Who the hell are you?"

Cece pushes off the wall, and that's when I see it. The shift into something different. *Someone* different. It's as though the carefully guarded rage that is always simmering just below the surface is seeping out of her.

Cece smiles, but it isn't kind or sweet—not like the ones she gives me. This one is vicious. "Me? I'm her revenge."

And it explodes.

Cece punches Danny in the face, clocking him in the corner of the jaw. Even from here, I can see that it's out of place now.

"Fucking bitch," he yells and takes a swing. She ducks in time and he punches the brick wall behind her. She throws her leg and kicks him in the side, nailing the perfect kidney shot. His hand immediately clutches his side.

"You're going to fucking get it, bitch."

He hurls himself toward her and tries to tackle her to the ground. Cece is quick, though, and she uses his momentum to push him headfirst into the dumpster. I hear his head crack against the metal, and he groans. But he isn't finished yet. He rights himself and comes at her again, swinging wide. Cece ducks and punches him twice in quick succession on his already injured side. There's no way that man isn't going to be pissing blood. When he grabs her hair, she sweeps his legs out from under him and they both fall to the ground, Cece landing on top. She throws another punch while he has her by her blonde locks, breaking his nose. He uses his hips to dislodge her, and she tumbles forward, landing in a low crouch. Danny rolls over, ready to go after her again, but I step out from behind the corner.

"What's going on here?" I ask casually, though I don't need his answer. I just need his attention off Cece for a moment.

Danny looks at me, but Cece never takes her eyes off him.

"What the fuck are you doing here? What is this?" he asks, his eyes darting between the both of us.

"Like the lady said," I say, walking closer. "Revenge."

He tries to stand, but before he can, my long strides eat up the distance between us, and I kick him in the chest. He falls back, moaning in pain. Pretty sure something in there is cracked now. Grabbing him by the front of the shirt, I twist, tightening the material around his throat.

"I hear you like to beat on women," I say.

"Fuck you," he spits at me.

A low chuckle escapes my throat. "You're the one who looks fucked, asshole."

My fist connects with the side of his face. Over and over again, I punch him. His mouth is bloody, and it looks like Cece's friend isn't the only one who is going to be having some reconstructive surgery.

When I stop, Danny is barely struggling anymore.

"Look at me, asshole," I say, shaking him a bit. "Look at my face."

He tries to focus, but it won't be long before he loses consciousness.

"If you go near Thea again, I'll find you. If you even think about hurting another woman, I'll find you. I'll have eyes on you until you take your last breath, and if anything happens to another woman at your hands, I'll be there when you take it. You get me, *buddy*?"

Danny coughs and mumbles, "Yeah, I get you."

"I didn't hear you, asshole," I say, giving him another rough shake.

"Yes," he says as clearly as he can. "I understand."

"Good. Night night, fucker," I say and punch him in the side of his head so hard I knock him out.

Tossing his body to the ground, I lift myself from the dirty pavement, and Cece is standing in front of me in the next heartbeat.

Both of us are breathing hard as I turn toward her. "Listen, I know I said I would only get involved if you were in danger of getting hurt, but—"

Cece throws her arms around my neck and smashes her mouth to mine. On instinct, I open, and her tongue invades, dueling with mine in a deliciously erotic dance. This is the complete opposite of the sweet kisses we've shared up until this moment. My fingers tunnel along the back of her head, tangling in her hair, and she winces.

"Shit," I say, pulling away, remembering that he had used her hair to try to take her down. "I'm sorry, sweetheart."

She shakes her head. "It's okay. Just a little tender right now."

My hands cup her beautiful face, and the blood on my knuckles looks bright red against her pale skin as I stare into her sparkling blue eyes. It's almost as though I'm seeing someone different staring back at me. But no, she's the same amazing girl she's always been; I'm just getting to see this other side of her. And it's done nothing to quell the emotions building inside me for months, hell, years. If anything, it's made me see clearly for the first time that there was no escaping this, escaping her. I never stood a chance.

"We should get out of here before he comes to," I say and let my hands drop before I take one of hers in mine, pulling her toward the street.

When we make it to my truck, I open her door and she hops in before I jog around to the driver's side. I start the engine and pull away from the curb, heading toward the highway that will take us back to Shine.

"I'm not mad," she starts, and I quickly look at her with a question in my eyes before refocusing on the road.

"Back there, you apologized for stepping in. I'm not mad about it. I mean, I had a handle on the situation and didn't need your help, but I'm not mad that you beat the shit out of him."

"You were amazing. One of the hardest things I've ever had to watch was him trying to hurt you." I exhale a harsh breath. "I couldn't stand by anymore."

"It's okay. I don't know if I ever really expected you to," she says with a light chuckle. "We should go back to the house so I can fix up your hand." She nods at my rapidly swelling fist that's gripping the steering wheel. "Do you think anything's broken?"

I flex my fingers a few times and shake my hand. "Nah, it'll be fine."

We get back to my house, and when I open the door, I head upstairs to the hallway bathroom to grab the first aid kit. When I turn around, Cece is standing behind me.

"Here," she says, holding out her hand, and I pass her the kit.

She sets it on the counter next to the sink and turns the water on. Grabbing my hand, she examines my knuckles then places it under the running water. The warm water stings at first, but her touch is the only thing I can really concentrate on. Cece grabs a couple paper towels from the roll sitting next to her and dabs them on my knuckles.

I've never been tended to like this. In the clubhouse, we're expected to deal with our own scrapes and bruises, which is perfectly fine with me. I can't really see any of my brothers playing nursemaid. But with Cece, it's more than just a quick wash and a Band-Aid. The way she carefully examines each cut makes me feel cared for, cherished even.

"Not too bad," she says, reexamining my wounds. She grabs a small package of alcohol wipes and rips it open, pressing the cold wipe against my skin. I hiss, and her lips tip up in a smirk.

"What? I don't care how tough you are, that shit stings," I tell her.

She chuckles and grabs the antibiotic ointment, spreading a decent amount across my skin before grabbing a few Band-Aids and covering her work.

"There, all better," she says and brings my hand to her mouth, kissing the back of it.

My uninjured hand reaches for the side of her face, and my fingers sweep her blonde hair away, tucking it behind her ear.

"Thank you," I say.

She leans up, taking my mouth in a kiss. It's not as frenzied as the one in the alley, but it's hardly sweet and innocent, either. She opens her mouth, and I swipe my tongue inside, slowly and gently playing with hers.

When she pulls away, her eyes are glowing with desire. I have to say it looks damn good on her.

"Cash," she whispers, looking away for a moment then back to me. "I'm done taking it slow."

CHAPTER TWELVE
CECE

That was probably one of the most vulnerable sentences I've ever uttered. But I want this. He could push me away and tell me we're still taking it slow. He could tell me he doesn't think I'm ready. I'm putting myself out there for him, hoping he grabs my hand and takes this step with me.

And he does.

When his mouth crashes to mine, the force nearly topples me over, but Cash bands his arm around my back.

This kiss is so much more. The one in the alleyway was fueled by intense emotion that I still haven't processed. The one moments ago was a question of sorts, me testing the waters a bit. This one, though? It's filled with the promise of more. And I really want more right now.

"Fuck, baby," he groans as I break the kiss and trail my lips over the skin of his neck. "That feels so good."

When my hands travel to the bottom of his T-shirt, I slip them under the fabric and run my palms up his toned stomach, which I've only had the pleasure of seeing once.

"I remember walking into this bathroom a few weeks ago and seeing you without your shirt for the first time," I whisper against his throat. "I've never had that kind of reaction to a man before."

"Oh yeah?" he moans as my tongue plays inside the little divot at the base of his throat. "What reaction was that?"

"It was like this ache exploded inside me. I wanted to reach out and touch you," I tell him as I do just that.

"I wish you would have," he says.

I shake my head and look into his lust-filled eyes. "No. It wouldn't have been the right time. This, though? This is the right time."

"I couldn't agree more, sweetheart."

Cash lifts his hands, cupping my face as he takes my mouth in another wild, passion-fueled kiss. I have no idea what to do or how to do this. In a lot of ways, this is a first for me. So I react with what feels natural. I press further into him, and his hands slide down my body to my hips before they come around to the front of my jeans and grip my upper thighs. His thumb brushes over my front seam, and that light touch has the muscles in my stomach tightening.

"If anything is too much, tell me right away. We can go at your pace, sweetheart."

I nod, biting my lip, and he lifts one hand to my mouth, pulling the abused flesh from between my teeth.

"I want to kiss you here," he says, his thumb still gently rubbing me through my jeans. "Is that okay?"

"I've never had someone do that," I tell him, again opening myself up to the man standing before me. The man who, time and time again, has refused to let the world swallow me whole.

"Are you going to let me taste you, sweetheart?"

I nod, but he shakes his head. "I need words."

"Yes, Cash. Please."

His lips slam into mine again, and his hand leaves my center, both moving to where my ass is sitting on the counter, and he lifts me. Instinctively, I wrap my legs around his waist and feel the effect I'm having on him. I squirm, liking the way it feels to be this close, having our bodies so connected.

"Fuck, baby," Cash groans out. "I'm going to come in my pants if you keep that up."

I don't stop, and he growls. I *really* like that sound.

Cash spins us toward the doorway and steps out of the bathroom, carrying me down the steps and into the living room. He gently sets me on the couch and stands, reaching behind the neck of his shirt and pulling it over his head. I get an unobstructed view of his chest and stomach, and the same flood of desire I had the first time rushes through me.

He stares at me and places his hand over his heart, rubbing the spot. "What you do to me, Cece." He shakes his head. "I've never felt this way. I can't even begin to describe it."

"I know," I whisper, looking up at him. "I feel it, too."

He kneels in front of me before gripping me around the waist as I lean forward and press my mouth to his. My hands tangle in his hair, gripping the thick strands in my fists. His fingers flex against my waist, and I lean back, lifting my arms in the air. Cash's needy gaze bores into me as he slides the shirt up my body, freeing me from the confines of my clothes. We stare at each other for a beat before his gaze travels down to my breasts covered in pink lace.

"You're breathtaking," he says, moving his hands to each of my breasts and filling his palms as his thumbs caress each nipple over the thin material. My overly sensitive buds scrape against the lace of my bra. It's not entirely uncomfortable, but I'd rather feel his touch skin to skin than through any fabric. Reaching behind my back, I unclasp the band and let the straps slip down my arms. The material covering my breasts falls away—leaving me exposed to the man on his knees in front of me.

"Fuck," he breathes out as one finger glides over and around my hard nipple.

Cash's eyes bounce between what his finger is doing and my face, gauging my reaction. Holding my half-lidded gaze, he leans forward and licks the peak, swirling his tongue around and around. My head falls back, and I let out a long moan. I never thought there could be so much pleasure in feeling his lips on my naked skin, but I was so, so wrong.

I feel dizzy and grounded at the same time as his hand comes to my other breast, and he scrapes his palm over my flesh. I'm writhing on the couch, the sound of my panting breaths filling the room. It's impossible for me to keep my hips still, but I'm unsure of what I need to quench this fire inside me that's quickly burning out of control.

"It's okay, baby. I got you." He licks once more then pulls my nipple into his hot mouth, sucking deep once before lifting his head.

The sensation makes my back bow, and he sits up before flicking the button of my jeans.

"If your skin tastes this good, I can't wait to taste your pussy."

"God, please," I beg, and he sends me an indecent smirk as his fingers grip the tab of my zipper and pull it down. If his mouth on my skin makes me feel this good, this out of control, I can't wait to feel what he can do with his tongue on my center.

Cash grips the waist of my jeans and shimmies the fabric down my thighs, then pulls them off completely. He stares at the pink fabric of my panties, and without looking, I'm positive there's a wet spot in the center.

"Goddamn, Cece. You are so fucking beautiful. I could stay here like this and stare at your perfect body all night."

A smile tips the corner of my mouth. "I hope you do more than stare, Cash."

He releases a deep chuckle. "Don't worry, baby. I plan on doing a lot more than just looking."

Cash leans forward and licks over the fabric of my panties. My body jerks, and he does it again.

"More," I beg.

"Shh. I've waited a long time for this, baby. I'm going to savor every moment."

He licks again, and I squirm under his tongue. He looks up at me once again to gauge my reaction.

"Please. I need more," I plead. Honestly, I'm not even sure what I'm begging for. I've never been in this kind of situation before, needing something I've never known, but craving it like my life depends on it all the same.

He finally takes some measure of mercy on me and slides my panties from my body, leaving me completely exposed and laid out in front of him.

Then his head dives to my center and he licks through my pussy as though he's filled with a thirst that can only be quenched with my body.

"Oh God," I cry, my head falling back against the couch. "Don't stop."

He growls into my pussy as his tongue flicks against my clit, then swirls around my entrance, dipping in every few rounds, tasting my core.

"That feels so good," I moan out and look down at him. There is something unbelievably erotic about seeing this man with his head between my legs, eating at me as though he can't get enough. "Fuck."

His eyes lift to mine, and he holds my gaze while he enters one finger—then two—inside me without lifting his mouth from my pussy. At every turn, every new thing Cash does to my body, he makes sure to gauge my reaction. If I wasn't already pretty sure I'm falling in love with the biker before me, I'd be damn sure now.

A tingling sensation that I've never felt before starts building where his mouth is connected to me. It quickly spreads through my legs and upper body. Moments later, the feeling detonates into an explosion of sensation, and I cry out. Cash never stops as I writhe beneath him, my hips jerking with every pulse, with every earth-shattering burst that comes when his tongue brushes over my clit.

"Holy shit," I breathe out.

Cash lifts his head, kneeling over my body and crashes his mouth to mine. I taste myself on his tongue, taste the indescribable pleasure he just pulled from my core.

"I've said it before, but you are devastatingly breathtaking, sweetheart. Especially when you come undone."

He kisses me again and again. I wrap my legs around his waist, rubbing myself against the bulge in his pants. I'm so incredibly sensitive after my orgasm, and the motion is building that sensation inside me again, but it's not quite enough.

I break the kiss and whisper, "I need more."

He doesn't waste a moment and lifts himself from my body, standing before me. Grabbing his wallet from his back pocket, Cash pulls out two foil packets and tosses them on the couch next to me, then drops his wallet on the floor. His hand reaches for the button of his worn jeans, and he undoes it. I feel his gaze boring into me as he slides the zipper down, but I don't look up. My eyes are firmly transfixed to the way he slides his jeans and underwear down his legs before standing straight and running his hand over his thick cock jutting out in front of him. I'm completely mesmerized by his movement and the bead of liquid at the tip.

"You still with me, baby?" he asks in a husky whisper.

"Yeah," I answer, nodding my head.

I look up and catch the smirk dancing on his lips.

He steps forward and grabs my waist, positioning me so my entire body lies across the wide couch, spread out before him.

Cash grabs one of the foil packets and kneels between my thighs, ripping it open with his teeth before he rolls the latex over his length. When he bends forward, his lips land on my breast, licking around the sensitive peak, then he sucks my nipple into his mouth, the tugging feeling causing my body to light up.

"Fuck, your skin tastes so good. I want to lick you from head to toe and taste all that sweetness," he says while he licks and sucks my skin.

"I wouldn't stop you," I breathe out as my fingers play in his hair.

He chuckles against my flesh, then lifts his head, bringing his lips to mine and kissing me, his tongue delving deep into my mouth. When he breaks the kiss, he has one elbow propped next to my head, his hand tangled in my messy hair, and the other reaches between us, positioning himself at my entrance. My hands slide from his waist around to his back. I grip him as he enters me, our gazes never breaking from one another. I release a keening moan as Cash's breath becomes shaky as he begins to move inside me.

"Holy shit, Cece. You feel so fucking good," he whispers. "I'll never get enough of you."

Tears prick the backs of my eyes. I've never felt this. This connection and absolute rightness with another person. It's all too much and not enough at the same time. I need more.

And he gives it to me.

He lifts his upper body, his strong arms holding himself over me as his hips change position. He wraps one hand around my calf, and he loops my leg around his waist. One of my hands grips his straining forearm and he takes the other in his, linking our fingers next to my head. He presses deeper, the change hitting a spot inside me that I've never felt. This is like when he had his mouth on me, but different, deeper.

"Oh God," I cry out as the walls of my pussy begin to pulse and that newly familiar feeling begins to spread from my core.

"That's it, baby. You're going to come for me again. Goddamn, you feel so good tightening that sweet cunt around my cock."

He moves inside me, hitting that spot over and over. Within moments, I'm crying out, and Cash keeps his pace as wave after wave of the most amazing feeling takes me under then pushes me back up, only to do it all over again.

"Fuck," Cash bellows, and I feel him jerk inside me, his gaze becoming slightly unfocused as he pumps a couple more times, then stills inside me.

Both of us are breathing hard as sweat drips down his flushed face.

He leans down, taking my mouth in a reverent kiss. Though he's still holding most of his weight with his arm, his damp chest brushes against mine and I shiver.

"You cold, sweetheart?"

I shake my head. "I'm perfect."

His gaze bores into me before he inclines his head and places another soft kiss against my lips. "That you definitely are. And mine."

There's no containing my wide smile that stretches from ear to ear. "And yours."

Cash presses a quick kiss against my smile that he says he loves to taste, and he lifts himself from the couch. Cash walks into the kitchen, naked as the day he was born. When he returns, he's rid himself of the condom, but he's holding one of the new towels we bought. He brushes the warm, damp fabric through my center, and I moan.

"Not sore then?" he asks with a small grin.

I shake my head. "I feel amazing."

Cash lies down on his side next to me and turns me to face him. His hand runs over my thigh, and he lifts it over his hip, settling us together like a naked pretzel.

He gently sweeps my hair from my face and over my shoulder. "I don't want you to leave me tonight," he says in a quiet voice.

My chest feels as though it's being cracked open with his words. "Then I won't."

His lips brush mine softly, like the first few weeks when we were taking things slowly. Guess that plan is shot out of the water. Not that I mind in the least. Nope, not at all.

"I need a bed in this house," he says, and I giggle.

"I like being this close to you." I wiggle my hips, and his face dives into my neck with a growl.

"You're going to kill me, sweetheart."

"Well, until you have a bed, the couch will have to do. At least you bought one big enough."

Cash lifts his head and smiles down at me. "When we were at the store and you had lain down on it to test it out, I knew I had to have it. You looked so beautiful and happy that day."

I smile up at him, and he kisses the tip of my nose.

"Actually, I have something that might work." He hops up from the couch and stares down at me with that same look on his face I saw earlier. "Damn, I'm really fucking glad I bought this couch."

Another giggle escapes me as he disappears down the hallway. A minute later, he's back with two plastic shopping bags.

"What's that?" I ask, sitting up to try to peer into the bags.

Cash chuckles as he starts pulling things out. "When Tanya found out I bought a house, she showed up at the clubhouse with a bunch of bedding. Said men never think about thread count or mattress covers, or some shit like that. I threw it in the closet and didn't think about it again."

He unzips the plastic packaging and pulls out a thick memory-foam mattress cover. "It's not quite the same, but it's better than nothing."

He lays out the large rectangular pad, then grabs the other plastic bag, pulling a set of sheets from it and laying one over the mattress cover. He stands naked and proud, looking down at his work. When he glances at me, he has an almost apologetic look in his gaze. "Sorry I don't have something more comfortable."

Rising from the couch, I pick up the top sheet from the floor. "This is perfect."

I sit down on the makeshift bed, turning to grab the pillows that had fallen from the couch, placing them behind me. Shaking the sheet out so it covers the rest of the pad, I let it fall over me.

Cash watches with a small grin on his face before he lies down next to me, pulling me so that half of my body is splayed over his chest. "Now it's perfect," he says, trailing his fingers up and down my back in a soothing motion.

It doesn't take long for my eyes to get heavy as I relax into the strong man underneath me.

He kisses the top of my head. "Good night, sweetheart," he whispers, and moments later, I'm fast asleep in his arms.

It's the incessant ringing that pulls me from slumber first. Then Cash's gravelly voice hits my ears.

"Hey," he says, listening to whoever is on the other end. "She's fine. She's right here." Silence for another second. "Yeah, hold on." He hands the phone to me. "It's your sister."

Shit.

After last night, I didn't even think to let Lucy know I wouldn't be home, not that I would have known how to explain it.

I bring the phone to my ear, still having no idea what to say.

"Hello?"

"Oh, Jesus Christ, Cece. Do you know how fucking worried I've been? I got up this morning and your bed is made with no note, no coffee made, nothing."

It's not unusual for me to be up and out the door before Lucy or Jude these days, but there's always some sign that I was home the night before.

"Sorry, I was trying out some new recipes at Cash's and fell asleep on the couch."

"You fell asleep?" she asks flatly.

"Yeah. It was a long day." Not a complete lie.

"And you didn't hear your phone the forty times I tried to call you?"

My sister tends to exaggerate when she's upset. Standing from the floor, I head into the kitchen and grab my phone from my purse. Forty-three missed calls. Okay, so maybe this isn't one of those times.

"Shit, I'm sorry. My phone was in the other room, and I didn't hear it."

Lucy scoffs. "Didn't hear it...I've been freaking the hell out over here, ready to call every brother to launch a manhunt—and all because you didn't hear your phone?"

She's really fucking pissed.

"Listen, I said I was sorry. I fucked up by not having my phone next to me, but there's no need to go nuclear on me," I say, trying to keep the irritation out of my voice.

There's silence for a beat, and then, "I was fucking terrified something happened to you!"

"I know. Jesus! I'm sorry. But you don't get to yell at me for one mistake."

"It's a lot more than one mistake, Cece. Don't act like I don't have every reason to be pissed at you."

"Lucy, I'm not dealing with this first thing in the morning." I take a calming breath in an attempt to calm myself and not fight with my sister. "You know where I am, and you know I'm fine. But you can't use shit that's in the past to fuel your anger over this. That's not fair."

I hear Jude say something to her, but can't make out his exact words.

"Fine," she grits out. "I'm glad I know everything is okay now. I was worried and may be overreacting a bit." Though she's saying the words, I'm not convinced she actually believes them. "Please let me know if you're going to be spending the night out in the future." Okay, she is one hundred percent being coached by her boyfriend. She exhales. "I was really worried, Cece," she says in a softer voice. "Can you please just let me know next time you stay out all night?" This version sounds more like my sister.

"I will. It was honestly an accident, but I'll be more careful next time. If I'm too tired to drive, I'll let you know. I'm really sorry I scared you," I tell her, and I mean it.

"Are you dropping anything off at Cool Beans today?" she asks.

"No, Betsy said she doesn't need anything until tomorrow, so I have the day off."

"Okay, I'll see you when you get home, then. I love you, sister."

I clear my throat, trying to get rid of the lump that's suddenly there. "I love you, too."

She hangs up and I drop my hands into my lap. "Shit," I breathe out.

Cash's hand rubs my back, soothing the tension that has my muscles tight. "You fell asleep baking? Wow, I feel like your dirty little secret," he says in a teasing voice.

I turn to him, worried that he's trying to cover his disappointment that I didn't tell my sister what was really going on.

"Are you upset I didn't tell her about us?"

Cash shakes his head. "You guys have a complicated relationship that I won't pretend to completely understand. But I'm not a fan of keeping secrets, either. We've been more than friends for weeks now. I think it's time we make it known what we are to each other."

That's completely fair, but I'm still hesitant. "What exactly are we?"

Cash sits up and presses his lips to mine. "You're mine, and I'm yours."

"Simple as that?"

He lets out a quiet laugh. "That simple and that complicated, I guess."

"I'm just not ready to announce it to the world. You heard how she reacted when I didn't come home last night. She's still really overprotective and is going to hate the idea of me getting involved with a brother. She still thinks I'm too fragile for that kind of life."

"Then she doesn't know you as well as she thinks she does." He tilts his head to the side. "But I don't think you show her all the sides of yourself, either."

I shake my head. "You're right. Sometimes it's easier to go with the flow rather than fight the current that is my sister."

"I hear you, sweetheart, but now you have me to help you swim."

I lean over and press my lips to his shoulder before resting my head against him. "Yeah. I do."

Chapter Thirteen
Cash

Waking up next to Cece was a fantasy I never thought would come true. Although at no point in said fantasy did her sister calling early as shit factor in.

After talking her sister down and having a discussion on where we stand, we clean up our makeshift bed off the floor.

"I wish I had a change of clothes," Cece says.

"Hold that thought," I tell her and pull my jeans on before I run upstairs, where I keep a couple extra T-shirts.

When I get back into the living room, I slide the shirt over her head, which looks more like a short dress on her.

"Not that I mind you walking around naked, but I really like the look of you in my clothes." I grab her around the waist and pull her flush against my body, my hand slipping under the hem of the shirt and squeezing her naked ass. "Feel free to not wear panties in my presence as well."

Cece giggles and pulls out of my hold. "Come on. I'm starving and need some coffee," she says, padding into the kitchen. When I follow her, she's reaching up inside the cabinet where the coffee grounds are. The shirt rides up, exposing the soft flesh of her delectable backside.

"Yeah, I *really* like you in my shirt."

She turns and throws me a saucy wink before getting back to her task at hand.

"French toast sound good?" she asks, pulling a frying pan from the lower cabinet.

"You don't have to cook for me, sweetheart. I can take you out for breakfast or go pick something up."

"I want to," she says, grabbing a loaf of bread I didn't know I had from the refrigerator. "I made brioche the other day, and it's the best kind of bread to use for French toast." She sets the bread on the counter and opens the fridge again, pulling out eggs, milk, and a bowl of berries. She opens the top cabinet next to the stove and rummages through it, grabbing a little bottle of vanilla extract and the cinnamon.

"What can I do to help?" I ask, standing in the doorway to the kitchen, feeling useless.

She smiles and shakes her head. "Nothing. I've got it."

I step toward her and loop my arm around her waist as she opens the egg carton. "Uh-uh. That's not how it works. If you're making breakfast for us, then I'm helping. I won't pretend to know the first thing about cooking, but I'm not going to sit around while you make me breakfast. Put me to work, Chef."

Cece looks up at me with something like wonder flashing in her blue eyes. "Okay," she nods toward the bowl of strawberries. "You can wash and cut those up for me."

"On it." I do as she says as she prepares the egg mixture. When I pop a berry into my mouth, the bright, sweet flavor invades my senses. "God, these are so good." I moan and grab another one, walking over to her as she places a piece of bread in the sizzling pan.

"Open," I command, holding the strawberry up. She does, and I place the berry on her tongue.

She chews with a small smile on her face. "Delicious."

I bend my head and take her mouth in a kiss, my tongue playing on her lips until she opens for me. When she does, our tongues tangle and tease, the taste of Cece and the sweetness of the strawberry mingling over my taste buds.

I pull away and lick my lips. "Mmm, my favorite."

Cece blushes, her eyes having gone a little hazy until she suddenly remembers the French toast frying in the pan. "Shit," she says and flips the bread over. "Okay, we're good, it didn't burn."

"Sweetheart, I'd take your lips on mine over a perfectly cooked breakfast any fucking day of the week."

She laughs. "Sorry. Old habits and all that."

My head tilts to the side. "What do you mean?"

She shakes her head, her blonde hair falling forward, shielding her face from me. "Nothing."

I don't like the sound of that. I swipe her hair behind her ear. "Tell me what that meant," I say softly.

"Those memories have no place here. It's just a thought that popped into my head when I was afraid I'd burned the toast." She places the first piece on a plate, then dips another piece of bread into the egg before placing it in the pan. She's not stalling per se, but she is taking her time telling me what that memory is.

"When I went to live with Otto, I was young. My mother had done most of the cooking, and I liked to bake. But Otto expected a full breakfast every morning, and he wanted it ready when he came downstairs. I was nervous to have so many things going at once, and I burned a pancake. When he came downstairs, he smelled the char and slapped me across the face. Told me I should have been more careful with the food he provided, and I was careless. That was the first and only time I burned anything in the house. Not that it stopped him from finding plenty of other ways where I fell short, so he could punish me."

She flips the bread, but doesn't look at me.

"Hey," I say, gently using her hand to tilt her face toward mine. "You don't ever have to worry about that with me. You know that, right?"

She nods and whispers, "I know."

"I wish I would have been the one to slice his throat," I say, thinking back to that day on the compound. "If I'd have known what he did to you, I don't think anyone could have stopped me from taking my pound of flesh."

"You didn't even know me then."

I shake my head. "The moment I laid eyes on you, I knew there was something special about you. When you held your sister's hand and watched everything you'd known your entire life burn to the ground, I knew you were the strongest woman I'd ever met. Even if I didn't feel that way, I still would have wanted to kill him myself. No man has the right to hurt a woman. Ever."

Cece clears her throat and gives me a watery smile. "Thank you."

"You don't have to thank me for wanting to kill that piece of shit."

She chuckles, but it doesn't hold any humor. "No. Thank you for believing in me even if I didn't believe in myself. Even when I felt like I was drowning."

"I told you, sweetheart—you've got me to help you swim now."

When breakfast is ready, we sit at the kitchen table, and I kiss my woman between taking bites of her delicious French toast. When we've both finished, I grab the plates and take them to the sink.

Cece stands, but I shoot her a look. "You cooked, I'll clean."

She holds her hands up and sits back down with a smile on her face. "Fine, I don't mind watching you do some work, especially when you're half-naked."

"Feel free to stare, sweetheart. This is all yours anytime you want it."

She laughs, and I shoot her a wink, then fill the sponge with soap and go about cleaning the plates and scrubbing out the pan. Cece keeps her eyes glued to me as she sips her coffee. Some people might feel a little awkward, a little on display, but not me. I fucking love the lust in my woman's eyes as she watches me freely. Love having her here in my house that's starting to feel more like *ours* with each passing day.

When I finish, I dry my hands on a towel and walk over to where Cece is sitting before I lean down and kiss her. My hands grip her waist, and she lets out a little squeal of surprise when I lift her from her chair and set her on the table.

"What are you doing?" she asks as I sit in the chair she was occupying.

My hands trail from her ankles to her knees, and I spread her legs in front of my face. Her already wet center makes my mouth fucking water.

"Having my dessert," I reply.

"No one has dessert after breakfast," she says, her breath hitching as my hand trails up the inside of her thigh.

"Then I'm thanking you for breakfast."

"You already thanked me." Her hips jerk when my thumb slides over her, a ghost of a touch teasing her clit.

"Fine. I'm going to eat my woman out on the kitchen table because I want to taste her sweet cunt." I dip my head and take a long lick up her pussy. "Mmm. Fucking delicious."

Cece lets out a shaky breath and leans back on her elbows. "That feels so good."

I lick again. "You like that?"

She nods. "When you moan against me. I feel the vibrations through my entire body."

I bend my head again and lick her wet opening, moaning as my tongue swirls her clit.

"Yes," she groans. "Just like that."

One hand tangles in my hair, and her hips begin to roll under my mouth as my tongue flicks her swollen bud.

Fuck, I love how she isn't afraid to tell me what she likes.

It's as though we've unlocked the goddess inside her who is free to tell me what she needs and what her desires are. When I enter two fingers and curl them, finding her G-spot, she cries out as my tongue plays with her clit, and the pads of my fingers rub the sensitive spot inside her.

"Oh God," she cries out. "I'm going to come."

Her hand tightens in my hair as her hips buck up into my face, and the walls of her pussy tighten around my fingers while she lets out a long moan. I keep licking her clit, and the orgasm rockets through her, her entire body becoming taut as her sweet cunt clamps hard around me. When her moans begin to fade, I slow my licks, following her down.

Cece collapses back on the table, a satiated smile on her flushed face.

"That was…" her breaths are still coming out in hard pants. "Quite the thank-you."

A low chuckle vibrates through my chest. "You make me breakfast, I eat you out. Seems like I get the better end of the deal on that."

"How do you figure?" A small smile plays on the corner of her mouth.

Taking her hands in mine, I pull her up and onto my lap. One of my hands tangles in her hair as the other wraps around her waist, pulling her flush against me. "Because I'm the one who gets to make you come, hear those breathy pleas from your lips, and taste your delicious pussy. It's become my new favorite pastime, and trust me when I tell you, I'll be making the most out of it every chance I get."

"I definitely won't be stopping you," she says and bends her head down, kissing me deeply. We stay in the chair, kissing and exploring each other's mouths. It isn't hurried or frantic. It's quiet, but just as passionate as any other kiss we've shared.

When I pull away, she has a dreamy look on her face. I wish we could spend the entire day touching and exploring each other's bodies, but there's something we need to take care of.

"I need you to do something for me," I say.

"What is it?"

"I need you to call Roman. I want to meet him."

She lifts a brow. "You're not going to threaten him or something, are you?"

The thought did cross my mind when Cece first told me about him, but I know the only thing that would've accomplished is pissing her the hell off. It's not that I think he's a bad guy with nefarious intentions when it comes to my girl—just the opposite, in fact. But I still want to meet the man who has been spending so much time with my woman and check out his operation.

"No, sweetheart. I wouldn't put you in that kind of position. But I need to see for myself what he's doing if you're going to keep working with him. Can we make that compromise?"

Cece stares into my eyes for a beat, her gaze full of appreciation with a touch of disbelief. I don't need to demand she stop training with him. I'm not going to try to control her. That's not my role in her life. But I am going to make sure I know who this guy is and make sure she's as safe as she can possibly be if she continues to work with him. Plus, I've always found the best way to get my point across is if someone knows *exactly* who they're dealing with.

She blows out a huff of air. "Okay. I'll call him."

I drop Cece at her house so she can shower and change, then I head to the clubhouse to do the same. When I walk in, Barrett is sitting at the bar nursing a cup of coffee, looking a little green around the gills.

"Morning," I say loudly, walking up behind him and giving his back a good slap.

"Why?" He groans, hanging his head.

"Rough night?" A chuckle escapes from my throat as I walk around him to pour myself another cup of coffee.

"Great night, actually. Rough morning. I must be getting old or some shit." He shakes his head and takes another sip of his coffee. "Nah, fuck that."

Rolling my eyes, I take a healthy swig from my cup.

"Where were you last night?"

"Spent the night at the house."

He arches one brow. "Alone?"

"Yup."

Barrett eyes me over the rim of his mug. "You're a shit liar."

I'm actually not, but he's known me for over a decade. Riding together and living in the same club-house gives him an advantage that most people wouldn't have.

"I don't know what you're talking about," I say.

He shakes his head. "All I'm going to say is, be careful. Whatever *isn't* going on is going to cause a shitstorm. I don't want to see a certain girl who has been through hell already getting caught in it."

I shrug, playing off his warning. I agreed to let Cece take the lead on when to tell her sister, but part of me knows Barrett is right. Cece and I are playing a dangerous game by not telling Lucy and everyone else what's going on.

"I need to get ready," I say and set my coffee on the bar.

When I start toward the hallway, Barrett calls, "For your funeral?"

"Fuck off," I holler back.

It doesn't take me more than twenty minutes to shower and change. I'm back at Cece's place with my bike less than an hour after I dropped her off.

"Hey," she says, walking out of her house and over to where I've pulled into her driveway. "I'm glad you brought the bike," she says, and I hand her a helmet.

I fucking love that my woman likes to ride almost as much as I do. Especially when she's feeling any kind of anxiety, which I'm sure is the case right now. This part of her life is something I've just come to know about, and now I'm inserting myself completely. But it's for her safety and my peace of mind, so no matter how nervous she is, it needs to get sorted.

"Thought we would take a trip to Ayre, then ride around for a while. I like having you wrapped around me," I tell her.

She smiles before putting the helmet over her head, then climbs on behind me.

We get to Ayre in thirty minutes, and when we pull up to the apartment building, a tall, broad man with salt-and-pepper hair is standing out front.

I park across the street, and Cece hops off the back before she removes her helmet.

"That's Roman," she says, nodding toward the man.

"What does he know so far?"

"I told him you were part of the Black Roses. He knows about the club. And I told him about you catching me with Danny and what I planned to do—which he was none too happy about—but that you stopped me. I also told him we went back last night, which he also wasn't thrilled about, but under-stood."

I nod and set my helmet on the seat before grab-bing her hand. "Let's go then."

When we walk up to Roman, he holds out a hand to me, and Cece handles the introductions. "Roman, Cash. Cash, Roman," she says.

"Heard you had quite the night," Roman says.

"Nothing particularly out of the ordinary for me," I reply, and he looks pointedly at my cut.

"I suppose not. Come on in," he says and opens the door. "Cyn and Colton aren't here, but I'll show you around upstairs first, then the gym," he says, leading us up the stairs.

When we step into the apartment, it doesn't look like anything much, save for the massive computer monitoring system set up in the living room and all of the fancy cameras sitting on the coffee table in front of a couch.

"So tell me about what you do exactly," I say. There's a whole day left, and I want to spend it alone with my woman, not in a little apartment in Ayre.

"I have contacts in various places—the police station, hospital, even a women's center in town. If one of my contacts sees someone coming in repeatedly with injuries that are suspicious, they give them my phone number and tell them I can help. They let me know, and if the woman calls, we help them."

"By beating the shit out of their abusers?"

Roman nods. "Sometimes. If they want to get away and start a new life, we help set them up. Give them a little seed money, and I've been known to dip my toe in helping people get a new identity. Sometimes we send a message to their abuser, then one of my associates will track them through bank accounts and various other means to make sure they're staying away. We keep an eye on things so they can feel safe again."

"What if the guys you go after don't get the hint?"

"Then we make our point more clear. But that's only happened twice since I've been doing this."

He doesn't go into detail, but he seems to be confident that his methods work.

"How much do you charge?" I ask.

Roman shakes his head. "I don't."

"So you're a vigilante out of the goodness of your heart? This is a pricey outfit you have here."

"Let's just say there are people out there who feel a call to support our work. I let them," he answers with a shrug.

I nod as I look around the room. "Tell me about you training Cece."

"Ah, that's what you really want to know about," Roman quips.

"She's my woman. I think I have the right to know how you were planning on using her in this."

"Cash..." Cece says. "You're making it sound like he was trying to take advantage or something."

"No, he's right to want to know," Roman answers. "And having a woman on the team does give us some advantage. They don't expect anything from you. However"—he gives Cece a pointed look—"I would have *never* sent you out by yourself. That's not how we do things. One of the guys does the fighting, but the other is always a lookout or will jump in if shit goes sideways. We work as a team, never alone."

Cece looks to the side then back to Roman with an apology clouding her normally bright eyes. "I fucked up."

He nods in agreement. "You fucked up."

"So she's going to have a partner when you send her out?" I ask.

"Absolutely," Roman replies.

"Great. Then I'm her partner."

"Cash, you aren't here to take over. Roman makes that decision," Cece tells me.

"When it comes to you? No, he doesn't." She narrows her eyes at me, not happy with my response. "Look," I tell her, cupping the side of her face. "If anyone is going to be responsible for making sure you're safe out there, there is no one I trust more than myself. I'm not trying to stop you from anything. I know why you need to do this, but I'm not going to hand off my responsibility as your man to anyone. Ever."

She blows out a breath and tips her mouth in a half smile. "I get it."

And I know she does. She's been around long enough to witness how the men in the club treat their women. We'll never stand in their way, but we'll always stand next to them and support them. If that means protecting them when they decide to go off and beat the shit out of people who abuse women, then that's what it means.

I kiss her lightly on the mouth, then turn back to Roman.

"That okay with you?" I ask, more for Cece's sake than mine.

"Happy to have the extra hands. Maybe you can join us in some training. What do you have experience in?"

I quirk my brow. "I've been in the club for fifteen years. Pretty sure that's all the training I need."

Roman chuckles. "Fair enough." He holds out his hand, and I shake it. "Glad to have you, Cash."

CHAPTER FOURTEEN
CECE

"Cece, watch me," Colby yells.

"I'm watching, buddy," I call back as he swings his bat at the ball Wyatt tosses him.

He hits it, and all the women sitting on the back patio of the clubhouse cheer for him when he runs around the pretend bases of the pretend baseball game that a few of the kids are playing.

Everyone is at the clubhouse for a family barbecue. Tanya likes to have one of these every month or so when the weather is nice. It's a great way to show the guys who work at the auto and bike shop and their families the club's appreciation. It's also a good excuse for everyone to get together. Plus, Tanya likes to make sure everyone working for the club feels like part of a big extended family.

"You look great, Cece," Charlie says, sitting next to me. She's sipping from a glass of wine, and it strikes me that I have no desire to have a glass in front of me. I'm perfectly happy with the watermelon concoction that I whipped up for myself. "You look happy."

"I am," I say. "I've been doing a lot of baking for Cool Beans at Cash's. His setup is perfect for the amount of pastries she orders." Not to mention the other various activities that have been taking place there over the last two weeks.

"I'm so glad you called her," Maizie says from across the table. "And that new strawberry and clotted-cream turnover you make is to die for. If I don't get there early enough, she sells out."

"Me too." Part of me wishes I wouldn't have waited so damn long to call Betsy, but the other part knows I did it at the exact right time for *me*. "If you ever want me to make you a special batch, it's no problem."

"I like supporting you, though." Maizie smiles. "*But* if you ever have any extras, feel free to drop them off at my house."

I laugh and sip my watermelon drink. "Consider it done."

"Girl, those giant peanut butter chocolate cookies you make are absolutely sinful," Mia chimes in.

"Thanks. She wanted to see how well the cookies move in her shop, so we did a little test run last week. She's been adding them to her daily order."

"Pretty soon, it might be time for you to open a shop of your own. Or maybe take over for Betsy when she retires. If you're ever interested in an investor, let me know." Mrs. Dawson says, sitting next to her granddaughter.

I never considered owning my own business, but I kind of like the idea of having something completely mine. Something that I actually own. I live in Lucy's house, drive a car Lucy and Jude bought for me and have been relying on them for money in an account they set up for me. I'm incredibly grateful, but would also really like to feel like I'm making it on my own at some point.

"Thank you, Mrs. Dawson," I reply.

"Now, honey, like I've told all the other girls—and you on a couple of occasions—call me Elaine. That missus stuff makes me feel old."

Colby comes running over to Maizie, and she wraps him in a big hug.

"Did you see my home run, Mommy?"

"I did, buddy. It was great!"

"You have quite the swing, Colby. It won't be long before the majors call you," Elaine says, smiling at her great-grandson.

"Thanks, Gigi," Colby says and turns back to his mom. "I gotta go practice some more. Daddy says practice makes perfect, and I want to be the best." Colby gives his mom a smacking kiss on the cheek and runs off in the direction of Wyatt and a few of the other guys.

"Daddy?" Lucy asks.

Maizie watches her son and her man get in position for another inning of their game. "He woke up last week and just started calling him that. You should have seen Wyatt's face. I've never seen a man with a bigger smile.

He was struck silent for a minute, and I almost started bawling on the spot."

"I fucking love that so much," my sister exclaims. "And to think you had that stupid no-biker rule."

Irritation flares in me. Lucy calls Maizie's old rule stupid, but she's the one who doesn't want me with a brother. I remember overhearing her say I wasn't cut out to be in this life. That I was too soft, too fragile. But it seems that it's good enough for everyone else except me. It's so fucking annoying sometimes that she still sees me as the broken girl she rescued from a cult. She has no idea what I went through. What I can handle.

I look toward where Cash is standing as he talks to Ozzy with one of the guys from the bike shop. His gaze finds mine, and he sends me a barely there smile. I need to tell Lucy what's going on between us. All day, we've had to pretend that we're just friends when what I really want to do is walk up to him and plant a kiss on his lips. I want him to be able to put his arm around me and keep me pressed into his side.

I discreetly return his smile and stand. "I'm going to get the desserts ready," I tell the group of women.

"Need some help?" Lucy offers.

"It's okay, I've got it."

I turn and head inside the clubhouse and into the kitchen. Opening the refrigerator door, I pull out the cupcakes I made and the ingredients for the frosting. I'm adding fresh fruit to the tops and didn't want it to dry out, so I opted to wait until it was time to serve them before frosting the desserts.

When I've finished making the frosting, I shovel it into the piping bag I brought and begin the process on all fifty. When I'm halfway through, Cash strolls into the kitchen with a devious smile stretched across his face.

"Hey, sweetheart. Do I get a taste?"

"Sure." I grab a spoon and add a little frosting to it.

His smile becomes more wicked, if that's even possible. "Not what I meant." He grabs the spoon and tosses it in the sink, then takes my mouth in a searing kiss. He trails his lips down my neck as he presses me against the counter. "Fuck, I've been dying to do that all day," he mumbles into my heated skin.

"Someone could walk in here," I say in a breathless whisper.

"At this point, I don't care. I can't be around you all afternoon and not be able to touch you."

I know that asking him to not tell anyone quite yet is unfair. He doesn't want to keep us a secret. I just need to break it to my sister first that I'm in love with a brother. Maybe I should tell Cash the same thing. We haven't said the words to each other yet, but I feel them. God, I feel so much for this man.

"I'm going to tell her tomorrow. I hate hiding too," I tell him.

He lifts his head from my neck and looks me in the eye. "Thank fuck. I don't think I could do this again and have to make it look like I'm not wholly and completely addicted to you."

I smile, and he leans down, taking my mouth in another kiss. I wrap one arm around him and clutch his shirt while my other hand still holds the piping bag.

"What in the actual fuck are you doing to my sister?" I hear Lucy scream from behind us.

I jerk away, though I can't get far, considering I'm between Cash's large frame and the counter.

Cash spins and stands with half of his body in front of mine. Lucy is standing in the doorway of the kitchen. Jude comes running in with Linc and Barrett, the three of them with wild looks in their eyes as though they think I'm being attacked. When they see Cash, the three men relax.

"I'm kissing my woman," Cash tells my sister in a firm and decisive voice.

"You're what?" she yells.

"Okay...this sounds like a family affair. I'm just going to..." Barrett hitches his thumb back toward the kitchen door.

"Yeah, I'm with you," Linc says, and the two of them turn and hightail it out of the room.

"You better start explaining, Cash." Lucy grits out the words through clenched teeth with a look of pure malevolence in her furious gaze. "And it better go something like how you are taking advantage of my sister and end with how you're going to fix your mistake and promise to *never* touch her again. She's in here putting together fucking desserts for Chrissake, and you...what? Followed her in here and decided now was a good opportunity for you to make a move? Not on your life, asshole."

"That's not what happened, Lucy. God, I'm not some precious little thing that you have to protect from him, or anyone, for that matter!" I stare at Lucy while she's having a ridiculous meltdown over something she clearly doesn't understand. And from the sound of it, she doesn't want to.

"Love, I don't think that's what's going on at all," Jude says, looking between Cash and me, noting the protective stance he's taken in front of me.

"That's my sister, Jude. And I trusted your brothers to look out for her. I trusted him"—she points an accusing finger at Cash—"to look out for her."

"He has. God, more than you could possibly know," I tell her, ready to push past the man blocking me.

"From where? Inside your pants?" she yells.

"Okay, that's enough." Cash crosses his arms over his broad chest and steels his spine. "You can be mad at me all you want, but you're not going to make those remarks to her."

"Who the hell do you think you are to tell me anything right now? You're nothing more than some dirty old man who saw a pretty young girl and decided to take advantage of the situation!" Lucy yells back at him.

"You're obviously pissed, love, and I can understand, but don't say anything you're going to regret," Jude interjects, trying to calm her down.

She whirls around and faces her man. "I want you to punch him in the face right now. He's taking advantage of the situation with Cece. My *sister*."

"It doesn't sound like Cece was opposed to the kiss, Lucifer."

"She doesn't know any better!" Lucy yells, waving her hand in my direction.

"Can you two please not talk about me like I'm not standing right fucking here," I say, moving around to stand next to Cash instead of behind him. "Everything you said about Cash is completely untrue, and you damn well know that. And for the record, *Cece* is perfectly capable of making her own decisions. *Cece* knows exactly what she's doing. *Cece* has been seeing Cash for weeks. *Cece* is fucking happy for once!"

"Sweetheart, let's calm down. We knew this was going to be rough. There's no need to fight." Funny, coming from the man who looks ready to defend me to the death. His gaze darts between my sister and me, obviously not wanting the situation to devolve further than it already has.

"Were you coaching her on what to say to me?" Lucy asks Cash. "Were you putting ideas in her head that I wouldn't understand? Is that why she hid this from me? Because of you?" I've seen my sister angry. I've seen her actually murder someone. She has that same look in her eye now. "You know what. You won't knock his teeth in? Fine. I'll fucking do it."

Before she finishes her sentence, she lunges toward Cash and throws her fist against his jaw. Cash's hand immediately clutches the side of his face with a curse falling from his lips. Before she can land the next punch, Jude grabs her around the waist and lifts her off the ground, spinning around as he bands his other arm around her.

"Calm the hell down, woman," Jude growls as Lucy struggles in his hold.

"I can't believe you just did that!" I scream. "What the hell is wrong with you? Why do you think I'm completely inept at taking care of myself or making decisions on my own? Cash never coached me on what to say to you. He wanted me to tell you what was between us from the start, but I didn't want *this*"—I wave a hand between Lucy and me—"exact scenario to play out. I was hoping you would be understanding. Maybe even a little happy for me." I knew it was a long shot, but a girl can dream.

"All I'm trying to do is protect you," she says with Jude's arm still wrapped around her.

"From what?" I throw my hands in the air. "From being happy?"

"From getting hurt," she says.

"Little late for that." I point a finger at my sister. "You left the compound, and I stayed. I thank God that you got away. You don't know the half of what they did to pretty girls there. What they did to me. We were so naive when we thought the worst thing they could do was kill you and bury you in an unmarked grave like they did to Bea. So fucking clueless."

My sister stops struggling in Jude's hold. "Cece," she chokes out with so much heartbreak in her eyes it almost brings tears to mine. But I'm too fucking pissed to cry right now.

"I need to get out of here," I say to Cash, and he gives me a nod.

"I got you, sweetheart."

"Cece, wait. Talk to me," Lucy begs.

"God, I'm so sick of you trying to get me to tell you things that will only break your heart. Can't you see I'm the one protecting *you*?"

I rush out of the kitchen and past Linc, Barrett, Charlie, and Maizie, who are all wearing varying degrees of pity on their faces.

I don't want their pity. No one needs to feel sorry for me.

When we get outside, Cash leads me over to his truck. "Your helmet is in my room," he says. "If you want to wait here for a second, I'll go grab it."

"You'd go back in there?"

He steps into my space and rests his warm palm against my cheek. "If you need to ride, I have no problem facing your crazy-ass sister again," he says. "What do you want?"

"Just you to get me the hell out of here right now."

"Truck it is, then."

He walks me over to the passenger side and opens the door for me before jogging to the driver's side.

When we make it to the clubhouse gate, he stops and looks at me. "Where to, sweetheart?"

"I need to scream," I tell him, and he nods, knowing exactly what I mean.

Cash pulls up to the old quarry, and we both hop out of the truck. I march to the edge of the pit, open my mouth and let out one of the loudest, longest screams I ever have. It's filled with all of the rage, hurt, and disappointment that was seeping from me on the way here. It wanted out, and now I can finally release it into the sky. Let the wind carry it from me.

"Cece," Cash says from behind me as I catch my breath.

My eyes squeeze shut. I know what he's going to ask me. As soon as the words left my mouth at the clubhouse, I knew he was going to want to know what I meant when I told Lucy that death wasn't the worst thing that happened on the compound.

I don't turn toward him as he comes to stand next to me, and he doesn't say anything for a few moments. He simply stands close, his silent support strong and unshakable beside me.

"I don't think Otto chose me for his own gain." I let out a caustic laugh. "Oh, he got what he wanted alright. A pretty young wife who he could fuck anytime he wanted. I was obedient, just like my mother and father taught me. I don't think my mother knew what went on when the Bone Breakers came to the compound, but I wasn't the only attractive wife of an elder. Other women knew. Other women went through it."

Cash takes a deep breath. "At the motel, I wondered if that was the first time you'd been attacked. When Nolan walked in, I don't know...he seemed too casual about knowing what that piece of shit was going to do to you. Like he expected him to."

I shake my head. "It wasn't the first time, no. And Nolan would have made sure to get his turn. He always did." I glance at Cash, and his jaw looks hard as granite. I'm not entirely certain he can handle hearing this, but I need to get it out.

My stomach is in tight knots, but I know I have to tell Cash this part of my story.

I stare into the quarry as I open my mouth to speak. "The first time it happened, I was led into a room where Red was. There were two other men there with him. Otto said it was time for me to do my duty as his wife. That these men were helping us, and in turn, I needed to show our appreciation. He left me with those sick bastards. I tried to run out of the room. I screamed until it felt like razors were cutting my throat. But the other two held me down while Red lifted my dress and unbuckled his filthy jeans. Then he gave his vice president and one of the prospects a turn. Told the man they liked to reward their prospects who worked hard for the club. The next time that man came to the compound, he was fully patched. And I was once again his reward."

"How long did that go on?" Cash asks.

Out of the corner of my eye, I can see Cash's chest rising with heavy inhales then collapsing with long exhales, trying to calm himself.

"About six years, give or take."

"That explains why you were scared to be around the brothers in the beginning."

"It didn't matter how many times Lucy told me you were safe. That the club was safe. I didn't believe her." I finally turn to face the man standing next to me. "Except for you. I always knew you were different from the men who hurt me. And it didn't take too long for me to realize that the rest of the Black Roses were different, too."

That first month was the hardest. I didn't want to leave my sister's house, but she was so happy and carefree around Jude. I knew in my heart these were good guys. Lucy didn't want me cooped up in the house. Coming to the clubhouse was sort of a way to test the waters, so to speak. But staying apart from them in the kitchen was the easiest and what felt like the safest way to do that. I knew at least Jude or my sister wouldn't let anything happen to me.

Then Cash started spending time there with me. It was as though I'd met a kindred spirit. Another person who needed a safe place to just *be*.

"What do you need from me right now, sweetheart?"

I love that he isn't asking me if I'm okay. He isn't saying how sorry he is that I went through that. He let me tell my story, get the words out, and he isn't trying to put a bandage over a wound that's scabbed over.

"I just want you to hold me," I tell him.

Cash wraps me in his arms, one hand around my waist and the other tangled in my hair as I press my face against his chest.

"Fuck, sweetheart. I'll hold you anytime you need. I don't know how I got so damn lucky, but I'm never letting you go. You amaze me every single day, Cece. You're one of the strongest women I've ever known, and I'm so fucking proud to be your man."

We stand here for a long time. Both of us lost in our thoughts. Mine aren't as horrible as I would have thought. I assumed that when I told another person what happened to me, when I let my mind go back there, I'd be stuck in it like I had been so many times before. But I'm not. I think about how I've not only survived, but I've found happiness. I found Cash. I found people who would lay down their lives for me.

"You know, you were my first kiss," I tell Cash, tilting my face toward his. "You were the first man I ever kissed back."

"I'm honored that it was me." He looks down at me with so much adoration shining in his blue eyes. "No one else's lips will touch yours. Not as long as I have breath in my body. I love you, Cece. I think I have for a long time. That first night when you gave me your body, I knew, down to my marrow, that I was never going to let you go."

Tears prick my eyes as I stare into his. We aren't perfect. We're messy, and things feel really fucking complicated right now. But we're us, and we're real.

"I love you too, Cash. So much."

He leans down and takes my mouth in a kiss that makes my toes curl and every nerve in my body light up.

"Take me home. To your house. I don't want to spend the night alone."

"Wasn't planning on letting you, sweetheart." His strong and steady hand cups my cheek. "You belong in my house, and in my bed, next to me. The same way I belong with you, and I always will."

CHAPTER FIFTEEN
CECE

Cash never takes his hand from my thigh the entire way back to the house. I was afraid that he would be scared to touch me after I told him what happened to me. I should have known better. Cash knows I don't need or want anyone tiptoeing around me. I've learned to deal with my past, and I've refused to let it define me or let it come between me and my happiness. Especially with the man sitting next to me. It has no place in my present or future, and I refuse to give it space.

"I had something delivered today. I wanted to surprise you, so I didn't say anything," Cash says as he opens the door.

That piques my curiosity as we walk inside his house. I look around the kitchen and the living room, but don't see anything out of the ordinary.

My eyes narrow, and I shoot him a questioning look as he stands in the doorway with a smirk on his lips.

"Upstairs," he says.

Cash has been working on a couple of the rooms upstairs. He had the carpet laid a few days ago, but he still needs to pick some paint colors and a million other little things.

I head up the stairs before him and look in the first guest room. "The carpet looks good."

He nods, "It does, but that's not the surprise."

I look in the bathroom and notice he hung the fixtures above the vanity. "Is it the lighting? I really like it."

"God no, but thank you for picking it out. I think I deserve a little more credit than you thinking your surprise is a light fixture."

I chuckle and walk into the primary bedroom. Sitting in the center is a giant bed. It's huge. Bigger than anything I've ever slept on. The mattress sits on a dark-gray tufted bedframe that looks straight out of a magazine. It looks so warm and inviting—exactly what Cash was going for when he talked about buying furniture for the house if he decided to keep it, that is. He still hasn't committed one way or the other.

"Did you pick this out?" I ask, walking over and sitting on the mattress that feels like a cloud.

"All by myself," he says with a grin. "You like it?"

Falling back onto the mattress with my arms spread out across the deep-green comforter, I smile so wide my cheeks feel like they're going to be stuck like this forever. "I love it, Cash. Oh my God, it's so comfortable. And huge!" I roll from one side to the other, demonstrating my point, and he chuckles next to the bed.

"I'm a big guy, and I like the thought of having you in bed with me. Figured we'll have plenty of room to stretch out."

"It's a lot more comfy than the floor, that's for sure." I hold out my arms. "Come here." Cash lies down next to me, and I roll over, draping half of my body over him. "But this is my favorite spot. I don't need more room than this."

The phone in his pocket dings with an incoming text. He pulls it out and holds it above us.

Jude: *You with Little Bit?*

I roll my eyes at the nickname Jude and Liam gave me the first night we met.

Cash: *Yeah. We're at the house. Gonna stay here tonight.*

Jude: *How's the jaw?*

Cash: *Sore.*

Jude: *At least it wasn't me punching you.*

Cash: *Wish it was. You hit like a bitch.*

I chuckle next to Cash, who is letting me see everything he says to his brother.

Jude: *Fuck you.*

Cash: *No thanks.*

Jude: *I'll let Lucy know where Cece is. And again, fuck you.*

He tosses his phone on the bed and looks at me. "We're going to have to deal with this at some point," he says, his hand brushing the hair from my face.

"I know." I let out a pained breath. "But not tonight."

Cash grins. "Not tonight."

I tilt my face up toward his and take his mouth in a slow, languid kiss. It isn't hurried—we have all night with each other. He lets me explore his mouth at my own pace, lets me run my hands under his shirt, feeling every inch of tight muscle and smooth skin.

Sitting up, I throw my leg over his waist and straddle him. "Up," I say, and he follows my instructions, lifting his torso from the mattress. My hands grab the hem of his black T-shirt, and I yank it over his head before pressing my palm against his chest, gently pushing him onto his back again. Leaning forward, my lips find his neck, and I run my tongue over the straining muscles and tendons. He swallows hard and grips my hips, pressing me into his growing length.

My hands cover his as I remove them from my hips and place them over his head. Bending over him, my hair falls around us like a blonde curtain. In here, in this space, it's just the two of us as he looks up at me with what I know now is love.

"Keep your hands here," I whisper, squeezing his wrists. "I want to play a bit."

Cash quirks his brow, and a salacious smile spreads across his face. "Be my guest."

Pressing a kiss to his lips, his mouth opens, allowing his tongue to slowly swirl and play with mine. Then I start my slow descent down his body, kissing his jaw, then moving farther down, swirling my tongue in the divot of his throat. Cash lets out a low hum, and I feel the vibration against my mouth. I continue to slide my body lower and lick my way across his chest, his muscles tightening as my tongue swirls his nipple. He lets out a quiet hiss.

"Do you like that?" I ask, and he moans when I do it again.

"Fuck yes," he whispers.

"What does it feel like?"

"Like every nerve in my body is on fire. Let me touch you," he pleads.

I smile and shake my head. "Not yet."

His fists clench the blanket above his head, and I lower my lips to his skin once again.

Cash keeps his gaze locked with mine as I continue my exploration. I place wet, open-mouthed kisses against the firm planes of his stomach, my tongue laving each band of muscle of his six-pack.

"Fuck, baby. I love having your mouth on me," he groans out.

My hands press against his thighs, and I push myself up into a sitting position, whipping my tank top over my head. When my bra comes off and I run my hands over my breasts, squeezing my nipples between my fingers, he groans.

"You're killing me, sweetheart. Fuck, I want to taste you."

"Me first," I say, scoring my nails down his chest and stomach before I reach the button of his jeans. "I've never done this before, so you're going to have to tell me how," I say, unbuttoning his jeans and sliding his zipper down. My hand reaches in, and I pull out his straining cock, wrapping my fingers around the base and pumping a couple of times like I've seen him do.

"Oh shit," he breathes out and squeezes his eyes shut. "Goddamn, that feels good."

I sit up and climb off the bed before I pull his boots off, then slide the denim from his legs.

Cash looks at me with such intensity, a shiver runs through my entire body.

"Yours too, sweetheart," he says, nodding toward my shorts.

I shoot him a smirk and quickly shimmy my shorts and panties down my legs before spreading his knees apart and climbing back on the bed, kneeling between his thighs. I grab his length again and wrap my fingers around it, holding it straight as I lick the bead of moisture at the tip.

"Holy shit," Cash groans, his hips jerking in response to my touch.

"Tell me what to do," I say, then take another lick.

"Goddamn, baby. That feels so good. Lick your tongue around the head."

I do what he says, my tongue swirling around where the head of his cock meets his thick shaft.

"You have no idea how hard it is not to touch you right now, Cece. I want to make you feel as good as you're making me."

"In a minute," I say, lifting my head up. "I'm not done playing." He growls, and I giggle. "What next?" I ask as I hold his stare and swirl my tongue around him again.

"Open your mouth, baby, and slide it over my cock." I do it, and he hisses again. "Wrap your lips around me tight. Yeah, like that," he says when I follow his instruction. "Now suck while you move your head up." His hips jerk again, and I glance at his eyes, intently watching me. His neck muscles strain as he holds his head up to get an unobstructed view of the pleasure I'm giving him.

"Just like that. Up and down. Holy shit, you're fucking perfect," he moans as I repeat the motion. "Can you take a little more?" I nod the best I can and move my mouth farther down his shaft until I feel my gag reflex, and I let out a little cough. "That's perfect, baby. We can work on you taking me down the back of your throat later. God, Cece, you're doing so good, baby."

My nipples are hard points scraping against the comforter between his thighs as I lie on my stomach and take Cash higher and higher with each pass over his shaft. I can't stop my hips from moving as I rub my pussy against the mattress, but I'm unable to position myself to find some relief from this ache in my core. I moan, and he hisses before he sits up, lifting me by the shoulders and crashing his mouth to mine.

"Why did you stop me? Was I doing it wrong?" I ask when I pull away, suddenly self-conscious.

"Are you kidding me? You are amazing." He kisses me. "Fucking perfect." He kisses me again. "But I don't want to come in your mouth. I want to watch your tits bounce and have my hands all over you when I come inside you."

My mouth opens, and I cry out when Cash lifts my hips and slides me onto his hard cock.

"Oh my God," I moan as his hands guide my hips up and down, over and over. The feeling of him inside me is incredible. I'm so full, more so than I've ever felt with him. This is the first time we've been in this position, and I can't believe how fucking good it feels. My hands clasp his shoulders, and I take over the rhythm, lifting myself up and slamming back down. Every time I do, the head of his cock scrapes along the spot inside me that makes me see stars.

"That's it, baby. Take what you need." He attaches his lips to my nipple, sucking it deep into his mouth while his hand reaches to where we're connected, and he begins rubbing furiously against my clit. Seconds later, I feel my pussy tightening in light pulses that get stronger and stronger until I clamp down around him, my body exploding in a rush of immeasurable bliss. I throw my head back as the orgasm careens through me, the mind-numbing euphoria making me feel dizzy.

Cash grips my hips and pumps deep inside me before I feel his cock jerking. He yells out words of praise as he comes deep inside me—telling me how good I feel, telling me I was made for him, telling me I'm perfect.

When he slows his movements, we're both panting hard, his arms wrapped around my middle and mine around his shoulders, with his head buried in my neck. We stay like this for several long moments, catching our breath and clinging to each other as the sweat cools against our skin.

He lifts his head and brushes his lips over mine once, then twice, before pressing his forehead against mine.

"I love you, Cece."

"I love you, too."

Cash lifts me off of him and gently sets me on the mattress. "I'll be right back." He walks into the bathroom and returns with a damp cloth. I reach to take it from him, but he shakes his head and tells me to lie back. "I like taking care of you," he says as he spreads my legs, wiping the cloth over my center. "We didn't use protection."

Every other time we've made love, Cash has worn a condom.

"I liked it better," I say.

He huffs out a laugh. "Me too, sweetheart, but I should have been more thoughtful. Not that I wouldn't mind seeing your belly round with my baby, but if that's not in the cards just yet, we should probably get you to the doctor for some birth control."

My breath catches when he mentions seeing me pregnant. He would want that? With me?

"What?" he asks when I don't say anything.

I shake my head, the lump in my throat making it hard to talk. "Nothing," I choke out. "I just...I love you so much."

He smiles and leans down, pressing his lips lightly against mine. "I love you, too." He looks to the side, his jaw tightening.

"What is it?" I ask.

Cash lies down on his side next to me with his head propped up in his hand. "It's something your sister said," he answers.

"She said a lot and was completely out of line with all of it."

He nods. "I get that you see it that way. But she did bring up something that I struggled with when I realized my feelings toward you were turning into more than friendship." He runs a finger down the side of my face. "I'm a lot older than you are, sweetheart. Over a decade."

"And?"

"And I want to know if you've ever...if you've ever thought there was a possibility that I've used that to my advantage. If our age difference has ever reminded you of—"

"No," I interject before he can finish his sentence, knowing where his thoughts have taken him. "No, Cash. I've never even considered that. I'm twenty-four, and you're thirty-five. I'm plenty old enough to make my own choices, even if my sister still sees me as the fifteen-year-old she left at the compound. The only thing

I see when I look at you is the man I love. The man who has been there with me through my darkest days. You are nothing like anyone I've known before. I don't give a shit about the years between us. I've lived two lives in my years on this earth. The first one nearly destroyed me. I'll be damned if I live the second one according to someone else's bullshit issues with our age difference."

Cash smiles and shakes his head back and forth. "Goddamn, woman, you are fucking incredible." He leans down and takes my mouth in a hard kiss. "I fucking love you."

A bark of laughter escapes me. "I fucking love you, too," I tell him.

Cash gets up and tosses the cloth in the bathroom. When he returns, he pulls the comforter down. I crawl up the bed, sliding between the sheets and under the soft blanket, before he lies down next to me and gathers me in his arms.

"So much better than the floor," he quips, and I smile against his chest.

I don't care where we are; if I'm wrapped in his arms, I'll be happy anywhere.

The alarm on my phone goes off before the sun has risen. Cash stirs, but I kiss him lightly on the cheek and tell him to go back to sleep. I grab his shirt from the floor and pull it over my body, then trudge down the stairs to start the coffee and my baking for Cool Beans. When Cash comes down, there's soft country music playing from the speaker, and I'm humming along while I put my last batch of fresh turnovers into the to-go container.

"I saved you a couple blackberry ones," I say, nodding to the cooling rack behind me.

Cash has a lazy, sweet smile on his face as he leans against the doorframe in the kitchen, his hand rubbing the spot over his heart. God, between the look in his eyes and the way his jeans hang low on his hips, I'm about to melt away on the spot.

"I like you in my shirt," he says as he prowls toward me, a playful glint in his blue eyes.

"I know."

"I really don't like waking up without you though." He wraps his arms around me from behind and nuzzles his face into my neck.

"Sorry, I wanted to let you sleep in."

"Don't care what time you get up, sweetheart," he says, his breath tickling me. "I don't want to miss a second with you."

"Noted."

He kisses his way down my neck and over my shoulder as he pulls the collar of the shirt away so his mouth has access to more skin. "How long until we have to leave?"

I look at the clock on the stove. "About twenty minutes."

"Perfect." He spins me around and lifts me in one motion, setting me on the counter.

I let out a surprised squeal. "What are you doing?" I ask on a laugh.

He spreads my knees and lowers himself to his. "Eating my breakfast."

When his mouth connects to my center, my head falls against the cabinet behind me.

Holy shit. Cash's mouth making me come before I've even had my second cup of coffee is quite the way to start my day. If I wasn't before, I'm thoroughly addicted to him now, and I have a feeling that's exactly the way he wants it.

Cash takes me to Cool Beans to drop off the pastries, then we head to my sister's house. He parks the truck against the curb, and I stare at the front of the house. The curtains of the kitchen window move, so I know someone is up, and they know we're here. So much for grabbing a change of clothes and making a quick exit.

"If you aren't ready, we can go back to the house. You really don't need clean clothes. We can just not wear any for the rest of the day."

I let out a surprised laugh, appreciating him trying to lighten my mood. I felt great this morning—after Cash made me come with his mouth before bending me over the counter and taking me from behind, making me come again.

I really love that kitchen. So many good memories in it.

On our way over, my mood slowly started to sour as I thought about running into Lucy, and I'm tempted to give in and say fuck it—Cash is right. We don't need clothes.

Still, I'll have to face my sister eventually.

Blowing out a breath, I shake my head. "They saw us. We can't just run away."

"We can do whatever you want, sweetheart. It's your life. You don't have to live it by anyone else's standards. Even Lucy's."

I look at Cash, then lean over and give him a particularly indecent kiss. It doesn't matter if anyone sees us. Cat's out of the bag now.

"I want to get it over with. She's going to have to accept it, and I'm not going to hide from her."

Cash nods and opens his door, walking around the front of his truck, then he opens mine. My hand is clasped in his as he leads us down the walkway and up the front porch steps.

"Here we go." I take a deep breath and exhale as I open the door and step into the quiet house.

I walk into the kitchen with Cash right behind me, his hand still holding mine. Jude and Lucy are sitting at the kitchen table.

"Morning," Jude says, his gaze darting between my sister and me. "Coffee?"

"Sure," Cash replies, and Jude gets up from his seat, looks me in the eye, and nods to the chair.

Cash gives my hand a reassuring squeeze, and I let go, walking over to the table to sit across from my sister.

"Hi," I say, and Lucy offers me a tight smile. "I know yesterday was a bit of a surprise—"

"Gee, you think? I walk into the kitchen and find this guy"—she nods at Cash, who is now standing on the other side of the counter next to Jude—"with his hands all over you."

"You overreacted," I tell her.

"How exactly was I supposed to react, Cece? I had no idea you were anything more than friends. Which I never had a problem with, may I remind you. Then to hear him call you his woman? You never told me anything about something more between you. You never tell me anything."

"I know. Talking isn't my strong suit. Opening up to people, especially you, doesn't come easily for me."

"Why?" she asks, her voice pleading. "You used to tell me everything when we were kids. I knew all of your secrets, and you knew mine. You kept them just like I did yours."

"That's why, Lu. A lot has changed since you left. I'm not the same person I was at fifteen. But it feels like you still see me as that little girl. You still treat me as though I'm her. I'm not, and I haven't been for a long time. You have this notion that you're the only one who can protect me. I don't need your protection. Not anymore."

"All I want is for you to be safe. I couldn't do it when we were kids, and I hate that I left you there. I hate what happened to you when I was on the run." A tear tracks down her face and I reach over, covering her hand with mine.

"You couldn't have known what would happen. No one uttered a word about it. And I meant it yesterday when I said I am so thankful you got away. It wouldn't have changed my story if you'd stayed, Lu. You would have just lived it alongside me." I shake my head. "And you wouldn't have shown up with the club and rescued me and all those other women. You wouldn't have been able to bring me here, where I have a shot at real happiness. A real life. Where both of us do."

"That's all I've ever wanted for you. But it seemed like you were dead set against it. You've been so angry, and I haven't been able to help you. I didn't know what to do."

"There was nothing you could have done, sister. I had to get through it. I may not have handled it the right way, but I can finally put the past behind me. I finally feel free."

Lucy looks at Cash. "Guess I have you to thank for that."

He shakes his head. "This is all her." He nods at me. "She's never needed me to save her. I'm just the lucky son of a bitch that gets to stand next to her."

"Do you love her?" she asks my man.

He nods once. "Yes."

Lucy looks at me. "Has he told you that?"

I smile. "He has."

She tilts her head back and lets out a breath. "Okay. I'm wrapping my head around this. It's not what I pictured, but I'm adjusting."

"I know you think I'm too soft for this life," I say with sadness tingeing my words.

Her head springs forward, and she looks at me. "I don't think you're too soft, Cece. I wanted your life to *be* soft. Be easy. I didn't want you wrapped up with a biker who, for the entire time I've known him, hasn't exactly screamed the type who wants a commitment to one woman."

"Hey now, I was never a manwhore. Jesus," Cash gripes.

"You weren't exactly ready to settle down, either. But I can see how much you love my sister. And lucky for you, she feels the same."

"Damn straight," Cash says.

"How's your face?" Lucy asks.

"You have quite the right hook," he replies, rubbing his hand over his slightly bruised jaw.

Her mouth twists into a self-satisfied smirk. "Sure as shit do. Keep that in mind if you ever even think of hurting her."

Jude laughs. "Jesus, Lucifer. Can you put a lid on it? The man is obviously smitten over Little Bit, and I, for one, couldn't be more thrilled." He walks over to Lucy and places a sweet kiss on her mouth. "I know what the love of a good woman does for men like us," he says softly, looking her in the eye.

It's always amazing to me the effect Jude has on my sister. She can be tough as nails, threatening anyone who looks at someone she loves wrong, but he utters sweet words, and she melts right into him. I guess it's not just her love that softens even the toughest people. It's his too.

"Alright. How about some breakfast?" Lucy says.

"You going to cook for me, Lucifer?"

My sister laughs as though she's just heard the funniest thing in her life. "Oh, you're hilarious. No, you're going to take us out to breakfast."

Cash's phone rings, and he pulls it from his pocket to answer it. "What's up, Oz?" He's silent as he listens to his president on the other end of the line. "Okay. I'm at Jude's. We'll grab Linc and be on our way." He disconnects the call and looks at Jude. "Ozzy called church. Liam waltzed into the clubhouse this morning. Time to make some plans, brother."

Jude nods and walks over to my sister, leaning down and kissing her. "Talk," he whispers in her ear before pressing another kiss against her cheek.

I stand as Cash makes his way over to me. When he wraps me in his strong arms, I inhale his fresh scent, and it helps calm the leftover nerves from earlier.

"You good here until I get back?" he asks.

"She's fine, lover boy," my sister answers for me.

I shoot her a look, but Lucy has a wide smile on her face as she sips her coffee.

"I'm fine." I lean up on my tiptoes and place a kiss on his lips. "See you when you get back."

He presses a kiss to my forehead and squeezes me just a little tighter before releasing me. "I'll be back in a bit," he says, and he and Jude walk out of the house, leaving my sister and me alone.

Lucy stands and walks over to the coffeepot, pouring another cup, adding some creamer and a dash of cinnamon on top before handing it back to me. "Let's go talk in the living room."

Grabbing the warm mug from her hands, I smile at the gesture and follow her out of the kitchen.

"I don't really know where to start," I say as I sit on her couch and pull my legs onto the cushion.

Lucy settles in on the other side, leaning her back against the opposite armrest and facing me. "Yesterday, you said you were protecting me."

I close my eyes and blow out a breath. "You don't want to know what I went through, Lu. It was..." I shake my head. "Horrific."

"You don't have to tell me details if you don't want to, or if you can't. But you don't have to protect me either."

I bite my bottom lip, readying myself for this conversation. "You were right that night at the church when you spoke of Otto raping me. He did. But he wasn't the only one."

Lucy's hand tightens around the mug. She looks out the window for a beat, then back to me. "Who?"

"The Bone Breakers. Red and the other members. Nolan Dawson," I answer.

"That motherfucker!" Lucy jumps up from the couch and paces in front of the coffee table for a few moments, taking deep breaths and releasing long exhales as she tries to calm herself down.

Finally, she sits back on the couch and looks at me with tears in her eyes. "I'm so sorry, Cece. God, I left you there." Tears track down her face as she reaches over and grabs my hand. "I'm so sorry I left you."

Shaking my head, I squeeze her hand. "No, sister. I'm not sorry you got away. I'll never be sorry for that. If you would have stayed, the same thing would have happened to you. There was no way you would have been able to protect me. Protect any of us. We would have never gotten out if it hadn't been for you and the club."

"Did they"—Lucy swallows hard—"do this to all of the women?"

"Not all, no. But there were a few other wives who would have this visible spike in fear every time the Bone Breakers showed up at the compound. I think it was only the young, pretty ones. Or maybe the women who they showed interest in when they would come to pick up the drugs. We were an added perk for their help in distributing the meth for Otto."

Lucy's head falls forward, and she silently cries while our hands are clasped together. She'd had no idea all the ways I'd been violated during our separation. The extent of the hell I lived through that she managed to escape.

She lifts her head and looks me in the eye. "I wish I would have made Otto's death more painful. Slitting his throat was too easy on him."

A huff of air escapes me. "I'm pretty sure destroying his entire life's work before killing him was torture enough."

Lucy shakes her head. "Nothing would ever be painful enough for him."

"I hope he relives that night over and over again from whatever pit of hell he was thrown in," I say. "And that he sees us happy and free. I'm damn certain there is no worse fate for him."

"We are happy, aren't we?" Lucy asks with a smile playing on her lips.

"Yes, sister. We are."

CHAPTER SIXTEEN
Cash

Tensions are high in the clubhouse when Linc, Jude, and I walk in. Not because of Liam being here, per se, but because of what it means.

We're going after the Bone Breakers, and soon.

After Cece telling me what those fucking bastards did to her, I'm more ready now than I ever was before. I had a feeling they'd hurt her. Especially after seeing that disgusting fuck on top of her when we walked into that motel a few months ago. But having her confirm it? Knowing for a fact what they did to her, what her husband made her endure? It makes me glad that son of a bitch is dead. And it has me chomping at the bit to send Red and the rest of those bastards to hell with him.

We all file into church, and my brothers have a seat at the table. For the first time in club history, we have more than just the brothers in the room with us. This is going to be a team effort, so Ozzy said, for one time—and one time only—he's allowing Liam and his team to join us. They are all standing against the wall, and Ozzy bangs the gavel, calling everyone's attention to him.

"I'm letting Liam and the rest of his guys in here because this is a family affair that includes them. The Bone Breakers need to be dealt with, and because Cece is Liam's little sister of sorts, he's going to help us."

"Glad to be allowed in the inner sanctum. Although I would have appreciated a seat at the table," Liam says.

"Only patched brothers get that. And as much as I appreciate your help, we aren't there. Unless you and your guys want to prospect?" Ozzy asks with a smirk.

Liam tilts his lips, returning the smirk with one of his own. "Thank you for the offer, but MC life suits my brother more than it does me. Too many rules."

"Meaning you don't make them," Jude says.

His brother chuckles. "Exactly."

"Alright. Sawyer, what can you tell us from the satellite images?" Ozzy asks.

Sawyer is Liam's resident hacker, which gives me an idea. Roman might be able to use his help on a couple things, whether he wants it or not.

Sawyer places several photos on the table and fans them out. "Their setup is pretty simple. Here"—he points to a larger building in the desert—"is their clubhouse. I pulled up the original plans. It looks like it was built similar to a small hotel with only a few rooms, but we can see from the photos that they've added on without permits. My sources tell me there are twelve members who live on site. Eight patched and four prospects."

The mention of their prospects has my blood boiling. I know the "reward" they used to get before patching in. *Fucking bastards.*

Sawyer continues. "These buildings"—he points to two smaller shanty-looking structures—"are where they took up their meth operation after the cult was...dismantled."

He means murdered and burned in the desert.

"It's a small operation, but it keeps them in the filth they've become accustomed to," he finishes.

"Are there any occupied houses out there? Encampments we need to concern ourselves with?" Ozzy asks.

"Nothing within a thirty-mile radius in each direction," Liam answers. "If they wanted to stay off law enforcement's radar, they picked a pretty good spot to do it. The men go into the little town closest to them to grab supplies and cause a little havoc while they're there. They aren't loved by the locals, but it's a poor town, and the residents don't like causing trouble. The closest police station is nearly an hour away, so if shit goes down, they know help won't arrive for a long time."

"How the hell are we going to get out there without them seeing us coming from a mile away?" Barrett asks.

"It would be nice if we had some ATVs or side-by-sides that didn't make a shit ton of noise. We could go in the middle of the night and take them by surprise," Braxton says, looking at the photos.

"Done," Liam says.

"Just like that?" our sergeant at arms asks.

Liam nods. "Just like that. A friend of mine specializes in low-profile ways to get in and out of certain situations without causing a fuss. I can have a few things here by tomorrow morning."

"Nice friends," Braxton mumbles.

"Okay. So, everything we have is here. How do we get it to Arizona? That's going to be a long drive across the country. There're a lot of eyes on the highways from here to there. Some eager local cops might pull us over and ask questions. This is a bigger operation than what we do for the Monaghans, with a lot more unknown variables," Wyatt, our road captain, chimes in.

"Lucky for us, we won't be driving," Liam says. "I have access to a cargo plane. It will fit all of our toys and weapons, plus the rest of us."

"Another friend?" Braxton asks.

Liam shrugs with a shit-eating grin on his face. "It's good to have people who owe you favors from time to time."

"What about a pilot?" Jude asks.

"I've been known to fly a plane or two," Liam says. "We also have Hendrix. He loves to fly the not-so-friendly skies."

As far as I know, Hendrix was never military like Liam or a couple of other guys on his team. Makes me wonder about his flying experience in those said skies. Not that I would ever get an answer. Liam and his guys only tell us what we need to know when we need to know it. I have a feeling he likes to think of himself as somewhat of a ghost, which, for all intents and purposes, he kind of is. I find it as annoying as Ozzy does, but I sure do get a kick out of Ozzy's reactions to him sometimes.

"Okay. When are we going to do this?" I ask, ready to fucking get out there and put some Bone Breakers to ground.

"Tomorrow too soon?" Liam asks.

I look around the table and each brother is shaking their head. We've been waiting for Liam to get back from wherever he was to help us out. All of us are more than ready to get out there.

"I have one ask," I say, looking around the room. "I want Red for myself. For...reasons."

I'm not going to divulge those reasons, not that my brothers need me to.

"Done," Ozzy says. "But before you take him out, I need information. I want to know who's been giving him intel about the club and our women. What they want with us or Shine. Think you can hold off long enough for me to get it?"

I tilt my head toward my president. "I'll do my best."

"That's all I ask, brother. We'll play this like we did with the Farinas."

"Go in and shoot anyone we see who isn't one of ours?" Knox asks.

Ozzy nods. "Exactly."

"How are we going to get rid of the bodies? Unless we have a pig farmer in Arizona that I don't know about," Linc asks.

Liam lifts his hand. "Leave that to me. Or rather Abel. He loves to make things go boom. What's another meth lab explosion in the desert?"

Abel dips his chin with a small smirk curling his lip.

"Anything else?" Ozzy asks.

No one voices any more concerns or questions, so he hits the gavel on the table, dismissing church.

We all file out to the main room of the clubhouse, where Freya is doing some work at one of the tables. Ozzy walks over to her and places a kiss on her mouth before whispering something in her ear that makes her blush. Instantly, I want Cece here with me. For the two of us to show the world that she's mine. I want everyone to know how fucking lucky I am to have such an amazing woman in my bed and by my side.

Liam walks up to me and stares at my face. "Heard you got clocked pretty good yesterday."

"Where did you hear that?" I ask.

"Lucy may have called me asking if I would be opposed to disappearing a body before Jude ripped the phone from her and told her in no uncertain terms that she is not allowed to try to take a hit out on one of his brothers."

"Jesus Christ. She was more pissed yesterday than I thought then."

"Just so you know, I wouldn't have done it," Liam says.

"Uh...thanks?"

He nods as though it makes perfect sense for me to thank him for not killing me. "Little Bit has been through too much. Lucy can be a little overprotective and tends to fly off the handle. Cece is different though. She has a calm rage that simmers because she rarely lets the steam off."

"I've been helping her with that," I say, my mind going back to the night in the alley when she beat the shit out of that asshole who hurt her friend.

"I've seen you with her. Seen how you two orbit around each other. I knew it was only a matter of time before one of you took your head out of your ass and saw what's been in front of your face."

"I couldn't rush her. Hell, I didn't even want to admit it to myself for far too long. But now that I have, I'm not letting anyone stand in my way."

"That so?" he asks, his brow in a high arch.

"It is."

A smile sweeps across Liam's face as he clamps my shoulder. I look at his hand and lift a brow of my own. *This touchy motherfucker.* He sees my expression but is completely unfazed, as I've come to realize he is with most things.

"That's good to hear. You'd be a right dumb arsehole if you gave up on something as special as what you two have. Then I really would have to bury you." Liam laughs, but I don't.

It's not that I mind the overprotective brother schtick from him, not as much as I do from Jude, at least, but I'm not a fan of anyone threatening my life. Especially when I know they have the means to follow through on that threat, and I'm not entirely sure they're joking.

"You didn't tell him what Lucifer said, did you?" Jude asks, walking up to us.

"That she wanted him murdered in his sleep? Nope, didn't mention it," Liam says with a sly grin.

"Really, Jude? Lucy is trying to call in favors to have me killed?" I ask, tilting my head to the side as I give him a look that screams, *This is out of the realm of okay.*

My brother shakes his head. "She didn't mean it. She was just really fucking pissed. It takes her a while to process things sometimes. And if she wanted you dead, she would've done it herself. We both know that. I think it was more of a tattling thing, if I'm being honest. Or she wanted someone to be as outraged as she was since I had a feeling something was going on, and you two were keeping it quiet. I wasn't pissed when I found out for sure, which really got under her skin."

"What are you talking about?" I ask.

"Man, I've known you for what? Ten years at least? You always liked to have a good time, and your bed was rarely empty. This last year or so, I haven't seen a woman do the walk of shame creeping out of your room when I show up in the morning."

"There was never any shame involved when a woman left my bed, asshole."

He's right, though. The partying, the revolving door of women—it got old. It wasn't what I wanted, but I didn't think I could have what I really craved, so I stopped pretending. Figured if it didn't happen with Cece, then I'd eventually meet someone. Or not. I didn't really think that far ahead.

"I'm just glad Little Bit has come around. It was breaking Lucy's heart watching her suffer and shutting everyone else out. Hearing that she went through more than what we thought had my woman up all night raging like nothing I've seen before."

"So it runs in the family. Good to know," I say, not wanting to get too deep in this conversation. If I think about what Cece told me yesterday, I'm liable to hop on the first flight out to Arizona and take care of those fucks by my damn self.

"Yeah, she thought with Otto gone, Cece could move on without fear he'd come after her. Lucy had no idea about the Bone Breakers," Jude says.

"They'll be dead soon enough, brother, you can count on that," Liam promises, looking Jude square in the eye.

"I'm going to go talk to Sawyer for a minute, then grab Cece and take her for a ride."

"Should I be expecting Little Bit home tonight?" Jude asks.

"If she is, it's going to be so she can grab her stuff and move it into my place."

Jude's eyebrows jump to his hairline. "She know that?"

"Not yet. But when we get back, expect her to have a new address."

"Alright then," Jude says with a wide smile.

I turn away from Jude and his brother and find Sawyer sitting at the bar with his eyes glued to his computer screen.

"Hey, can I talk to you?" I ask, walking up and having a seat next to him.

"Sure. What's up?" He turns his full attention to me.

"How good are you with hacking into shit?"

"I'm the best," he replies.

"You don't even know what I need you to break into."

He shrugs. "Doesn't matter. I'll still be the best. What are you thinking?"

This fucking guy.

"I was wondering, if I gave you a name, could you put together a paper trail going from his bank account to some dark web shit? Shit that would be flagged by the FBI and have him investigated. If you could make it look real enough that they'd be knocking down his door and the charges would stick?"

Sawyer scoffs. "Fucking child's play. I'll even get a hold of my contact at the bureau and put them on the trail. How dark are we talking?"

"I'll leave that up to you, but dark enough that it's a long fucking while before he breathes free air."

Sawyer nods. "Give me a name and consider it done."

"Danny Crispin. He's a guard out at the state prison. He's a fucking asshole who likes to hurt women."

Sawyer types some shit on his keyboard and pulls up a photo that looks like it's from a law enforcement database. "This the prick?"

I nod. "Yeah, that's him." Though I'd imagine he looks a little different after the beating my woman and I gave him not too long ago.

"I'll work on it."

"And if I gave you another name in the future?" I ask.

If he can do it with this Danny asshole, maybe Roman will have a few more names for me at some point.

"Just let me know. I can do this shit in my sleep."

"Thanks, Sawyer."

He nods and turns back to his computer, typing away. I take that as my cue to leave him alone and let him work.

I head over to where Ozzy and Freya are sitting. "I'm going to head out unless you need me for anything else today."

"Nah. I think I'm going to make my woman close her laptop and go on a ride with me anyhow."

Freya straightens her spine and quirks her brow at my prez. "Make me?"

"Beg you?" he asks with a smile.

"Much better." She leans over and places a quick kiss on his mouth.

"I'll see you tomorrow," I say and wave as I head out the door into the warm summer afternoon.

The only thing I want at this moment is to have my woman on my bike, then take her back to our house and enjoy her body until we leave in the morning. And that's exactly what I plan to do.

CHAPTER SEVENTEEN
CECE

When Cash shows up at the house, he takes the bag I packed and puts it in one of his saddlebags before I pull my helmet over my head and climb on his bike behind him. I love wearing his shirt in the morning, but I'm a little tired of not having something clean to change into after spending the night.

"How about a ride?" he asks.

"Perfect," I reply.

God, I love being on the back of his motorcycle with him. When he would take me out before anything started between us, I would fantasize about being with him, *really* being with him. That I was his woman, and after the ride, he would take me home and kiss me for the rest of the night. Now, that fantasy is a reality, and it's better than I could have ever imagined. And I have a *very* vivid imagination.

We ride through the windy country roads with my arms wrapped around Cash, his hand resting on my thigh pressed against his. It's peaceful and exciting all at the same time, the way most things are between us.

We stop at a diner about an hour from Shine and grab some lunch. It's summertime and the weather is perfect today, so the patio is busy as we eat our food. He leans over and kisses me sweetly on the mouth.

"What was that for?" I ask.

"I fucking love that I get to kiss you any damn time I please. Especially now that everyone knows you're mine."

"It's not like anyone here knows who we are," I say with a laugh.

"Doesn't matter. There's no need to sneak around or go for rides under the pretense of being just friends, or you being at my house only to bake for Betsy. Now everyone knows you're on the back of my bike because you're mine. I can kiss you whenever I want, and you're at my house because you can't stand to be away from me." He tosses me a wicked smile.

"Oh, is that why I'm over there?" I mean, the answer is obviously yes, but still, it's awfully bold of him to assume.

His eyebrow quirks, but that damn smile remains on his face. "You trying to tell me it's not? That you aren't as addicted to me as I am to you?"

"I would, but that would make me a liar, so..." I lean over and kiss him like I've wanted to be free to do so many times in the last month. A lot longer than that, if I'm being honest.

We finish lunch, then Cash and I ride out to the quarry. It's late afternoon, but there's still plenty of time before the sun sets.

He gets off the bike and grabs a roll that's attached to the back.

"Figured we could spend some time here and not have rocks cutting into our asses," he says as he lays a blanket on the ground.

Cash sits down and pats the spot between his legs. Instead of sitting on the blanket, though, I move my leg over his hips, then sit on his lap, facing him.

"That's a much better idea," he says, leaning forward to kiss me.

"I thought so, too."

My arms are draped over his shoulders as Cash runs his hands up and down my back lightly, tasting the skin at my neck.

"I swear I didn't bring you out here to make out with you like a horny teenager, but fuck, sweetheart, I can't seem to keep my hands off you." He lowers his head to my shoulder and places a wet kiss there. "Or my lips." He runs his tongue along my throat until it reaches my chin, then he bites gently. "Or my tongue."

"You don't hear me complaining," I say, and his deep chuckle reverberates from his chest into mine. "However, I did want to come here and make out."

Cash chuckles again, and I decide it's one of my favorite sounds in the entire world.

We continue our lazy, unhurried strokes, but it doesn't take much for the heat to begin building inside me. I gasp when he lightly nibbles on my ear, then let out a quiet moan when his hand cups my breast over my shirt, his thumb brushing my nipple in a soft, sweeping motion.

He leans his head back and stares at me through hooded eyes, and my hips begin to rotate slightly over his hardening length as if they have a mind of their own. Anytime Cash touches me like this, an instinctual part of my brain takes over, and my body moves in whatever way feels natural, whatever feels good. I don't even have to think about it because I know nothing happens between Cash and me that isn't absolutely spectacular.

"You look so fucking pretty sitting on me while you rub yourself against me," he says, leaning back a bit more, allowing his gaze to slowly travel up and down my body. "Fuck, sweetheart, we need to pack up and get back to the house, or I'm going to end up taking you on this blanket."

A ghost of a smile sweeps across my lips as my hands travel to the hem of his shirt. "I wouldn't mind. This is our place, after all."

"You make it easy to lose control," he says, still looking at me.

"And yet you haven't," I taunt.

I should have known better.

Cash shoots forward, taking my mouth in an all-consuming kiss. "I fucking love your lips," he pants when he briefly breaks the kiss, then dives back in as though he's starving for them. His hands grip the hem of my shirt, and he whips it over my head, letting it fall to the blanket. "And your perfect tits." He dips his head and sucks my nipple in his mouth over the white cotton of my bra. When he pulls away, I look down, and the fabric is wet from his mouth, my nipple poking through.

He moves to the other side and does the same while he twists the one that was just in his mouth. The sensation makes my center throb with need as I rub myself over his hard cock through our jeans.

Cash undoes the clasp of my bra, letting the material fall from my body, then rolls forward, laying us on the blanket. When he takes my naked breast in his mouth again, I moan in pleasure, my back arching. His hand trails down my stomach, and he flicks the button of my jeans open. His fingers immediately find me wet as he strums my pussy like the fucking expert he's become at bringing me to unimaginable heights within moments of touching me. Cash has become so attuned to me that touching me exactly where I need is almost second nature to him.

"Fuck, baby. You're so wet for me already," he says, sliding one finger, then two, into my core.

I cry out as his fingers expertly move inside me while his thumb rubs my swollen clit. His face hovers over mine, and my mouth falls open, moan after moan tumbling from my throat.

"You're so fucking beautiful, Cece, riding my hand like this. I want you to drench my fingers, baby."

Pressure builds fast as his hand moves inside my panties with his eyes on me, his breath tickling my face. He must feel the moment my walls begin to tighten because his grin turns absolutely feral as both of our breaths come out in hard pants.

"That's it, baby. Right there?"

I nod furiously. "Don't stop. Oh God, don't stop."

"I got you, sweetheart. Fuck," he moans as my pussy squeezes his talented fingers, and I let out a cry of pure pleasure. His motions never cease as I ride his hand through my orgasm, stars bursting behind my eyelids when I squeeze them shut.

"Open your eyes, baby. Let me see how good I make you feel," Cash commands.

When I do, there's so much love in his that it nearly brings me to happy tears as my body comes down.

"I need to be inside you," he says and removes his hand from my pants, licking his fingers clean before he grips the waist of my jeans and pulls them down my legs.

"God, I don't think I've ever needed anything more." He has my boots and jeans off and tossed to the side in record time before he shoves his over his hips. It takes a couple of frustrating moments for him to undress. When he does, he kneels between my thighs and wraps my legs around his waist. Cash lifts my hips, and in one swift motion, he's buried so deep inside me all I can feel is him pumping in and out of me at a furious pace, so intense, and so, so right.

One of his hands grips my hip as the other finds my clit, and he begins rubbing, the delicious friction quickly bringing me to the brink of what I know is going to be another earth-shattering high.

"Fuck, Cece. Are you going to come for me again? Let me hear it, baby."

My head tilts toward the sky, and I let out a scream, my second orgasm burning through me so furiously I feel like I may actually ignite right here.

Cash bands an arm around my waist and pulls me up, smashing his chest against mine as he roars out his own release. I feel him jerk inside me over and over, coming deep inside me. God, I've never felt so full to my very soul than I do when I'm connected to him, both of us finding such mind-bending pleasure in each other.

His hand is tangled in my hair, massaging the back of my head as we both catch our breath.

"I love you," he says against my mouth. "So fucking much, Cece."

"I love you, too."

Once again, his lips connect with mine, but this kiss is languid and slow as though we have all the time in the world to get lost in each other.

He pulls his mouth away and looks me in the eye, kissing my damp forehead. "We should probably get back to the house at some point. At least put some clothes on so I'm not showing the entire world my ass."

"It's only me and the birds out here, and I don't know about them, but I personally love seeing your ass."

Cash chuckles into my neck, and I smile.

Nothing could possibly take me down from this high today. Absolutely nothing.

When we get back to the house, I go upstairs and hang the few clothes I have with me. I step back and take a look at my clothes alongside the ones he keeps here. They look good next to each other. I jog back down the stairs and find Cash on the front porch, rocking in his chair and looking out over the front of his property. It's dusk, which is my favorite time of day to spend out here.

He looks at me in the doorway, a smile creeping across his mouth and holds out his arm in invitation. I walk over to him and sit on his lap before he wraps his arms around my middle.

"I have to take a trip tomorrow," he tells me.

I'm accustomed to the brothers having to go on runs, but they don't usually call them "trips." That term piques my interest.

"Where are you going?"

"Arizona."

The breath stalls in my chest, and my body becomes as rigid as a plank of wood.

"Why?" I ask, already knowing the answer.

"It's time to take care of the Bone Breakers. We're done waiting for them to make another move. We were waiting for Liam to get back from wherever he was, and now that he is, we're leaving tomorrow."

"Did you...did you tell Liam and the rest of your brothers what they did to me?"

His hand rubs my arm in an attempt to comfort me. "No, sweetheart. And I won't. They only know what they saw in the hotel room. That's your story, and I won't ever repeat it."

"I want to go with you," I say, and he immediately shakes his head.

"No, baby. It's way too dangerous. There are too many variables, and I can't have you as one of them."

"Cash, you know I can handle myself," I argue. "I want to be there when those assholes take their last breaths."

"Cece, I'm not going to budge."

I jump up from his lap and start pacing the front porch. Anger, hurt and disappointment in the fact that he's telling me what I can and can't do flow through me at rapid-fire speed.

"What makes you think you can tell me what I can do? You've seen me fight. Even Roman knows how skilled I am. Why don't you see it?"

Cash leans forward. "I don't give a shit what Roman says," he replies, his jaw tightening. "He's never walked into a clubhouse filled with armed, sadistic fucks like I have."

"You think you can stop me? I'm coming!"

"I'm the one with the plane, and I say no." His tone leaves no room for argument. Not that it's going to stop me from trying.

"What are you talking about? What plane?"

Cash blows out a breath and sits back in his chair. "Liam knows a guy who knows a guy. We're taking off in the morning."

I cross my arms over my chest and stare into the front yard, stewing in silence and going through every possibility in my head.

"So what am I supposed to do, huh? Sit around and wait for you to get back like a good little woman?" I finally ask.

He shakes his head and stands, walking over to me and putting his arms around my waist. I don't uncross my arms, and I'm still stiff, but I let him hold me, even though I'm pissed as hell.

"You're going to stay here where it's safe. Where those assholes have no shot of getting to you again. If you came with us, they'd have a chance to hurt you. There's no way in hell I'm going to allow you to be put in that situation."

I understand what he's saying. Truly. But Cash will never understand the soul-deep need I have for vengeance. He'll never fully understand what I went through. And that's okay. There's no way for him to know. But because of that, he'll never see where I'm coming from. It's not a question of putting myself in danger. There is no way to stay completely safe one hundred percent of the time on this planet. This is a matter of me weighing the potential outcome of that danger. Regardless of what he says or how much he begs, this is a decision I have to make for myself.

"I hate this," I say, which is not a lie at all.

"I know you do, sweetheart. But you have to understand this is a different situation than what you do with Roman. These guys won't hesitate to shoot first and ask questions later. We don't know exactly what we're walking into, but it's going to be ugly, I'm certain of at least that."

I drop my arms and wrap them around Cash.

"When we get back, I can promise you there will be nothing left of that fucking club."

He's right. When *we* get back, there won't be.

Chapter Eighteen
Cash

Cece and I spent the night in each other's arms. I could feel something off with her, but I suppose that's to be expected. She was pissed when I told her there was no way in hell I'd be okay with her coming with us, but it didn't take long for her to see reason. She was still quiet, though, lost in her thoughts. I did what I always used to and remained by her side for when she was ready to talk—*if* she wanted to talk about it.

We get up before dawn. She insisted that she go to the clubhouse with me to see me off. Lucy, Charlie, and Freya are here as well. This is the first time I get to hold my woman like I've been wishing I could around everyone.

When Liam walks in, he smiles at me and Cece, nodding his approval.

"Alright, boys, plane's ready to go when you are. If you're hungry, I'd suggest getting breakfast now since, unfortunately for you, I don't offer in-flight service."

"On it," Charlie says as she and Freya head to the kitchen.

"You doing okay, Little Bit?" Liam asks when he walks up to where Cece and I are sitting at the bar.

"I'm okay." She checks the time on her phone. "Just have a lot of stuff to do today. Figured it was a good day to keep busy and all that."

"Do you have to do some baking for Betsy today?" I ask, knowing the answer is probably yes.

Cece nods. "It's okay, though. I can be late," she says, chewing her lip.

"Sweetheart, go back to the house and do what you need to do. We're going to eat and head out to the airfield in a few minutes."

"Are you sure?"

"Of course," I reply, swiping a kiss across her lips. "We'll be back before you know it." I can feel her anxiety running away with itself, and I'm not sure being here is what's best for her. Baking always helps center her, so I'd rather she do that than sit here for five more minutes, watching me eat a fucking breakfast sandwich.

"Don't worry. I'll make sure your man returns to you safe and sound," Liam says, and Cece gives him an appreciative smile.

"I want everyone to come back safe," she says and stands up from her chair.

"I'll walk you out to your car," I say, since I took my bike here.

Cece nods, and we head out the front door into the cool morning. The sun is barely peaking over the horizon as I open her door.

"I love you," I tell her and wrap her in my arms.

Cece places her head against my chest. I still feel a lot of tension radiating from her, but this is the first time since we've been a couple that I've had to take off for something like this, so it's to be expected. Not that I would know. This is also the first time I've done something like this and had someone waiting for me at home. I have to say, it's a good feeling.

"I love you, Cash. So much." She lifts her face toward mine, and I lower my mouth to hers, kissing her in a way that I hope conveys everything I'm pouring into it. *I love you. I'll be safe. I'll come home to you.*

We break apart, and Cece gets in her car.

"Save me a couple scones for when I get back. Oh, and that chocolate thing you make, too," I say with a smile.

She returns the smile, but I can tell it's forced. Fuck, I hate this so much. I want this to be over so I can see a real smile on her face again.

She starts the car, and I close her door, watching as her taillights disappear from view before heading back to the clubhouse.

"She okay?" Liam asks, and I shake my head.

"No, but she will be. When this is over, she'll never have to worry about those sons of bitches again."

Thirty minutes later and we're in the air. Liam decided to play pilot again, and we're all sitting in the back of the huge cargo plane strapped to jump seats. It's a tight fit with giant cases upon cases of everything we'll need. There're three side-by-sides and four ATVs. All electric. All much quieter than the gas-powered alternatives.

"You doing okay over there?" I ask Barrett, who isn't his normal chipper self.

"I hate flying."

I bark out a laugh. "But you're okay with walking into a potential death trap. Or taking trips out to the pig farm with Knox?"

"Totally different, man. We could plummet to the ground from thirty thousand feet in the air. None of us would survive. When I go to the farm, I know I'm not the one being fed to the pigs. And when we have to handle some shit, I know every brother has my back, so my odds of survival are pretty high. Planes, though? I'd rather never step foot on one if I don't have to."

"How did I not know this about you?" I ask, shaking my head. "You were fine the first time we came out West." That was the trip we took to rescue Lucy from that fucking cult. The first time I laid eyes on Cece and my fate was sealed.

"Trust me, brother, I wasn't. But this ride is a little bumpier than the last," he says right as we go through a pocket of turbulence that lasts several minutes. The groan that comes from him has me cackling, but I take pity on the fucker and don't try to talk to him again.

Instead, I rest my head against the shitty padding behind me and close my eyes, thinking about the night ahead. I picture myself walking into that clubhouse and putting bullets in as many Bone Breakers as I can. I imagine riding back to the safe house Liam secured for us and getting the information we need out of Red before I slice open the fucker's throat and watch the life drain from him.

Then I think about getting on this plane and landing at the airstrip back in Shine. I imagine Cece's face when I walk through the door and crawl into bed next to her, holding her close and knowing her nightmare has been eliminated. That the men who hurt her are no longer breathing. These thoughts carry me through the next several hours as I listen to my brothers chatting around me. All the while, with a smile on my face.

We land six hours later on an airstrip in the middle of the desert. Liam emerges from the cockpit with Hendrix behind him.

"Alright. We'll pack up the vehicles and unload here. The safe house is about five minutes away. I have a van there in case we're transporting anyone back," he informs the group.

"Red's coming back with us. He has information we need, so I'll be questioning him," Ozzy says.

"And I want to make sure his death is slow and painful," I chime in.

"Fair enough," Liam says.

I look over at Jude, who is staring at his phone, which he's just turned back on after the flight.

He presses the screen and brings the phone to his ear. "Lucy, what the hell is going on?" He's silent as he listens to her. "Okay, love, slow down. What time was that?" Silence again. He looks at me and mouths for me to check my phone. I shoot him a questioning look, but do it regardless.

There are several missed calls from Lucy, and I look back at Jude. "What's going on?"

"Little Bit is missing. Betsy couldn't get a hold of her this morning, so she called Lucy. She drove out to the house, and her car wasn't there, so she drove around and found it parked on the side of the road about a mile from the airstrip."

Jude puts the phone on speaker.

"Lucy, were there signs of a struggle? Tire marks on the road, or anything like that?" I ask, fear and adrenaline coursing through my blood. Were the Bone Breakers waiting for us to leave so they could make a move? Sawyer had some fancy spy shit tracking their phones, but what if it failed? What if they discovered it was there?

"No, nothing. I'm so fucking scared, and no one is here. What do I do? I tried calling her a million times, but she's not answering."

"Tell her I'm okay."

I hear the one voice I should absolutely *not* be hearing behind me right now.

Slowly, I turn around, and standing behind a crate of weapons is my fucking woman. The woman I kissed goodbye less than seven hours ago. The woman who should be in *Shine*, not on a fucking plane with us in goddamn *Arizona*.

"Jude, what's going on? Who do I hear? Is that Cece?" Lucy screams into the phone.

"Sure is, Lucifer," Jude replies. "Seems we had a stowaway."

"I'm going to kill her!" Lucy screams into the phone. "Cece, what the hell are you doing?"

Cece doesn't answer her sister. Her gaze is firmly locked on my very angry one as Lucy continues to scream into the phone about how, when she's done murdering her, she's never going to let her out of her sight again.

"Love, I have to go," Jude says, taking Lucy off speakerphone. "Yes, I'll tell her." Silence. "Yes, I'll tell her that too." Silence. "No, I'm definitely leaving that one for you. I really have to go. Cash looks like he's about to pass out, and that's the last thing any of us needs right now." He disconnects the call, then turns his attention to Cece. "What is it with you and your sister? She hides in a van to get out of the desert, and you hide in a plane to go back to one? I swear someone needs to put a bell on you."

I'm staring at Cece. She hasn't moved, nor does she acknowledge Jude in any way. Just holds my steely gaze. She's waiting for me to have some sort of reaction. Bracing herself for what she thinks is going to be an explosion.

"What. Are. You. Doing here?" I grit out slowly.

"I told you I wasn't staying behind," she replies with her chin lifted.

I scoff. "You told me you…" I shake my head back and forth. "Everyone out!"

Liam quickly heads back into the cockpit, and the ramp of the plane descends, landing on the dusty ground. My brothers and Liam's men walk out of the plane. I'm certain they can still hear everything, but I don't care.

All the while, Cece and I don't take our eyes off each other.

"Listen—"

"No. You do not speak yet," I say, cutting her off. "I can't believe you did this, Cece. Do you have any idea what you've done by coming here? How badly you scared your sister? She thought something awful happened to you, and we're thousands of miles away. What did you think was going to happen when we landed here? That I was going to see you and not give a shit that you directly defied me? Once again, you're jumping into something completely half-cocked without any thought to yourself or the people who care about you."

"I get that you're pissed, but I had to come," she says without any remorse or acknowledgment that she royally fucked up. "I have to see with my own eyes that Red is dead. I should be here. I should be a witness to his last breath, so he knows that he didn't break me. I have the chance to finally fight back, and this time, I'm the one who gets to make him hurt. Make him suffer. I deserve that."

"What about me? Don't I deserve to be able to trust that you're safe, that you're where you fucking said you were going to be?"

She crosses her arms over her chest. "To be fair, I never agreed to stay."

I open and shut my mouth several times. "Are you seriously standing there trying to justify your actions by telling me you didn't *explicitly* say you wouldn't come? Is that what's actually happening right now?"

Cece throws her arms to her sides. "I'm standing here telling you that you don't get to make my decisions for me. I told you I wanted to come. You know why I need to be here."

I shake my head, too angry for my thoughts to make sense, for words to form.

"Let's go. We need to unload and get this shit to the safe house."

"Cash—"

I shake my head. "No. I can't listen to you right now, Cece."

I walk off the plane, and Cece follows.

"That was sneaky as hell, Little Bit," Liam says when we walk up to the group waiting on the ground. "I like it."

I shoot him a glare that I wish would incinerate him on the spot. Of course he would be proud of her for pulling this asinine bullshit.

We pack up the vehicles and the ATVs with the weapons from the cases. And I get the pleasure of finding Cece's little hiding spot. She must have pried the side off the crate and snuck inside before repositioning the wood so no one would notice. That was fucking sneaky all right.

Seven of us drive the loaded-down vehicles off the plane. Cece moves to get into the side-by-side with Jude.

"Absolutely not. You're riding with me," I call to her.

"Jude is perfectly capable," she answers.

"I don't give a flying fuck. Get in here." I turn my gaze to the dirt road in front of me, waiting for her to get her sweet little ass over here.

When she does, I tell her to strap in, then we take off for the safe house.

When we pull up, it's only late morning. We have hours before we'll be hitting the Bone Breakers clubhouse. The plan was for us all to get here, go over the attack, get some rest, then hit them in the middle of the night. Now I have no idea what the plan is. I have no idea what the hell is going on, period.

We get out of the side-by-side and walk over to where everyone else has parked.

There're twelve men standing around, not knowing what the hell to say about how the situation has changed. And one woman who is still holding herself with way too much attitude for being completely in the wrong.

"What do you want to do?" Ozzy asks.

"I want Liam to get on that plane with Cece and take her back to Shine. We can do this without him."

"Absolutely not," Cece says, standing next to me. "Nothing has to change."

"Everything's changed!" I yell, then take a breath in an attempt to compose myself. The last thing I want to do is fight with my woman in front of my brothers and Liam's team. "She can't stay."

"I'm not leaving," she says.

If it were anyone else and this were any other situation, I would probably laugh at the way everyone's heads swivel between Cece and me. But it's not, and I don't find anything about this remotely funny.

"I say she stays," Liam chimes in.

What the fuck?

"She's already here. She knows how to use a weapon, and she can stay in the house until we bring Red back."

"I'm not staying in the house," Cece states.

"I'm trying to help you out here, Little Bit. Could you maybe do the same?" Liam asks.

"I'm not useless. I've been training to fight, and I'm damn good. Ask Cash."

Everyone looks at me.

"How do you know that?" Jude asks. "Have you been training her?"

"Not exactly," I reply. I don't want to get into the whole situation with Roman right now. "But she's right. She is good." I can at least admit that.

"So it's settled. I'll go with you," Cece says.

"It absolutely is not settled," I say. "Since this asshole doesn't want to take you back," I say, nodding toward Liam, "you'll stay in the house like he said."

She tilts her head and glares at me. "And I said no."

"Goddammit, woman." I throw my hands in the air. "Would you listen to reason?"

She doesn't cower, doesn't budge when I raise my voice. It's like trying to reason with a brick fucking wall.

"Are you going to chain me up, Cash? Because that's what you're going to have to do to keep me here."

"The thought crossed my mind," I mumble.

"She can drive the van. I was going to, but since she's here, I'll go in with you guys. That way, we have an even number of men to what we think they have at their compound, and we still have a driver," Sawyer chimes in. "Win-win."

I look at Cece, and she nods in agreement.

It definitely isn't a *win-win*, but apparently, it's the best I can hope for.

And it looks like that's all I'm going to get.

When we walk into the house, there are two bedrooms and a couple couches in the main room, which isn't saying much. The place is small and looks like any random run-down house you would expect to find out here. Dingy white paint, outdated kitchen appliances, scarred wooden kitchen table and chairs, and a layer of dust that covers every surface.

We all spread out. Linc, Jude, and Barrett take one of the rooms. All of us are tired from our early start, and we need to get some rest. Cece and I take the other room, and we leave the rest of the guys to figure it out for themselves. The bedroom contains nothing more than a mattress on box springs pushed against a wall and an old dresser on the other side of the room. At least there are blackout curtains hanging from the window, so we don't have to try to sleep in a bright room.

"Cash, I know you're angry with me," Cece says, sitting on the bed

I shake my head, leaning against the closed door. "Angry doesn't even begin to cut it, sweetheart."

I'm pissed as hell. But the longer I think about what she did, the more I respect her for it, begrudgingly as it may be. Cece is a force. I knew it from the first time I met her. It's the quiet kind. The kind that's unmovable, unbreakable. Part of me wants to strangle her, and the other part wants to kiss the hell out of her for being so fucking brave. She didn't cower once when I was doing everything in my power to send her packing. She stood firm in her resolve to see this through.

"I'm sorry I lied," she says.

"Oh, you admit it now?"

A ghost of a smile ticks up the side of her mouth. "Yeah, I admit it. You thought I would stay in Shine, and I let you believe that. But do you understand why I'm here? Why I *have* to be here?"

"Part of me does." I blow out a long breath. "It's why I want to be the one to kill the bastard myself."

"I guess we aren't so different then," she says.

I walk across the small room and sit next to her. "The difference is, I'm always one-hundred-percent up front with you. You still keep things from me."

"I've told you more than anyone else in my life."

"True. But I need more than that. I need trust. I need you to do what you say you're going to do, not go behind my back." It's not as though this is the first time she's let me believe she was doing one thing when she went and did another.

"I get that. I really am sorry."

"I know. But Cece, if anything happens to you..."

She shakes her head. "It won't. I didn't come all this way to fail now."

Neither did I.

Chapter Nineteen
Cece

I wake before Cash. We didn't talk much after coming into the bedroom. It was just more of me explaining why I need to be here and trying to get him to understand. I don't know if he really does. I honestly don't think he can. Me being here goes against everything inside him that screams he needs to protect me. Part of me feels bad for putting him in this situation. I don't want him scared. But the bigger part is determined to see this through, consequences be damned. There's something to be said for the notion that it's better to ask for forgiveness rather than permission.

Cash is facing me as I stare at him while he sleeps. His face is serene. I want to trace my fingers over his brow and down his cheek. Feel the smooth skin of his face. Then he opens his eyes. At first, there's a small smile on his lips when he sees me. But then I watch as it registers where we are, and his smile fades, his eyes shuttering.

"You're still angry with me," I state. It's not a question, because I know the answer.

He sits up and scrubs a hand over his face. "Not as mad as I was earlier, but yeah. I'm still upset."

I sit up as well and lean against the wall. "I can't keep explaining why I'm here. I don't think it will make a difference. All I can do is apologize again for misleading you."

"I know. And honestly, I respect you for what you're doing. I hate it, and I'm pissed because I don't want you in harm's way, but I respect your determination. And that's kind of fucking with my head right now."

"I am a multifaceted woman," I say, smiling to myself, remembering when I spoke those words to Roman.

"That you are, sweetheart." Cash turns and looks at me. Really looks at me, as though he needs to make sure I hear and understand what he says next. "You have to stay in the van, Cece. I hate you going, and I really wish you would just agree to stay here until we get back. But you've come this far, and I would rather not hold you prisoner. I don't think I could live with myself, even if my head is telling me to damn the consequences."

"I know the feeling."

He shakes his head. "Please. Promise me—in clear, concise words—that you won't get out of the van tonight."

"I promise you I won't get out of the van tonight," I reply, imploring him to see the honesty in my eyes.

His eyes close as he takes a calming breath. "Thank you."

We venture out into the house where most of the guys are sitting around on the couches or chairs in the kitchen.

"Where's Sawyer?" Cash asks the room.

"Making sure all the comms are working properly and double-checking some satellite footage to make sure nothing has changed since he last took a look," Liam answers. "It's his own little routine he does before every mission. Not that I would ever complain about my men being overprepared." He looks at me and arches a brow. "Having you tag along sure is a surprise, though."

"One that you signed off on," Cash mumbles.

Liam smirks. "I didn't say it was a bad one."

My eyes wander around the room, and I don't see Jude.

"Where's your brother?" I ask Liam.

"Outside having a smoke," he answers, tilting his head toward the front door.

I nod and make my way outside, following the trail of smoke around the corner of the house.

Jude has a cigarette in one hand and his phone in the other, staring at the screen.

"How mad is she?" I ask, walking over to him.

He looks up and shakes his head. "Fucking fuming. Threatened to charter a plane herself to come take your arse back to Shine."

"And how mad are you?"

He narrows his eyes and looks toward the vast desert, silent for a few moments as he considers his next words. "We live a violent life. Lord knows your sister isn't immune to it." He looks at me. "Did I ever tell you about the first time I saw her shoot a man? Or, I should say, he was dead when I got there, but it was Lucy who put him to ground."

"I didn't know there was more than Otto," I reply, a little taken aback by this new information.

"When I saw how hard she fought back against those fucking assholes, I think I fell a little in love with her on the spot." He grins. Only Jude would fall for someone after he cleaned up the murder scene. "She's never shied away from violence. From protecting herself and the people she loves. But she never wanted you to be involved like you are right now."

"That's why she was pissed when she found out about me and Cash."

Jude shakes his head. "It's not just the fact that you're with a brother, it's the fact that she can't protect you. That she feels like she failed you." Jude takes a drag from his cigarette then throws it to the ground and stomps it out. "I love you like family, Little Bit. But you're putting my woman and my brother through hell. I'll protect you with my life, because that's what we do for family, but you need to stop this bullshit. If your man tells you to stay behind, you stay behind. If your sister is pissed that you keep things from her, then stop keeping things from her. No one here is the enemy. No one wants to control you. But you need to stop putting yourself in risky situations without caring about the fact that it would destroy the people we both love if something happened to you that you didn't come back from. For everyone's sanity."

His brows are raised, waiting for me to say something.

"You're right."

"Of course I am," he quips, and I roll my eyes.

"I'm not sorry that I'm here though, Jude. I'm sorry that I did it in a deceitful way. But I'm not sorry that I get to see Red take his last breath."

"I know. Which is why I'm going along with this crazy plan. You deserve that, Little Bit. I won't be the one to deny you."

"Thank you," I say. "And thank you for talking Lucy out of flying here."

"Well, all I did was refuse to give her the coordinates. Can't charter a plane without knowing where you're going. I fully expect to pay for it when I get home."

"Sorry about that."

He shrugs. "Your sister likes to argue. I like to make up. It works for us."

I eye him with skepticism. "You guys have a weird relationship."

"You aren't the first to point that out and probably won't be the last," he says with a wide grin and walks back toward the front of the house.

Night has fallen, and it's time to head to the Bone Breakers clubhouse. Nerves dance through my stomach as we drive out to the middle of the desert, where Sawyer has designated the drop spot.

"Okay, everyone, let's test the comms again," Sawyer says.

"We tested them not even two hours ago," Jude grouses.

"I don't give a shit. The man says do it again, we do it again," Ozzy says, quieting the complaints that anyone else might have.

Liam's team, along with all of the brothers, places the comms in their ears, and I do the same. A round of checks comes through the tiny earpiece, and Sawyer nods.

"Everyone clear on the plan?" Liam asks, his gaze traveling over each brother and his team as they nod in confirmation. "What about you, Little Bit?"

"Stay in the van," I reply.

"No matter what you hear through the comms?" he questions for clarification.

I nod.

"Words, please," Liam tells me. "You seem to be in the habit of making people think you agree with something without actually vocalizing your agreement, and then you use that as some sort of loophole." He arches a brow and shoots me a knowing smirk.

"No matter what I hear through the comms, I swear, I won't get out of the van," I confirm.

"Thank you," Liam replies.

"Okay, brothers. Time to blow some shit up," Ozzy says and heads to the side-by-side he'll be taking along with Knox, Linc, and Cash.

Cash walks over to me and cups my cheeks in his warm palms. "I love you."

These nerves are really playing with my emotions because it takes everything in me not to break down in tears right now. His anger from earlier is gone, and the only thing shining in his blue eyes is love.

"I love you, too. I'll be right here when you get back," I whisper, and he bends, giving me a firm kiss on the mouth.

When he breaks the kiss, he presses his forehead against mine for a moment before he turns and heads toward the side-by-side, holding on to the roll bar as Ozzy drives away. Two more side-by-sides drive past me, then the four ATVs quietly move to follow.

Then I'm alone next to a van in the middle of the desert, waiting for the man I love more than anything in this world to return with the one I hate. The one I'm here to see die.

It takes less than three minutes before I hear Ozzy quietly come across the comm in my ear.

"Clubhouse is in view. Everyone, take your positions."

Another minute passes.

I hear Braxton through the comms. "Cruiser two in position."

The rest of the men in the side-by-sides and the ATVs all check in and confirm that they're in position.

"Abel," I hear Liam say. "If you will."

Moments later, there's a loud bang and a flash of light in the distance.

"Door's gone. Let's go," Abel confirms.

The noise of gunshots and screams comes through the comms. Someone who isn't one of the Black Roses, or with Liam, yells, "We're under attack!"

My heart beats wildly in my chest as I stare toward where I saw the flash of the explosion. More gunshots, more screaming and yelling. It seems to go on for hours, but in reality, it isn't more than a few minutes.

Then it's quiet.

"Everyone check in," Ozzy says, his voice sounding out of breath.

I hear Jude first. "Two down. Linc and I are whole."

Abel, Hendrix, Liam, and Sawyer are next, confirming their kills and their safety.

When I hear Cash's voice, tears spring to my eyes. "I got two in the head. I'm whole." I let out a choked sob of relief. "Who has eyes on Red?"

A chorus of no's sounds through the comms.

"Fuck," I hear Cash say. "We need to find him. That fucker isn't getting away from me."

"Well, look what we have here," I hear someone say from the other side of the van.

"Who is that?" I hear Liam call.

When I turn, I see the man responsible for so much pain, so many nightmares that I was awake for and had to live through, staring at me with a gun pointed at my head.

"Red," I say.

"Cece!" Cash yells. "I'm on my way, baby. You're going to be okay."

"Cece," Liam says in a calm voice. "I'm going to cut the power to the engine. We're less than two minutes out. Don't give him any indication that you have a comm in your ear. It's dark, so chances are he won't see it."

"It's been a long time, Cecilia," Red says, his bloodshot eyes traveling over me. "What fucking stupid son of a bitch let you come with them while those assholes murdered my club?"

"Murdered? You mean someone finally gave your club what was coming?" I say.

"Looks like Otto's little whore went and got a mouth on her. That's okay. There are plenty of useful things your mouth can do. None of them includes you talking."

"I'll fucking kill him," Cash roars through the comm, and I squeeze my eyes shut, swallowing hard. I hate that he can hear everything Red is saying to me. The vile way he talks to me. That much hasn't changed.

"Cece," Liam says. "One more minute."

Red walks around the front of the van, keeping his gun trained on me. "Open the door," he says.

"The van won't start, Cece. I've disabled the engine. Play along until we get there," Liam instructs.

I put a shaky hand on the handle and open it.

"Slide over, bitch. We're getting the hell out of here."

I move to the passenger seat, and Red gets behind the wheel. When he tries to start the van, nothing happens.

"What the fuck? What did you do?"

"Nothing, I swear." Not a lie.

He grabs me by the arm and pulls me from the passenger side as he jumps out of the van. I fall to the ground, and he yanks me up.

"Let's go," he growls.

"We're in the middle of the desert, Red. Where do you think we're going?"

"I have a bike stashed out here in case something like this happened. See, I'm not as stupid as your new family thinks I am."

He starts dragging me away from the van, and I stumble along for a few brief moments before headlights are seen coming toward us.

"Shit," Red yells and grabs me around the waist, pulling me against the front of his chest with his gun pressed against my temple, the hard metal digging into my skin.

The side-by-sides come to a halt about ten feet in front of us, with the ATVs scattered between them.

"Where do you think you're going, asshole?" Cash yells, stepping out of the side-by-side.

I look around at the men here to save me with tears in my eyes. Some of them have blood splattered on their faces—evidence of the massacre they were responsible for just minutes ago. A small smile creeps across my mouth, knowing that they sent those assholes to hell.

No matter what happens to me, at least I know they can't hurt anyone else.

"Take another step, and I put a bullet in her," Red yells, jerking his head back and forth, looking at the twelve men before him.

"You won't make it out of this alive, Red," Ozzy calls. "Put the gun down, and I promise to make your death quick."

"Nah, I don't like that offer. How about you hand over one of those fancy side-by-sides and I get the hell out of here? I'll give the girl back when I'm safe."

"Not going to happen," Cash growls. He knows Red is full of shit. I'll be dead when they find my body.

"Well, then we seem to be at a crossroads," Red hollers. "But if I go, I'm taking this bitch with me."

Not without a fight, he isn't.

I dip my head forward, then slam it back into Red's face. He yells, and I drop to my knees. Since he isn't expecting the sudden movement, he loses his grip on me. I swipe my leg out and connect with the back of his, sending him flying to the ground. The force of landing on his back knocks the air from him, but I know it won't last long.

I quickly scramble over his prone body and grab the gun, but he still has a hold of it. I send one elbow flying into his temple while my other hand wraps around his wrist, slamming it onto the ground with every ounce of strength I have in me. His hand loosens around the handle of the weapon, and I grab it from him, quickly rolling off of him and into a crouched position as I aim the pistol at his head.

"Fuck you, fuck you, fuck you!" I scream at the man who is moaning on the ground.

From the corner of my eye, I see Cash run over to me. He skids to a stop at my side, crouching down next to me and wrapping me in his arms. At the same time, Ozzy, Jude, and Knox rush over to Red, pulling him from the ground. Ozzy steps in front of the man who hurt me so many times and punches him twice in quick succession. Red's head flies backward with the force of each blow. He's knocked out cold.

"Shh, sweetheart. I got you," Cash murmurs. "Can I have the gun?" His hand slips over mine, and he takes it from my loose grip, shoving it in the waist of his pants. I collapse against him, sobs racking my body as I let out an anguished cry.

"You're safe, baby. You're safe." He repeats the words over and over as he lifts me from the ground and takes me to the side-by-side. He sits down with me in his lap, holding me tightly.

"Someone put him in the van. Let's get the fuck out of here," he calls to anyone who's listening. I register someone getting behind the wheel, and they drive us back to the house. But my head stays pressed against Cash's chest, and he never lets me go.

When we get back to the house, Cash carries me inside. The van transporting Red followed us, but it drove around to the back, where I saw what looked to be a dilapidated shack behind the house.

He carries me to the bedroom and sits down with me still clutched to his chest.

"I'm okay," I say, looking up at his dusty face. "I'll be okay."

"I know, sweetheart." He presses a kiss to my forehead. "We all will."

"What are they going to do with him?"

"Ozzy needs some questions answered, then he's going to kill him," he answers honestly.

"I want to be there."

"Cece..."

"No, Cash. I've come this far. There's no way he's going to be able to get to me with all of you there. I want my face to be the one he sees when he takes his last breath."

Cash stares at me for several long beats then nods. "Okay."

I stand, still feeling a little shaky, but Cash puts his arm around my waist as we walk out of the house and into the shed. It looks just as bad from the outside as it does inside.

Red is tied to a chair, and there's an old workbench across from him. Several syringes and bottles of liquid sit on the bench, as well as a mean-as-hell-looking knife.

Jude walks over to Red and waves smelling salts under his nose, and his head jerks back.

"Wakey, wakey, asshole," Jude says and gives him a couple slaps on the cheek for good measure.

Red struggles in his restraints for a moment before looking around the room. It's just the brothers here. And me. When his eyes land on me, a nasty sneer appears on his battered face.

"You everyone's whore now, Cecilia?"

"Fuck you," Cash says, lunging forward and punching him in the jaw.

Red lets out a caustic laugh as he moves his jaw from side to side. "Just yours, then."

My man lunges again, but Braxton pulls him back. "No good killing him now, brother. Not until we have answers."

"I ain't telling you shit," Red says.

Ozzy chuckles, and when I look over at him, he has his arms folded across his chest as he leans casually against the wall. "That's what they all say." He looks at Jude and nods toward Red. "Let's get some answers."

Jude strolls over to the workbench and picks up the knife, holding it eye level and inspecting the blade. "I used a knife just like this when I sliced your brothers who tried to take my woman," he says, walking up to

Red. "That's a nice tattoo on your hand." Red struggles again, but Jude grabs his wrist that's tied to the arm of what looks like an old office chair. The knife easily cuts under the skin of Red's hand, slicing the Bone Breakers insignia from his body. Jude tosses the bloody chunk of skin onto Red's lap.

"Who've you been talking to in Shine, Red?" Ozzy asks.

"Fuck you," Red spits, and Ozzy chuckles, nodding at Jude once more.

Jude walks over to the other side of him, where he has a tattoo of a naked woman on his forearm. I remember being trapped under him with my head tilted to the side, and my gaze would be glued to that arm as he moved his disgusting body over mine.

"This your mum?" Jude asks with a chuckle, and Ozzy rolls his eyes.

"I can do without the jokes," Ozzy tells him, but that only serves to make Jude laugh harder.

"But we're having so much fun, Oz," he says, then turns the knife in his hand, slicing Red's tattoo from his arm and tossing another piece of mutilated flesh on his lap. Red howls in pain, and Jude laughs more.

I should be sickened. Hell, I should be scared that my sister sleeps next to Jude every night, but I'm not. Everyone has a dark side that comes out to play every once in a while. This is Jude's.

"Who are you working with?" Ozzy yells over Red's cries.

"Fuck you!" the soon-to-be-dead man wails.

Ozzy nods at Jude again. When he walks over to the table, he picks up a glass bottle containing some sort of liquid.

"This one's going to hurt," Jude comments with a sadistic smile on his face. He opens the bottle and pours the contents on the bloody wound of Red's hand, and it begins to sizzle and bubble.

The stench of burning flesh hits my nostrils, and I quickly bring my hand to my nose.

"You okay?" Cash whispers next to me.

Clearing my throat, I nod and drop my hand back to my side. I won't show any weakness in front of the piece of shit in the chair less than five feet from me.

Red screams seem to last for hours as he cries and begs for the acid to stop eating away at his hand.

"Tell me what I want to know. Jude can make the pain stop, Red. Tell me who you've been working with," Ozzy yells over the screaming.

"Okay, okay, I'll tell you," Red finally chokes out.

Jude walks over to the table and grabs another bottle. He pours the liquid over his hand, and the bubbling ceases. I'm pretty sure I can see bone from here.

Red takes several deep breaths, his pain etched on his face. "When you were involved with what happened to that Farina asshole, it pissed some people off. Some Russians from New York."

"Petrov runs New York," Ozzy says.

The only man named Petrov I'm aware of is the new head of the Russian Bratva in New York. But I thought he and the Monaghans had called a truce since his sister is involved with Finn Monaghan's brother.

"Yeah, but there're some guys who don't like how he's running things. They were pissed that you killed their supplier. This is personal. They want you out of Shine. They want to send a message to anyone who tries to stop them. They know you're working with the Monaghans, and they thought you would be the weaker of the two organizations."

"Give me a name," Ozzy says.

"Damien Sokolov."

Ozzy nods. "Now was that so hard?" He nods toward Cash. "He's all yours."

Cash steps forward.

"Let me ask you one question first," Red says, and Cash pauses his steps. "Is her pussy still as tight as when I had her?" He lets out an evil laugh, and rage like I've never felt before explodes from me.

I lunge to the table and grab Jude's knife, then step in front of Red. "Tell Otto I said hello."

The blade slices across his throat before anyone can stop me. I revel in the shocked look in Red's eyes as his throat is left with a gaping wound stretched from ear to ear. His blood pours from his body, staining his shirt and the floor around him with a dark, viscous liquid.

I drop the knife to the ground and turn, facing Cash.

"It's over," I say.

He stares at me for a beat, then wraps me in his strong arms without a care for the blood on my hands.

"Yeah, sweetheart. It is."

CHAPTER TWENTY
CASH

I keep Cece's hand firmly clasped in mine as we walk back to the house. I'd rather carry her in my arms like I did when we got back from the Bone Breakers' clubhouse, but I got the sense that she needed to walk out of that shed on her own two feet.

She says nothing as we walk inside, nothing as I lead her to the room we're occupying, and she remains silent as I walk into the bathroom and turn the shower on. Thank the gods there's running water.

"You need a shower, sweetheart," I say as she stands in the middle of the bedroom.

"Will you take one with me? I don't want to be without you."

I nod. "Of course."

We walk into the small bathroom, and I take her shirt off her, then her bra. Next, I slide her jeans and panties down before gathering all of her clothes in my arms.

"These need to be destroyed. Is it okay if I leave for just a second?" She nods. "I'll be right back," I say and head out of the house.

Jude is standing outside, smoking a cigarette. "She okay?" he asks.

"Yeah. Can you get rid of these?" I hold out the filthy clothes to him.

"Yeah. I'll scrounge up something for her to change into, too." He takes the clothes and walks over to an old oil colander that looks like someone had burned some shit in it at one point.

I walk back into the house and to the bedroom, finding Cece still standing in the middle of the small bathroom.

"I didn't want to touch anything," she says, holding her bloodstained hands out.

I strip out of my clothes and throw them in the corner. I can deal with those later. Right now, my woman needs me.

Stepping into the bathroom, I shut the door behind me and clasp her bloody hands. "Come on, sweetheart. Let's get cleaned up."

We step into the beige-tiled shower, and I put her hands under the stream of hot water, watching the red swirl in the water before it goes down the drain.

"I killed him." She shakes her head. "I should feel bad. At least, I think I should. I took a life. But I don't feel bad about it."

"What do you feel?" I ask as I turn her around to look at me.

"Free. Like the weight I've been carrying is gone. I didn't even realize how heavy it was, but now I know.

Now that he's dead, I know for certain I'm safe." She looks at me with worry in her gaze. "Do you think I'm a monster?"

I shake my head. "No, sweetheart. No, I think you're a vengeful goddess who slayed her demon. I think you're amazing."

She lets out a sigh and tilts her head back in the spray. Dirt and water circle the drain, and I grab a bottle of cheap shampoo from the corner of the shower, pouring some into my hand.

"Tell me if I'm doing this wrong," I say and bring my hands to her head. "I've never washed a woman's hair before." I massage the shampoo into her scalp. I need to take care of her. Need to show her my devotion and love by doing something for her.

"That feels amazing," she says and lets out a little moan.

I ignore my hardening cock and rinse the suds from her hair, then grab the soap and run it over her wet skin. When she's finished rinsing, she places her hands on my hips and turns us so that I'm now the one under the spray.

"Your turn," she says and grabs the shampoo bottle. "You're going to have to help me out here." I tip my head forward and let her run her soapy hands through my hair.

"You're right, that does feel good," I say then tilt my head back to rinse out my hair.

Next, she grabs the soap and creates a thick lather in her hands before running them over my chest and down my arms.

"This is the first time I've washed a man's body," she says, her hands reaching behind me and running up and down my back. "How am I doing?"

Her wet, naked body pressed against mine is causing the wires in my brain to fritz the fuck out, but I answer her. "Good, sweetheart. Perfect."

She smiles up at me and stands on her tiptoes, pressing her mouth to mine. I wrap my arms around her waist and open my mouth, letting our tongues tangle in a slow, erotic kiss.

"I need you," she whispers. "I need you inside me."

I pull back and search her eyes. They're filled with nothing but love and adoration, but I still pause.

"Please, Cash. I need to feel something real. Something good."

It's the *please* that does it for me.

I crash my mouth to hers, taking her face in my palms and stroking my tongue inside her eager mouth.

"You have to stay quiet. Can you do that?" I ask.

"Yes," she breathes out.

One hand leaves her face, and I trail it down the smooth planes of her stomach, running it over her pussy, then dip my finger inside her. She's so hot and wet already, and we've barely started. I pull my finger out and find her clit, swirling over it again and again. Cece's breath quickens as does my finger.

"Fuck, that feels so good," she whimpers, looking down at my hand then back to my eyes. "I love you."

"I love you, too, baby," I reply, and then I slide two fingers inside her and place my thumb over her clit. They pump in and out of her while the pressure from my thumb has her walls quivering in hardly any time at all.

"I'm going to come," she whispers, and I crash my mouth to hers, swallowing every throaty moan that falls from her mouth. When those moans turn into soft whimpers, I remove my hand and bring my fingers to my mouth, sucking each one clean. She watches me with hooded eyes, and a grin tips the corner of my mouth. "Fucking delicious," I say, then take her mouth in another kiss. I love the taste of her on my lips as I swirl my tongue with hers.

Without breaking the kiss, I wrap her legs around my hips, lining her center with my hard cock. "Hold on to me, sweetheart," I say as I band one arm around her waist and the other against the wall behind her to hold us steady. Her hand reaches for me, and she grips my length as I push inside her. The feeling nearly brings me to my knees as my hips thrust upward, dragging myself in and out of her perfect heat.

The muscles of my arms strain from holding her up, but I need to see her face, need to look into the depths of her blue eyes as I take her against the shower wall.

"Goddamn, baby, you feel so fucking good," I whisper as the water beats down on our bodies, and I pump my hips over and over.

"Don't stop," she pleads. "God, don't stop."

Her pussy clamps down, and quiet gasps fall from her kiss-swollen lips as she comes. I thrust inside one, two, three more times before I explode inside her. My mouth crashes to hers again, and I let out a quiet groan. Fuck, she feels too good to stay silent. I don't know what my brothers and Liam's team are doing right now, but I hope to hell they didn't just hear me make my woman come all over my dick.

My kisses slow, and when I pull away, Cece has a glow to her bright eyes.

"What is it, sweetheart?" I ask as she stares up at me when I set her on her feet.

"I feel on top of the world right now. So happy I could scream. That's because of you."

I shake my head. "No. That's all you. I'm just the lucky bastard who gets to see that smile."

I kiss her forehead and rinse myself off, then cup my hand to collect water and help Cece rinse me from her body.

"I love how you always take care of me," she says with a smile when I turn the shower off.

Leaning down, I kiss my woman again, unable to keep my lips from her skin.

"I always will, sweetheart."

Two hours later, Cece and I are curled up on the couch together. Jude left a change of clothes for her outside the bedroom door. I don't love having Cece in another man's clothes, but I only brought one extra set. Apparently, Sawyer, being Sawyer, had a few changes stashed away, so he lent them to her. He'll be getting those back as soon as humanly fucking possible.

Jude, Linc, and Braxton walk in and see me on the couch with Cece curled up, asleep on my chest.

"We're about done," Braxton says. "All of us need a shower and to change before we get on the plane, though."

"Feel free," I say, nodding toward the bedroom.

"I wasn't asking permission. There're only two bathrooms in this place and I'm not about to hose off outside like Liam's team seems perfectly content to do."

They've probably had to clean up in worse places than this through the years.

Braxton heads into the bedroom Cece and I used and Linc heads into the other one.

Jude sits on the couch across from us.

"We'll be wheels up within the hour," he says.

"You must be happy getting back to Lucy," I say, knowing how fucking pissed she is at this entire situation.

Jude waves his hand. "I'm excited to calm her down with my dick," he replies with a salacious grin.

"Fucking gross, Jude. That's my sister," Cece mumbles against my chest.

"Sorry, Little Bit. Thought you were asleep."

"I was until you started talking about my sister and your dick."

I chuckle and Cece looks up at me with smiling eyes. "Hi," she whispers, and I lean down and kiss her softly on the mouth.

"Hi, baby."

"Speaking of sisters, could you not make out with mine in front of me?"

My smile broadens, and I kiss my woman again. "No."

"Fucking wanker."

When the plane touches down on the old airstrip not far from the clubhouse, Cece's knee is bouncing up and down.

"Don't be nervous, sweetheart. You guys will work it out."

Cece hasn't asked to call Lucy, and Lucy hasn't tried to get in contact with her, either. The silence has my woman nervous as hell.

"I've never heard her so angry," she says, referring to when Lucy threatened to kill her. Obviously, it wasn't a real threat of actual murder, but yeah, she was angrier at Cece than I've ever heard her. "I think I may have really fucked it up this time."

"I think it's time the two of you got to know each other. The real people you are today, not the sisters you were ten years ago."

"Hopefully she'll talk to me."

"Cece, your sister loves you with a fierceness I've never seen from her. She'll talk to you. She may yell, but she'll talk. Eventually."

Cece blows out a breath as the ramp descends. Lucy, Charlie, Maizie, Mia, and Freya start walking toward the plane. My brothers rush out of the cargo plane toward their women, wrapping them in their arms.

All except Jude. No, that cocky bastard strolls down the ramp with a wide smile on his face as he approaches his woman.

"You still pissed?" he asks, and she sends him a glare that would have most men cupping their balls out of protective instinct.

"Am I still mad? Jude Ashcroft, you haven't even seen mad, you fucking son of a—"

Before she can finish her sentence, he grabs her around the waist and kisses her so hard she bends backward. Her hands grab him by the back of his shirt—I'm sure to tear him away. But it only takes moments before her palms flatten against him, and she clings to him as he makes out with her in front of everyone.

"Get a room. Jesus, no one needs to see that shite," Liam says, striding off the plane.

Jude sets his woman back to rights and moves to stand beside her as Cece and I make our way over.

"Hi," Cece says meekly.

"Jude told me what you did. How you ended it. Are you okay?" Lucy asks her sister. "I know, I know, I'm not supposed to keep asking you that."

Cece steps forward and wraps her arms around her sister. Immediately, Lucy does the same and they stand, holding each other as Cece cries. I even see Lucy's eyes fill with tears, and that's a first for me.

"I love you, sister," Cece says. "I had to go, but I'm so sorry I scared you. But you understand, right? Why I had to be there?"

"Honestly, if you would have told me your plan, I would have come with you," Lucy replies. Jude groans, standing next to me. "You're my sister. I would walk through fire for you. Don't ever doubt that. And don't ever do that again."

Cece shakes her head. "I won't. I promise."

Lucy nods and releases Cece from her hold. "Okay then. Let's get out of here and grab some lunch. I'm starving."

"I'm disappointed, Lucifer. I thought you would have lunch ready for me when I got home," Jude jokes.

Lucy turns her head toward Jude. "It's your goddamn fault I'm hungry all the time now, so you can cook your own fucking meals."

Jude looks at her with a confused expression, and Cece gasps.

"What the hell is going on?" Jude asks.

"Your demon spawn has implanted itself in my uterus, and I'm pregnant," Lucy says.

Jude's eyes nearly bulge out of his head as he opens and closes his mouth several times, struck completely speechless.

"Charlie made me take a test yesterday. She said I was even crazier than usual lately."

"Lucy, you called Liam to have Cash taken out. That's a little much, even for you," Charlie says, standing with Linc's arm draped over her shoulders.

Lucy turns to me. "Sorry about that."

I shrug. "No big deal. But maybe don't go around punching people for the next nine months."

"Fair enough," she replies.

"I'm going to be a father?" Jude whispers, staring at his woman's still flat stomach. "I'm going to be a father!" He grabs her around the waist and kisses her indecently on the mouth. "I love you so much, Lucifer. Fuck, I can't wait to see you swell with my baby," he says and places his palms over her belly.

Cece comes to stand next to me and wraps her arm around my waist as I throw mine over her shoulder.

"I love you too, you fucking caveman. Now feed us, please. The baby wants a giant cheeseburger."

He kisses her again, and they start toward the cars parked about a hundred feet from the plane.

"I get to be an auntie," Cece says with tears in her eyes. "I get to see my sister become a mom. I never thought..." She shakes her head and clears her throat. "I never thought life would be this good. That I would have this family. Or you."

"Until I take my last breath, sweetheart. I'm yours until the day I die."

EPILOGUE
CECE

"**F**uck, you feel so good. God, I can't get enough of you," Cash moans as he pumps his cock in and out of me against the kitchen counter.

Have I mentioned how much I love this kitchen?

"Right there. Oh God, I'm going to come," I cry.

Cash wraps his hand around my chin and turns my head to the side so he can reach my mouth from where he stands behind me. The kiss is frenzied and deep as I tighten around him. I moan into his mouth and my pussy pulses hard as the orgasm washes through me, each wave as intense as the last. His movements become hurried, and moments later, he spills inside me on a roar.

When his hips stop moving, he takes a step back, running his palms over my naked ass.

"Fuck, you're so goddamn perfect," he pants out.

"Mmm, I wish we could stay here for the rest of the day, but we have to get all this stuff to the clubhouse," I say, looking at the to-go containers sitting on the other counter. "Lucy might actually barge in here if I don't get these lemon curd cupcakes to her."

Cash chuckles and grabs a wet paper towel, dipping it between my legs to clean up our mess.

Since moving into the house, Cash has been absolutely insatiable. I think seeing my things all over the place fills him with what my sister likes to call "caveman tendencies." He can't keep his hands off me.

I was packing up and ready to head out the door a half an hour ago, but Cash strolled in the kitchen and saw me in my sundress with my hair pulled up. He couldn't resist kissing my bare skin. Which turned into him getting on his knees and going under said dress before he turned me around and flipped up the back, taking me against the counter in our kitchen.

"I can't help it. You look too good to not eat out," Cash says with a smile.

"I don't think that's how the saying goes," I tell him, and he laughs.

We pack up his truck and make our way to the clubhouse. I walk into the kitchen and put everything away while Cash heads outside to say hello to his brothers and wish Barrett a happy birthday. Grabbing the blender, I pull out the container of watermelon from my bag and go about making two of my favorite watermelon drinks. One for me, and one for my pregnant sister. I still haven't touched a drop of alcohol in the two months that we've been back, and I don't plan to. I don't need to numb any of my feelings. Even the bad ones. Those I take out at Roman's gym when we work out together.

Walking outside, I see my sister and the other old ladies sitting around a table under the patio cover.

"Hey, sister. How's the demon?" I ask, handing her the watermelon concoction.

"Still making me puke every morning," she replies with a smile and takes a sip of the pink drink. "This helps, though. I mean, I'd prefer it contained vodka, but..."

"Lucy," Charlie admonishes, shaking her head.

"What? I didn't say I was going to put it in there. I would never do anything to hurt the spawn growing inside me. All I'm saying is vodka would be a nice addition after he or she comes screaming from my vagina."

"Wow, you paint such a lovely picture, Lucy," Mia says across from her.

"It'll be magical, I'm sure," my sister deadpans. "How are you?" she asks me. "I feel like I never see you anymore."

"You see me all the time. Probably more than when I lived with you."

The day we got back—after we took Lucy for food, of course—Cash and I showed up with his truck, and he moved all of my things into his house. Not that I had much of my own, but now all of it is at the house Cash decided to keep.

"But it's not the same. Jude misses your music."

I bark out a laugh. "I'm sure that's not true."

My relationship with my sister has gotten better these last couple months. Now I spend time with her like we used to, sitting and talking and getting to know each other again. And I still use her kitchen to bake on occasion because, according to my sister, the baby likes the smell of fresh-baked bread.

The guys are in the backyard playing cornhole as classic rock plays from the speakers. Barrett is three sheets to the wind since, apparently, it's club tradition that every time someone wishes him a happy birthday, he has to take a shot. Sounds like a one-way ticket to alcohol poisoning if you ask me.

The hour is getting late, which means the dancers from the strip club are going to start showing up, and the party is going to *really* get going. In fact, as soon as the thought crosses my mind, a couple of the girls from the club walk through the back patio door and straight to the birthday boy. The man can barely stand straight, but that doesn't stop him from grabbing each girl around the waist and pulling them to his side.

"Ladies," he booms. "Now it's a party."

The girls titter out laughter, and Lucy stands. "Okay. Time to go. I'm way too sober to think he's funny right now."

Another girl walks through the door, younger than the ones from the club. *Much* younger.

"What the hell?" Mia says as we see the girl look around, her determined gaze landing on Barrett.

She marches up to him while he's laughing at something one of the dancers whispers in his ear. Naturally, all of us walk over to where they are to find out what on earth is going on.

"Are you Barrett O'Neil?" the girl asks. She can't be older than fifteen, and that's being generous. He stops talking to the dancers and looks at the girl who has long dark hair under the black beanie she's wearing. She's swimming in her baggy T-shirt, and her jeans look two sizes too big. Lucy says that's the fashion for young girls nowadays, but what do I know? That's certainly nothing I would have been allowed to wear growing up.

"Yeah," he answers, looking confused.

Jude comes to stand next to him and the dancers, nodding toward them to go somewhere else.

"You knew my mom. Samantha Fuller." The girl pulls out a picture and shows it to him. "See. That's you, and that's my mom. I'm her daughter, Sydney. And you're my dad."

If it weren't for the low music playing in the background, it would be dead silent. I'm not even sure if Barrett is breathing. His gaze travels down to the picture Sydney is holding, then back to her face.

"Holy shit," Jude says, slapping Barrett on the back, nearly knocking the man over. "Congratulations. It's a girl."

The End

Thank you so much for reading Cash and Cece's story. Her happy ending was so important to me. I really put her through the wringer and knew she needed someone who would never waver by her side. And I knew Cash was going to be that man for her.

If you enjoyed their story, I would be forever grateful if you left a review where you purchased the book. They're so important for indie authors, and it helps us more than you could possibly imagine.

Do you want to read about what ist was like for a few of my guys to grow up in Shine? My free prequel novella **Rose Colored Glasses** can be downloaded when you sign up for my newsletter at katerandallauthor.com or by scanning the QR code below. Don't worry, I'll never spam you.

Stalk me on my socials!

TikTok
Instagram
Facebook

BookBub
Goodreads

Or you can scan the QR code below for links to all of my socials and to sign up for my newsletter!

ALSO BY KATE

<u>The Ones Series</u>
The Good One
The Fragile One
The Other One

<u>The Black Roses MC</u>
Linc
Jude
Ozzy
Knox
Wyatt
Cash
Barrett

<u>The Boston Syndicate</u>
Finn
Luca
Eoghan
Cillian

ABOUT KATE

Kate is a lover of all things books. It doesn't matter what sub-genre, as long as there's a HEA, she's in. She started reading romance in high school and would hide novels in textbooks to read during class. Becoming an author was always a dream she had and finally decided to put pen to paper (or finger to keyboard) and write what she loves. She grew up in the beautiful upper peninsula of Michigan then became a West Coast girl where she lives with her amazing husband and hilarious son. She would love to hear from readers so check out all her socials and sign up for her newsletter so she can keep you up to date on her books and whatever other ramblings come to mind.

Acknowledgements

First off, I want to thank YOU for reading this story. Without my amazing readers, I wouldn't be writing in this crazy outlaw world. I love my anti-heroes, and I'm so damn happy you do, too.

Kiki, Megan, and Anna with The Next Step PR- you three are the best at what you do at helping me spread the word about my books and keeping me organized the whole way. I'm so happy to know you!

Victoria, my amazing editor. I'm pretty sure you were sent to me by the gods. You take my words and polish them up perfectly. And you're never getting rid of me! LOL!

Megan, my beta-reader extraordinaire. I am so happy we met and you wanted to be on my team of one. LOL. You know my world and love my guys as much as I do. I absolutely adore you and love getting to swoon over fictional men together!

And last but never least, my amazing husband. You're the best signing assistant/bodyguard/wrangler I could ever ask for. You do this with me every single day, and just like my fictional men, you support me in every way imaginable. Even when I came to you with a crazy idea to become an author. LOL! I couldn't and wouldn't want to do this without you next to me.